FISH WIELDER

J.R.R.R. (Jim) Hardison

FIERY SEAS PUBLISHING

Visit our website at www.fieryseaspublishing.com
This book is a work of fiction. Names, characters, places, and incidents either are products of the author's imagination or are used fictitiously. Any resemblance to actual persons, living or dead, events, or locales is entirely coincidental.
Fish Wielder
Copyright © 2016, Jim Hardison
Cover Art by Herb Apon and Jess Small
Editing by Charlie Tate
Interior Design by Merwin Loquias (www.mlgraphicdesigns.tk)
ISBN-13: 978-0-9968943-1-9
Library of Congress Control Number: 2015959645
All rights reserved.
No part of this publication may be used or reproduced in any manner whatsoever without written permission, except in the case of brief quotations embodied in critical articles and reviews. Requests for permission should be addressed to Fiery Seas Publishing.
Printed in the United States of America
First Edition:
10 9 8 7 6 5 4 3 2

Dedication

For the thirteen-year-old versions of
Jim Raymond, Jon Kendzie and Randy Savada,
who daydreamed of writing fantasy novels with me
when we were supposed to be studying in class,
and for my awesome wife and ingenious girls,
who put up with endless lame ideas and
rewarded me with brilliant, hilarious suggestions
and more love and support than I deserve.

Acknowledgement

Special thanks to: Rachelle Ramirez, Dave Land, Brian Reid, Mike Wellins, Phil Amara, David Altschul, Wayne Rowe, Herb Apon, Dave Stewart, Amy Arendts, Rachel Miller, Lucy Vosmek, Mark Gottlieb at Trident Media Group and Charlie Tate & Misty Williams at Fiery Seas.

Fish Wielder

ROWLETT PUBLIC LIBRARY
3900 MAIN STREET
ROWLETT, TX 75088
WITHDRAWN

J.R.R.R. (Jim) Hardison

"This is a work of fiction.
Everything in this book is fake."

Map of the Lands of Grome

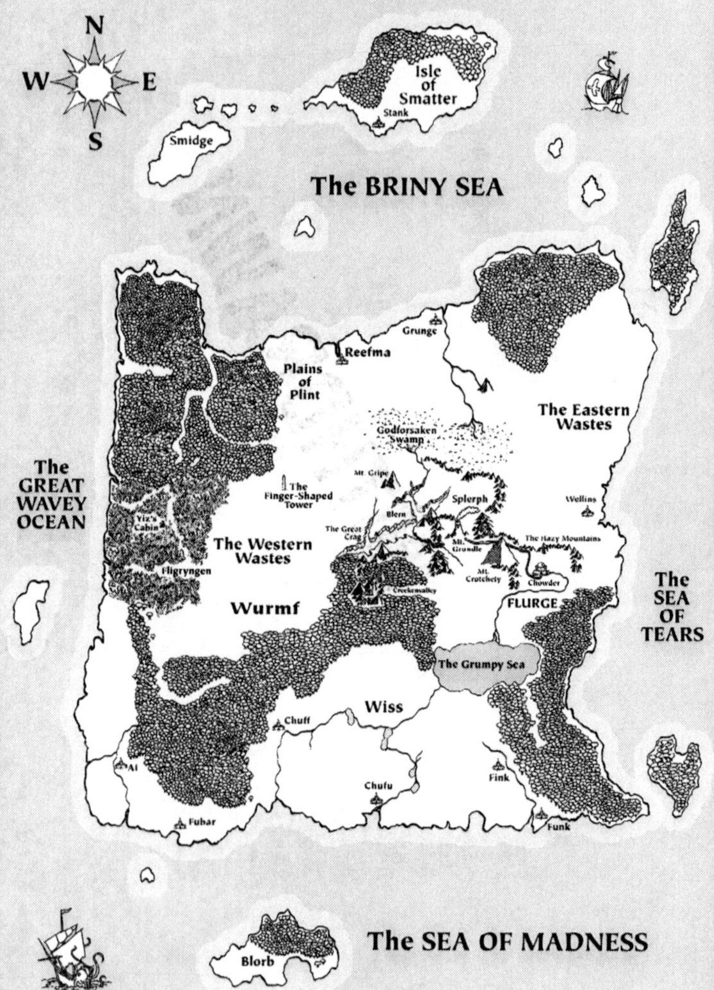

CHAPTER ONE

The Fist Wielder

It was the anniversary of something bad.

Thoral Mighty Fist, perhaps the toughest, most mysterious and manly fighter in all the mystical world of Grome, sat in the Inn of the Gruesomely Gashed Gnome in a dark corner, weeping into his tankard of warm ale. He hated ale, especially when it was warm, although he'd been swilling the stuff since before breakfast. Now it was well after dinner, and all he'd eaten the entire day was a piece of dry toast and a couple of olives as black as his mood. He raised his mug for another bitter sip and the jeweled hilt of the magic broadsword, *Blurmflard*, poked him in the side like a reminder of past mistakes. It was awkward to sit at a table with a broadsword at your belt, but the mighty barbarian had kept *Blurmflard* with him at all times ever since the blade was lent to him by his wizard mentor, Yiz. He even slept with it.

As Thoral sat brooding and trying to adjust his position to more comfortably accommodate the blade, a twelve-inch-long orange koi fish walked into the bar on his tail fins. Standing in the entryway, the koi peered around the crowded, dim interior until his bulging eyes fell on Thoral. The fish frowned.

At six feet, Thoral was a head taller than most other human inhabitants of the world of Grome and was so powerfully built that he barely fit at the heavy wooden table at which he sat. He was dressed pirate-style, with a black leather vest buttoned over his otherwise bare chest, tight, plum-colored breeches and knee-high, iron-toed boots. A wide crimson belt bore the magic sword as well as an assortment of leather and velvet pouches. A less attractive or more effeminate man would never have been able to pull off such an outfit, but for Thoral it was no problem. He had chiseled features and a head of thick, golden hair that curled to his massive shoulders. The few strands of gray made him even more handsome–in a seasoned and mature way, of course. His glorious hair notwithstanding, his most striking feature was his piercing gaze. So intense, so smoldering was his stare, that those on the receiving end often felt the need to look away for fear that they would catch fire. There was no word in Gromish for the vibrant purple color of his eyes, but they were violet.

The koi contemplated the warrior. Given his charisma, strength and fighting abilities, Thoral could easily have conquered his own kingdom. But Thoral didn't seem to care about that kind of thing. He mostly liked to drink and fight and brood and wander around in forests looking at trees. As the fish watched, the mighty warrior burped. The hot gas seemed to sear his manly nostrils so that he blinked as his striking violet eyes watered.

Thoral looked up from his drink and squinted around the bar to see if anyone had noticed his tears and if there was anyone worth fighting. He failed to detect the fish, who was hidden behind the legs of a passing barmaid. The other patrons were humans, except a few half-elves and a handful of drunken gnomes. He could take them all on single-handedly, but he knew from experience that he'd feel even worse after beating them. Especially the gnomes. It was better to do nothing, to sit and drink and wish things were different.

Thoral closed his eyes and hunched forward to lay his tawny-maned head on the table. The rough-hewn planks, though, smelled as if they had been wiped with a mildew-y rag, so he sat back up. He fumbled in one of his many belt pouches for the last of his dried herbs, crushed them between his long, calloused fingers and inhaled their fading minty fragrance. It wasn't quite strong enough to clear the lingering scent of the mildew.

As Thoral sniffled at his mint leaves, the fish sighed. Shaking his head, he stalked across the sticky floor on his tail fins. The barbarian noticed him with a wince.

"This is the end, Bradfast," Thoral grumbled at the fish in his outlandish accent, his rough voice heavy with melancholy. Thoral tended to transpose the sounds of *v* and *w* and to pronounce *th* at the beginning of words as *z* because he was foreign.

"Here we go again," Brad commented dryly, leaping up onto the bench and then the table. He picked his way across the tabletop and stopped before the warrior. "This isn't the end, Thoral. It's just the beginning…or maybe the middle or something. The point is, it's not over. It's never over until you give up—or you're dead."

"I dost wonder about death," the barbarian said, as if to himself. He also used outdated words like *dost* because he spoke High Gromish even though most everybody else spoke the low version. This was also because he was foreign. "Would it truly bring an end? Or just a transition to another world?"

"You've had too much to drink, Thoral," the fish cautioned. "You always get morose when you drink. It's time we get moving. Maybe go on another adventure or something."

"I am tired of adventures," the warrior sighed. "I wish only to go home." He burped again, and the fish staggered back, blinking.

"Come on, pal. Let's get out of here," Brad suggested, fanning himself with a fin. "We'll fight a monster or go on a quest or steal the jeweled eye from an idol or something. It'll be fun."

"My heart is too…" Thoral trailed off. "What is that word that means when something has substantial weight?"

"Heavy," the fish supplied. Thoral always had trouble remembering that one.

"Heavy. Yes. My heart is too heavy for adventure," Thoral complained.

"Well, maybe if we pick something really hard, you'll get killed," the fish offered.

"A hero's death?" Thoral asked, perking up just a bit.

"Yeah, sure. A hero's death."

"And then I couldst be done with this world," Thoral murmured.

"Exactly," Brad affirmed.

"Then let us go," Thoral said, "this very instant." He slammed his drink down on the table so hard that some of the ale sloshed out of the tankard, splashing at the fish. The koi danced back, just missing a soaking.

"Up to bed first and we'll hit the road in the morning," Brad countered, stepping around the puddle of spilled drink.

"No, we will leave now." There was a dangerous edge to the warrior's tone that drew the attention of everyone in the room even though he had not raised his voice. The bar went silent.

"Look, Thoral," the koi answered, "it's getting late. I'm tired. You're drunk. We could both use some sleep. Let's not make a rash decision that might lead to all kinds of unexpected complications."

Every eye turned to see the barbarian's reaction.

"We will leave now," Thoral insisted. The warrior and the fish stared at each other.

"Be reasonable," Brad tried again. "Just give me one good reason why we shouldn't wait until morning."

"We will leave now," the barbarian declared, "because *I am Thoral Mighty Fist!*"

Everyone gasped. Brad sagged, defeated. Once Thoral noted that he was Thoral, there was no point in arguing further. Everyone knew it. That's just how it was.

With that, Thoral drained his pewter tankard and crushed it one-handed. He got unsteadily to his feet, massive muscles rippling under sun-bronzed, battle-scarred skin, and transferred Brad from the tabletop into a belt pouch. Then he tossed a gold coin to the hideously disfigured gnomish innkeeper to pay for the mug he'd ruined even though it couldn't have been worth more than a few coppers. The gnome had been engrossed in restocking a spice rack over the bar, so the coin struck him in the head and then clattered to the floor. He stepped on it with his clubfoot before it rolled away and then pinched it between his stubby, ring-clad fingers.

"Many thanks, Fist Wielder," the innkeeper croaked, his one eye glittering from his gashed face as the warrior strode past him. "Where are you headed now? Not to the Godforsaken Swamp, I hope. You should steer clear of that place for a while. There is nothing there but death."

"I am eager for it," the barbarian whispered as he strode past the gnome, who frowned and wrung his tiny hands.

Thoral staggered from the bar into the dark, filthy street. Although it was well past sundown, the city was still bustling with all kinds of criminals and cutthroats and that sort of riffraff. They all cleared out of the big barbarian's way. Three figures, cloaked and hooded in the black robes of the Bad Religion, watched from the shadows as Thoral went to the tavern's hitching post to untie his massive tiger-striped steed, Warlordhorse. He fumbled with the knot, his fingers clumsy from the ale. He shook his head and tried again.

"Let us attack now," the leader of the Dark Brothers whispered. "We will take him unawares."

"Uh…are you sure?" one of his subordinates asked, his voice quavering. "Have you heard the stories about him?"

"We have our orders," the leader countered tersely. "Besides, he is inebriated, there are three of us, and we have the ultimate advantage…" He trailed off, sliding a dagger from a fold of his robe. The curved blade was slick with oily, black poison. He leered at his minions for a moment, and they reluctantly drew their own poison-coated daggers. The three of them started toward the barbarian while he was distracted.

Thoral was still having no luck with Warlordhorse's tether, and grew frustrated. He put his face close to the rope, trying to get a better look in the dim light of the moon, and made another attempt. The Dark Brothers crept closer, raising their poisoned blades in unison.

Just one scratch and Thoral would be paralyzed before he even felt the wound. Agonizing death would follow within hours, but not before they had had time to drag the warrior before the master of their order to find out how much Thoral knew of their plans.

The Dark Brothers closed in on the unsuspecting champion, swift and silent as death itself.

CHAPTER TWO

Foul Magics

Just as the Dark Brothers sprang at Thoral, the big barbarian, still thwarted by the knot in the tether, roared in anger and whipped his magic blade from its sheath to cut the horse free. His furious backswing clanged against the lead attacker's poison dagger, deflecting it back into the Brother's own neck with such force that it opened the entire left side of his throat. Thoral spun to see what he'd hit as hot blood geysered into the faces of the other two. The leader's body convulsed, then collapsed to the ground like a black bag of meat. One of the remaining Brothers jerked a hand up to wipe the gouts of blood from his eyes, nicking his own cheek with his poisoned blade. He gave one strangled gasp, staggered a half step and collapsed across his partially beheaded companion, stabbing the third guy in the shin as he fell. Thoral gaped at the carnage he'd caused, then turned to apologize to the third man. The poison had already done its work. The last Dark Brother dropped to the ground before Thoral's eyes, apparently dead.

The big barbarian stood contemplating the bodies for a long moment, his head buzzing.

"It's OK. I think they were trying to kill us," Brad noted from Thoral's belt pouch, startling the warrior. "I mean, they were springing on you from behind with poisoned daggers, right?"

Thoral blinked slowly. Without a word, he turned and hacked through the hitching post so that Warlordhorse's tether swung free. Then he vaulted onto the back of the stallion. He sat swaying in the saddle for a minute, slumped a bit, his eyelids drooping. He shook himself, sat up straight and howled mournfully at the moon. Several people walking nearby jumped at the unexpected sound and shot him angry looks, but he ignored them.

"Why do you do that?" Brad asked, exasperated. "You know it's annoying."

"I howl in sadness because this moon is almost always…" The warrior trailed off, screwing up his face with mental effort. "What is that word used to indicate when the moon is more than half full so that it appears convex at both edges?"

"Humpbacked?" Brad offered.

"No. The astronomical term."

"Gibbous?" the fish supplied.

Thoral gave a terse nod then urged Warlordhorse to a gallop while the koi rolled his eyes at the barbarian's drama. Thoral ignored him, his flowing, tawny locks streaming heroically behind him as he clattered along the cobbled street and out of the southeast gate of Reefma, the city known to the elves as the Black Gem because the elves always had to have their own names for everything.

"I shall head for the Godforsaken Swamp," Thoral intoned. "There a man can find adventure, treasure, and beasts to fight. Perhaps enough battle to drown one's sorrows or end them entirely."

"The Godforsaken Swamp!" Brad complained from Thoral's belt pouch. It was tricked out for him to sit in, as he had a tendency to slip off the saddle when he tried to ride the more conventional way.

Thoral narrowed his violet eyes at the koi. "I was talking to myself, Brad."

"Fine, whatever," the fish shrugged. "Hey, what do you make of those guys who were trying to kill us? Did any of them look familiar to you? Did you owe them money, or did you insult them before I got to the inn or something?"

"I wish they had not been so inept," Thoral grumbled.

When the fish realized there was no further comment coming, he shook his head. Frowning, he ducked back into the pouch and tried to get comfortable. If Thoral wasn't going to worry about it, he wasn't either. He sighed, resigned to his fate. There was an ancient koi genealogy scroll he was eager to peruse over the many boring miles between their current position and the swamp, but he knew from experience that he'd get motion sick if he read it while they cantered. Instead, he adjusted his position and tried to settle in for a nap.

***

Thoral reined in Warlordhorse at the edge of the Godforsaken Swamp as the sun was setting behind its vast, rotty expanse. He and Brad had been riding for three days. Thoral's spirits had not lifted. A ground-crawling fog of stinking swamp gas seethed around the horse's hooves. A dead frog floated, belly up, on the scummy surface of a stagnant pool. Thoral clicked his tongue and tried to urge Warlordhorse forward, but the great beast rolled his eyes and laid his ears back. He was the last of the mighty Brendylschmylyn, the horses that can smell danger, and the swamp was full of it.

"Do not be afraid," Thoral soothed. "I shall protect you as you have so often protected me, my friend." Warlordhorse glanced over his shoulder at Thoral, then back at the swamp. He narrowed his eyes but headed into the desolate marshland despite his misgivings. Then the sun set, and some kind of bird cried ominously to the onrushing shadows of the glooming night.

***

Many hours later, as the constellation of the celestial gopher crested the dome of the midnight sky, Thoral allowed Warlordhorse a brief moment to grab a mouthful of black marsh grass. Thoral, Brad and the tiger-striped steed were tired, sore and splattered with smelly muck from the miles they had slogged through the swamp. It was the muck that bothered Thoral most.

"Mayhap this was not such a great idea," he confessed, but the fish tapped him on the thigh with one flipper.

"Over there," Brad said, pointing off into the misty darkness. Squinting, Thoral could just make out the hulk of a castle in the distance, its crumbling walls edged with the wan light of the gibbous moon.

"A castle," Thoral mused. "And it appears to be abandoned."

"They always appear that way, don't they?" Brad asked rhetorically.

"Perhaps some small pool of untainted water has collected within," Thoral speculated, a wistful note in his voice. "Or maybe there is a well with some unpolluted water in it or even some kind of cistern containing unsullied water that I might splash upon my person in order that I might restore myself to a relatively clean and fresh-smelling state. Mayhap there is even a forgotten sliver of soap, left over from happier times." He wiped some of the muck from his brow but didn't have a great place to clean it off his hand. He wanted to stop to get out a towel but suspected he would just get dirty again before they arrived at the castle. He knew better than to rub the mud on Warlordhorse. His eyes fell on the fish.

"Don't even," Brad cautioned with a stern look.

Thoral frowned but spurred his steed toward the dark and foreboding ruin, hoping for water and trying not to think about his filthy hand.

After struggling through yet another pool of muck and hacking past some thorny blackberry bushes, they found their way to the overgrown remains of a road that led toward the crumbling and ruined castle. On the road lay a human skull with a snake poking its head out of an eye socket. Thoral glared at it, still brooding about the muck. The serpent, startled by the purple fire of his gaze, slunk back into the skull but continued to watch them with its own jewel-black eyes.

Warlordhorse flared his nostrils as he whiffed the air. The scent of evil was overpowering and peculiar, like cumin mixed with cocoa, and it was coming from the castle. Warlordhorse couldn't place the odor, but it was the smell of an evil sorcerer.

***

The sorcerer sat in the cold and empty throne room of the castle stroking his dark beard. The castle was otherwise empty because he had killed the good and noble king of that land with his foul magics and had taken over the stronghold and ruined the kingdom. There was more to it than that, but that's the short version. He wore the old king's stolen crown, which was a little too tight for him, and read a blasphemous recipe from a book bound in the skin of babies. Following these instructions, he spooned the gelatinous contents from two malformed and blackened pudding cups into a golden chalice worked with an uncouth octopus motif. The mixture bubbled with a greenish vapor that rose and writhed like a handful of worms. The sorcerer pulled a disgusted face as the fumes reached his nostrils. He gulped once, shuddered, and then set to devouring the dark result.

Just outside the ruin, Warlordhorse nickered and rolled his eyes as the unusual odor intensified. The mighty equine shuddered and laid his ears back.

Thoral, who could be as gentle as he was strong, fed Warlordhorse lumps of sugar and patted his striped neck. "Do not fear. Now that I am forewarned, I will overmatch whatever evil may lie within that castle, last Lord of the Brendylschmylyn," he promised. Then he got a faraway look in his eyes and recited a poem:

"Last Lord of the Brendylschmylyn,
King of horses, swift and bold,
Best to heed thy danger feelin'
Worth its weight in precious..."

He trailed off.

"Gold?" suggested the fish from his belt pouch.

"Mayhap," Thoral gruffed.

"Of course it's gold," Brad snapped.

"Mayhap," Thoral grumbled, reining in Warlordhorse before the ruined gate of the castle. The gate gaped like the mouth of a monster. It was obvious someone had gone to great expense to have it built that way. Warlordhorse snorted as Thoral squinted into the void. The light of the moon did not penetrate the inky blackness of the fortress. Damn gibbous moons. Thoral swung down from the saddle and unpacked and lit a torch. Its flame flickered like a dancing wraith as thunder rumbled in the distance.

"I'm telling you, lanterns are better," Brad commented, still in the pouch.

"This torch is more than serviceable," the warrior answered.

"It's all flickery and eerie," the fish huffed at his side. "Lanterns give more consistent light for the money."

"Enough," Thoral growled.

He led Warlordhorse through the door and into the courtyard beyond. Once inside, he tied Warlordhorse to the testicles of a crumbling sculpture and looked around. It was dark and gloomy enough that it was hard to see even with a torch, but Thoral decided not to say anything about the poor lighting. He didn't want to give Brad the satisfaction. Instead, he strode unconcerned through a door that hung half off its hinges, stumbled over a whole human skeleton and dropped the torch. It went out.

Recovering with the agility of an acrobatic dancing cat trained in martial arts, the warrior drew *Blurmflard* from its sheath and pronounced the magic word that made the rune-covered blade glow with a bright pink radiance. They were in a small antechamber from which many doors led. The floor was littered with bones. Thoral glanced down at Brad, who glared back at him from the belt pouch, furious. Before the fish could say anything, however, a soft scrabbling sound came from behind them. The Fist Wielder whirled round, roaring a battle cry, and slashing the darkness with *Blurmflard*.

A little rat squeaked at him from the bone-strewn floor, blinking in the magic pink light.

"It's just a rat," Brad sighed with relief.

"A mere rodent." Thoral forced a chuckle. Then he relaxed.

Of course, that's when the evil sorcerer sprang on him. The

sorcerer slashed Thoral's sword arm with a wickedly curved dagger. He hacked into it so deeply that the arm almost came off at the elbow and was left hanging by a mere thread of gristle. Thoral bellowed in anger and pain. Brad gagged at the sight. The sorcerer cackled like a madman as he ran off into the twisting maze of corridors that he had enchanted with a confounding spell to make them as confusing as possible.

CHAPTER THREE

Necrogrond

Thoral's arm dangled uselessly as his blood pumped in spurts onto the dusty floor of the ruined castle. Although he was still clutching *Blurmflard* because his grasp was so amazingly powerful, he couldn't really use the blade like that, so he fumbled in one of his belt pouches with the other hand. Brad pushed a bottle of green pudding into the barbarian's groping fingers. Thoral pulled out the cork with his unnaturally white, evenly spaced teeth and spat it into the pool of his own blood. Then he slurped down the contents, even though he didn't enjoy pudding. The creamy green gel burned like fire but tasted like vanilla cream pie. Over the course of the next few minutes, it healed his arm and left a cool-looking scar. The magic of the pudding even replaced the blood he had lost. It was a convenient pudding.

Thoral went after the sorcerer.

In his secret room in a shattered tower of the ruined castle, the sorcerer conjured a giant spider. It was gross. "Go!" he told the spider. "Go and destroy my enemy! I, the sorcerer Necrogrond, command it!"

The evil magic spider nodded and then teleported himself right behind Thoral.

Thoral stood lost in the maze conferring with Brad, who was poking his head up out of the barbarian's belt pouch. Thoral heard the spider, but thinking it to be another rat and not wanting to look foolish again in front of Brad, he did not turn around. Mistake. The spider sprang onto his back.

"AAHHHHH!" shouted the fish in terror.

Thoral was silent. He almost never screamed when startled.

The spider's pincers clacked together as it tried to bite him, but the barbarian managed to twist around and block the jaws with his blade because his reflexes were significantly better than those of a praying mantis. Thoral punched the spider in one of its multifaceted eyes with his mighty fist and three of the facets burst. The spider squeaked in rage, but Thoral did not relent. He punched it twice in its abdomen and once in its thorax. Then he punched it in the eye again despite the gick that splattered everywhere.

"Use the *magic sword* for God's sake!" shouted Brad.

Before Thoral could bring his blade to bear, the spider sprayed the warrior in the face with a gob of sticky webbing. As he staggered back, struggling to clear the web from his eyes, it seemed as if he was going to lose the battle. It seriously seemed that way. But then he cleared his eyes and cleaved the spider with his magic sword. Its head tumbled through the air, spraying green ichor everywhere. The goo even got on Thoral.

Necrogrond watched the view from the spider's dead eyes in a crystal ball as the mighty barbarian dug a towel out of one of his belt pouches and began meticulously cleaning the goop off himself.

"He killed my magic arachnid! I didn't see that coming," the sorcerer said to himself out loud. "Could this be that guy from the Goomy Prophecy of Doom, the Chosen One that my mysterious evil master is always warning me about?" He stroked his dark beard until he realized he was doing it again and stopped. "Eh, what are the chances? And I'm safe here anyway. No one could find the way through my enchanted maze to this chamber."

Brad could. Once Thoral got himself clean, the fish closed his eyes and used the vibrations of his koi whiskers to lead the warrior through the maze of twisting corridors, up the spiral staircase of the ruined tower and right to the iron door of the secret, hidden room. "He's in there," the fish whispered. Thoral kicked the door off its hinges.

Taken by surprise, Necrogrond screamed like a child and dropped his crystal ball on the floor so that it shattered on the flagstones. There was only a big pile of powder left. Necrogrond looked up from the ruined crystal ball dust at the hulking warrior. He pressed the heel of one hand to his eye and shook his head. He wasn't really interested in having a fair fight with Thoral right then; he had other evil to get up to. He whispered a spell that should have teleported him out of the room, but nothing happened.

"Oh, great," he snarled, eyeing Thoral's glowing pink sword.

Sucking up the energy from other people's teleportation spells so that its wielder could teleport was one of the enchanted blade's many powers. However, to his everlasting sadness, Thoral had long ago forgotten the word to trigger the teleportation spell. The barbarian glowered at the magician as the blade thrummed in his hand.

"Prepare to meet whatever maker made thee," Thoral spat.

"No, *you*!" the sorcerer shot back.

Then the two ran at each other. Necrogrond swung his wickedly curved dagger, and Thoral blocked the blow with his magic sword so that blue sparks showered around him. The sorcerer pirouetted like a dancer dancing a dance of death and slashed at the barbarian's heaving chest. Thoral jumped backwards, avoiding a nasty cut. Then he sprang forward and punched the sorcerer in the ear. Necrogrond was spun round by the force of Thoral's mighty fist, and his ear tore right off and fell on the floor with a wet plop. He howled in pain and clutched at the side of his head.

"You'll pay for that, barbarian!" the sorcerer screeched and made a big flash of magic light that had Thoral seeing spots.

When the Fist Wielder's vision returned, Necrogrond appeared to be gone. Actually, he was in the air above Thoral, hovering in a way that made the magician look as if he were floating underwater. Even his hair rippled as if he were underwater. It was pretty creepy, but the effect was wasted on Thoral because he didn't see it.

"Where art thou, FOUL WIZARD?!" Thoral roared, turning

this way and that as Necrogrond descended. The sorcerer was a mere foot above him when a single drop of blood dripped from his severed ear and splashed onto the top of Brad's head as he peered from inside Thoral's belt pouch.

"He's hovering above us!" the fish shouted.

Thoral looked up, but too late. The sorcerer plopped down on him, seizing the warrior's neck between his powerful thighs. He squeeze until Thoral's face turned red and veins bulged at his temples. The barbarian staggered and fell to his knees, gasping for breath and grasping for the sorcerer. And then it really seemed as if Thoral might lose. Really this time.

Only guess what? With the last of his oxygen running out and the capillaries beginning to burst in the whites of his violet eyes, Thoral summoned all of his strength and shrugged his shoulders with such explosive force that Necrogrond was thrown up into the air. As the wicked wizard tumbled head over tail toward the vaulted ceiling, Thoral leapt to his feet and swung *Blurmflard* in a glittering, two-handed arc. The magic blade sliced through the sorcerer's neck at the exact middle. Necrogrond's severed head spun through the air, spraying bright blood everywhere. The warrior sprang from the ground in a flying cartwheel and kicked it with his iron-toed boot so that it sailed right out a small window of the tower without even nicking the frame.

Thoral stuck the landing and shot out a hand to catch Brad a split second before the fish slapped to the floor. The koi had fallen from Thoral's belt pouch during the acrobatics. The two blood-slathered companions eyed each other.

"Did you see the expression on that guy's face as his head went through the window?" the fish asked.

"What is that word that indicates the impossibility of fixing a value to something?" Thoral asked.

"Priceless," the fish supplied, deadpan.

The two of them burst into wild laughter, Brad slapping the gory flagstones with a fin while the brilliant white of Thoral's perfect teeth flashed in the pink light of his sword. The sounds of their uproarious mirth echoed around the ruin so that even in the courtyard, Warlordhorse raised his head from munching black swamp grass and looked about in mild confusion.

***

Seven minutes later, the fish still lay giggling on the floor, but the big barbarian had sobered. The warrior's purple gaze was distant, his face clouding with its typical brooding expression. As Brad watched, his own smile fading, Thoral unslung a wineskin from his belt and chugged half the contents in a single go. He offered the koi a swig, but the fish declined. The warrior drained the rest, then set about wiping the gore off himself with a piece of cloth torn from Necrogrond's robe. He would have used his towel, but it was already soggy with spider ichor. When he finished, he tore off another swatch and tossed it to Brad.

Sufficiently clean, Thoral and Brad poked around the chamber a bit and discovered an iron-banded treasure chest. Thoral broke it open with *Blurmflard.* The contents were hundreds of gold coins and the book bound in baby skin and marked with a many-tentacled face. Thoral threw the book out the window with a shudder, then noticed a small pile of other items that had the smell of magic. Thoral was always keenly interested in magical relics for reasons he didn't talk about. He picked through the pile as Brad wandered off to search elsewhere. A small cylindrical crystal caught Thoral's eye. He plucked it up and tentatively touched one end of it to his tongue, but nothing happened. He made a disappointed face and tossed it aside. He also spent a few minutes examining a brass compass in minute detail. It was an ancient thing, engraved on the back of the case with an intricate motif of vines that encircled the worn initials *L.E.* Thoral was curious because the needle didn't seem to point north. He experimented by walking around with it a bit, then checked to see if the needle moved when he was stationary. It didn't.

"Do you think this could be a Walking-Door Tree Compass?" Thoral asked, holding up the device for Brad to see.

The fish glanced over from where he was knocking on the wall on the other side of the chamber to see if there were any hidden doors. "Maybe," the koi responded, distracted. "I don't know."

Thoral gave the compass a last look and then put it in the bag of magic stuff that held his dearest possessions, including two tiny blue orbs, a coil of what appeared to be white string, a metal wand he very rarely used and a thin, black, rectangular box that hadn't worked in years.

"Whoa!" Brad called out. He had found a secret room with a young woman in it. She was chained up and had on hardly any clothes. Raven haired and fine featured, her pointy ears suggested she might be an elf. She looked as if she couldn't have been more than seventeen, but she eyed Thoral defiantly, her eyes flashing, and tried to draw herself up to her full height despite the hampering shackles.

"Who art thou?" she demanded, afraid but doing her best not to show it. "And what is thine intention?"

"I suppose I am rescuing you," the warrior gruffed. "And I am Thoral Mighty Fist."

Relief replaced her previous defensiveness, and tears welled in her green eyes, though to her credit, she held them back. "The Fist Wielder?" she whispered, her voice trembling.

"The one and only," Brad interjected. "And I'm Bradfast. *The* Bradfast." He peered up at her from near Thoral's war boot, taking in her scanty red-velvet loincloth and brassiere.

"The necromancer dressed me like this," the girl declared, suddenly self-conscious. "He said…he said he was going to…to eat me."

Thoral used his magic sword to sever her thick chains as if they were made of room-temperature butter. As the heavy links dropped away, she swooned and fell. He caught her a second before her head hit the floor. Thoral was always smooth like that.

Safe in the embrace of his massively muscled arms, the elf peered up at him through a tangled cascade of midnight hair that created an attractive contrast with her flawless, creamy skin. Her eyes were a deep emerald green that would have been unrealistic on a human. She was a looker. And she was looking at Thoral with burning intensity now—his big muscles, his striking violet eyes, his almost unnaturally even white teeth. (Most everybody on Grome had bad teeth.) Her pale cheeks flushed.

Thoral brushed her hair aside so he could get a better view of her eyes and make sure there wasn't any discrepancy in the size of her pupils that might indicate she was suffering from a concussion. The elf misread the gesture and pulled herself toward him, her full, sensual lips pursed for a kiss. Thoral frowned as he fended her off. He hadn't had time to check her hair for lice.

Brad rolled his eyes. Women.

Outside the castle, Necrogrond's head glared up at the pink glow of the tower windows. He wished he still had a body so he could retrieve the priceless baby-skin spell book, which had bounced off his forehead before sinking into the muck, but he'd have to worry about that later. With a supreme effort, he began to roll away, careful not to snag his crown on any weeds. "Oh, how you will pay, barbarian!" he raged, unable to make anything but lip-smacking sounds because his torn vocal cords were no longer connected to lungs. The creeping fog parted around the rolling head and swallowed it up without a trace as lightning flashed in the distance and thunder rumbled ominously.

CHAPTER FOUR

Something Fishy

Thoral sat in the Inn of the Gruesomely Gashed Gnome, drinking warm ale and gambling what was left of his haul from the necromancer's castle with a dozen other adventurers. He laid down his cards and won the last of their money. The other adventurers were getting pretty mad as this was the tenth time in a row he'd beaten them and they had been hoping to use their winnings to finance an expedition to find and destroy the withered soul of the evil lich king terrorizing the distant land of Wiss.

Their leader, Wyse of Wiss, gave Thoral the stink eye.

"Something's fishy," he hissed. Wyse was a cocky warrior with silver hair and an enchanted sword forged by ghosts. He was pretty famous in Wiss and had his own trilogy of epic poems that the bards were always singing, but he still probably shouldn't have said that.

"Dost thou insult my friend, Brad?" Thoral asked, narrowing his startling violet eyes.

"Let it go, Thoral," Brad cautioned, peering over the top of his own cards. "You've had too much to drink. He's not insulting me; he's accusing you of cheating."

"Is this true?" Thoral barked at Wyse. "Dost thou accuse me of cheating?"

"Let it go, Thoral," Brad suggested again.

"I will not be accused of cheating by an *unwashed* ruffian," Thoral told his friend. He turned back to Wyse. "So, art thou accusing me of cheating?"

"I thought I made that pretty clear," the hero of Wiss exclaimed, looking around to his fellows for support.

"Not really," Thoral noted. "And let me caution you before you say anything else. I am in a surly mood, and I do not like the way you smell."

"Then let me make it clearer," Wyse growled. "I think you're a cheat!"

Thoral slapped Wyse so hard that one of his eyeballs flew out. Then everyone started fighting. One of Wyse's men smashed a chair across the back of a tall, skinny guy who didn't have anything to do with the scuffle. A saucy barmaid winked at Brad and broke a bottle of wine on a fat adventurer's head as he prepared to throw a knife at the fish. Two gnomes who looked like twins but had never met before punched each other at exactly the same second and knocked each other out. But Thoral did the most fighting. At one point, ten of the adventurers jumped on him, and he went down under the pile. It really seemed as if he were defeated. That's how it seemed. Then he struggled back to his feet and spun around so fast the men flew off him and crashed into the nearby tables. The innkeeper shielded his spice rack with his little body and watched with a worried expression to see what would happen next.

Thoral stood in the middle of the room and wiped a little trickle of blood from the corner of his sensuous but masculine lips. He narrowed his violet eyes as he examined the blood on the back of his hand, and a fire seemed to kindle in their depths. Then he fell upon Wyse's men with his mighty fists flying.

A few moments later, Thoral stood in a pile of wreckage and unconscious adventurers. Wyse, the cocky warrior from Wiss, lay on the floor with his own eyeball staring at him from a pool of eyeball juice.

"This is why you can't drink," Brad chided Thoral. The barbarian shook his head as if trying to clear it.

"I hate warm ale," Thoral mumbled, more to himself than anyone else. He looked up from the wreckage. "I hope this pays for any damage," he said, throwing all the gambling money to the horribly disfigured innkeeper. The coins went everywhere, but it was the thought that counted. "If there is anything left over, give it to Wyse so he can buy an eye patch to match your own. If there is anything left after that, tell him he can use it to fight the lich king."

"Thank you, Fist Wielder," the gnome replied, his gruesomely gashed face twisting with what was meant to be a smile. "And where are you headed now?"

"Away," the barbarian grumbled, scooping up Brad and leaving the bar.

"That's a little vague," the innkeeper called after him, wringing his chubby hands, but the warrior was already gone.

Outside, Thoral staggered to his tiger-striped steed and mounted, but almost fell off the far side of the saddle before finding his balance. He sat swaying astride the massive horse and rubbed his eyes with the heels of his hands.

"What's troubling you, Thoral?" Brad asked. "You always seem to get depressed around this time of year."

"Memories," the warrior grunted.

"Care to elaborate?"

"No." Thoral teetered so that the saddle squeaked, as if impatient. Warlordhorse stamped his foot, actually impatient.

"I have spent too much time thinking," Thoral complained, patting the horse's striped neck.

"You have spent too much time *drinking*," Brad corrected him. Thoral dismissed the comment with a wave of his hand, then gave Warlordhorse a gentle prod. The mighty steed surged forward. Brad climbed onto Warlordhorse's head as they rode so that he could feel the wind on his face. They left Reefma through the south gate this time (the one called Schinthis, the Bile Gate, by the elves) and thundered off along the Wildering Road. Three figures that were robed and hooded all in black, watched them in sinister silence from the walls of the city.

"That wasn't the guy we weren't supposed to let leave the city alive, was it?" the first of the three asked the other two.

"I think…I think maybe it was," the second one replied.

"Dang it!" the first guy cursed as Thoral and his companions rounded a bend and vanished from sight.

CHAPTER FIVE

The Unknown Force

The companions trotted along for several weeks, taking only the occasional break to make wee. Brad chose their course, as Thoral was drinking too much to be trusted with deciding and professed to feeling too moody to care where they went anyway. Soon they were in the mostly uninhabited area, where even adventurers seldom went, on the outskirts of the vile, ruined kingdom of Splerph. It was a rough region of rolling wooded hills, dotted here and there with disquieting ruins overlooking unappealing vistas of stunted trees and murky ponds. They had to stop messing around then and really pay attention because that territory was dangerous, full of ogres and barfarts and whatnot.

Turning right to avoid the dread land of Flurge, they passed into the dark land of Blern under the shadows of Mount Gripe. There they crossed the Extremely Deep Abyss on a swaying rope bridge, which was problematic because Warlordhorse had trouble with heights. He wasn't afraid; he just had an inner-ear condition that made him susceptible to spells of dizziness.

Two days later, as they picked their way through the Great Crag where the battle of Sklounge had been fought, they were attacked by drawths, those legendary, giant-boulder-dropping birds. Warlordhorse was nearly squished, but Thoral managed to snap the neck of the king drawth with a leaping punch when it swooped too low. The companions ate that night until their bellies groaned and still had plenty left to replenish their dwindling stores with great slabs of roasted drawth breast that Thoral preserved with a spell his wizard mentor, Yiz, had taught him when he was a lad.

For the next week, the three followed the meandering course of the Chumble River until they came to the feet of the Towering Cliffs. They could have made better time if Thoral didn't insist on bathing every morning, but the warrior was a stickler for personal hygiene. Eventually, they entered the Gap of Goosh, which few men know of and fewer still care to seek. The Gap led them through to the Cavern Made Mostly of Bones. They tippy-toed through its inky hollows while Thoral kept an arrow nocked in his great yew bow, *Fwang*, and the fish whispered charms of protection against the vile mertalizers that crouched in the hungry shadows of that foul passage. Finally, tired and completely out of mead, they arrived at Windendale, the secret valley where the elves live. Brad made a big point of telling Thoral he hadn't been planning to go there; it's just how it worked out.

What to say of Windendale, which the elves call Creekenvalley? It is an ancient kingdom and last of the elvish strongholds of Grome. Fair yet perilous, its alabaster citadels and delicate soapstone towers wear the rainbow-hued mists of the thundering Glimmerwimmer Falls like a delicate veil. Always that city is filled with the singing of high, fair voices and the annoying tinkling of wind chimes and door harps.

The elves were mostly pleased to see Thoral again, and they laid out a lavish feast in the great high hall of the royal palace. The King of the Elves, Elfrod, welcomed the companions and bade Thoral sit at his right hand. Elfrod was tall and trim and serious looking because he was about two thousand years old, but his sea-green eyes still had some twinkle in them.

"Many thanks do I continue to shower upon thee, Thoral," Elfrod spake as he cast his eyes upon his only daughter, the elfish princess that Thoral and Brad had rescued from Necrogrond in the Godforsaken Swamp. The warrior likewise turned his startling violet eyes upon her, and she blushed because she had totally been staring at him. She was wearing a flowing green dress of a shimmery cloth that only the elves know how to make, and she had amethyst earrings that were cut into miniature likenesses of Thoral dangling from her pointy ears. He acknowledged her with a slight nod, but she gazed on him with such a smolder that even the fish could feel it. It was Thoral's turn to blush. Brad shifted his gaze to Elfrod, noting the king noting the smolder. Elfrod's noble brow creased with a hint of concern or annoyance.

"We're honored to have been able to help," the koi said from Thoral's belt pouch, rushing to draw the king's attention.

Elfrod looked from the fish to his daughter to Thoral. He eyed the barbarian speculatively. After a moment, he nodded sagely, then clapped his long-fingered hands. With that, musicians started playing, and everyone got down to eating. There were all kinds of dishes that didn't sound appetizing but were rare delicacies and, as Elfrod pointed out more than once, insanely expensive. Things like baked eel stuffed with bluebirds stuffed with salamanders stuffed with ground dragon tongue. Thoral usually scorned such rich fare, and feasts always depressed him, but he made a show of enjoying everything so as not to embarrass the fish. Brad loved this kind of cuisine and sat on the table beside Thoral gorging himself. The koi had been pleased as punch when they first returned the princess to her father, and Elfrod had insisted on hosting them for a week of lavish feasts and parties. As Thoral watched the fish tucking into the collection of delicacies, it occurred to him that maybe Brad *had* led them back here on purpose.

An elf waiter interrupted Thoral's reverie to offer him a steaming slice of roasted hedgehog, but the barbarian waved him off with a tight smile. What Thoral wanted was some strong wine or hard alcohol to dull his memories, but the elves were only serving water, as was their wont. At least it was cold.

All through the meal, the princess kept trying to catch Thoral's eye from across the table, but he had a massive headache building and didn't notice her. He wished there were at least a loaf of bread to nibble, but elves are gluten intolerant.

As the gathered host was starting in on dessert, Elfrod told Thoral that there was trouble in the land.

"It is true," admitted the king, his expression grave. "My people are being killed by an unknown force. I need a hero to stop it."

At those words, Thoral dropped his confection spoon. He set his sherbet aside, unfinished, although it was the only food he had enjoyed all night. The Elves of Windendale were famous for their sherbets. Truth be told, they didn't compare with the great gelatos of ancient Flurge, but they were still pretty tasty. Regardless, the barbarian pushed back from the table, scooped up Brad and strode from the feasting hall. The music ground to a halt, and a lot of the elves followed him out to see what was going on, including Elfrod and the princess.

"I will destroy this unknown force or die trying," Thoral vowed, his voice ringing as he mounted Warlordhorse in the alabaster courtyard. "That will most likely stop it."

The elves sang a song as he rode away. It was long and didn't have much of a tune to it, but it made the elfish princess sad. The upshot was that nobody knew where Thoral was from, although there was some speculation he might have been from the distant kingdom of Fligryngen. He was an enigma. Even to the elves.

"You have sent him to his death," the princess complained to her father.

"He is Thoral Mighty Fist," the king noted sagely, putting an arm around her shoulders. A slight smile touched his lips.

CHAPTER SIX

The Sinister Tower

They rode for two weeks searching here and there and following various clues. Thoral managed to trade the last of their drawth meat for a small barrel of mead when they encountered a traveling band of gnomes, but other than that, they saw no one. As dusk fell on the fourteenth day since leaving Windendale, they were beginning to wonder if maybe they should go back and ask Elfrod for more explicit directions. Just then the fish spotted a sinister tower, poking up like a black finger etched against the setting sun. It wasn't on any of their maps. When they got close, they could see that it was made out of a single piece of obsidian, but that it wasn't literally carved in the shape of a finger. There were scorched and blackened bones all around it. Brad scrambled down Thoral's leg and hung from a stirrup by his tail to examine them more closely.

"Elf bones," the fish confirmed after brushing one with his whiskers. He dropped it with a clatter and climbed back up to Thoral's lap.

"Hmmmm," Thoral murmured.

"You think it's a trap, don't you?" Brad asked, trying to read his companion's expression.

"Mayhap," Thoral returned.

"I mean, it's got to be a trap. Look at all these bones," Brad pressed, gesturing to the impressive field of desolation.

"Mayhap," Thoral grumbled.

"Definitely a trap," Brad concluded. "Proceed with caution."

Without a word, Thoral spurred Warlordhorse toward the tower at a full gallop.

Giant wolves attacked. They seemed to materialize out of nowhere, coming so fast that they managed to strike just as Warlordhorse was about to whinny to indicate that he smelled danger. It was ridiculous how fast they were. There was a whole pack of them, and they were twice as big as regular wolves and each had two heads. Both heads were in the front. They didn't have one at the front and one at the back. That would have been stupid.

Warlordhorse reared and kicked at the wolves, but they snapped at his iron-shod hooves so that he had to dance back on his hind legs. Even the horse could tell that there were just too many of them, what with the extra heads. So Thoral vaulted from the saddle and fought the wolves with his bare hands. He probably should have used his magic sword, but he was primarily a fist guy, so he just grabbed them by the scruffs of their filthy necks and shook them to break their backs. He killed a score of them, but twenty more jumped on him all at once. He went down under the pile, borne to the ground beneath the snarling, twisting mass.

It really seemed as if Thoral was defeated. Then he struggled back to his feet and spun around so fast that the wolves flew off and were impaled on leg bones and smashed against trees and the side of the obsidian tower. He stood in the middle of the pack as the surviving wolves snarled and circled him, spit dripping from their yellowed fangs. At least thirty of them remained. Thoral wiped a little trickle of blood from the corner of his left nostril. His eyes narrowed, and fire seemed to kindle in their violet depths as he examined the blood on the tip of his finger. Then he fell on the wolves with his mighty fists flying.

Two minutes later, Thoral stood upon a pile of dead giant two-headed wolves.

"These wolves are not…" he trailed off.

Warlordhorse and Brad shot him questioning looks.

"What is that word for when something is not the way it is supposed to be? How do you say that?" Thoral asked.

"Normal?" Brad supplied.

Warlordhorse looked from the fish to the warrior to see if the guess was correct.

"No. Not that. It is that word that indicates when something is not right according to the laws of the world," Thoral pressed, a frown creasing his manly brow.

Warlordhorse looked back to the fish.

"Regular? Ordinary? Typical?" Brad suggested.

Thoral shook his head in frustration at each descriptor. The three friends stood there, thinking, amid the pile of dead two-headed wolves.

"Natural?" Brad offered finally.

"Natural," Thoral nodded, smiling. "These wolves are not natural."

"Perhaps they are agents of the unknown force?" posited Brad.

Thoral nodded, frowning this time.

As the last rays of the dying day were swallowed alive by the hungry darkness of the rising night, Thoral stood before the ancient bronze door of the ancient tower trying to locate a doorknob. Words were engraved on the metal portal in a language he could not read. Probably Dwarfish. Finding no handle or knob or anything, he wedged the tip of his magic blade into the crack around the door's edge to force it. A normal sword would break, but *Blurmflard* was supposed to be unbreakable, and over the years Thoral had pretty much stopped worrying about snapping it. There was a deafening crack as the lock broke, and then the door creaked open. Behind it was a small chamber with nothing but a black wrought-iron staircase winding up into darkness. Thoral entered and sniffed the air.

"Cumin?" queried the fish in a whisper from Thoral's belt pouch. The warrior nodded and put a finger to his lips, signaling Brad to be quiet. The koi made a face because he felt as if he *had* been quiet. He resolved to say nothing else, not even to shout a warning if Thoral was about to get killed.

Totally missing the Brad drama, Thoral tiptoed to the bottom of the stairs and peered up. He couldn't see anything, so he started to climb, one hand on the handrail, the other holding his magic sword. As he ascended, his magic sword began to emit a pale-pink glow that reflected in his eyes. He stopped as soon as he noticed. He hadn't used the magic word that made it glow. It was glowing because unknown evil was near. That was another thing it did—but only sometimes. He hadn't quite figured out that bit.

"Evil is likely near," Thoral whispered, glancing down at Brad. "Be on your guard."

The fish held a flipper to his lips in childish retaliation, but then his eyes widened in sudden terror. The repellent figure of a terrible monstrosity was reflected in them, but Thoral didn't notice. He was shaking his head at Brad's reprimand. The creature standing on the stairs just above him was very large, with the body of a giant blond gorilla and elephant trunks for arms. Its face was so high up it was hidden in shadows that were not brightened by the flaming war hammer it clutched with the end of one elephant trunk.

Despite his earlier pissiness, Brad was about to shout a warning. Before he could, the beast smote Thoral on the head with the hammer. Thoral fell down the stairs, his tawny locks leaving a spiral trail of bad-smelling smoke as they smoldered. At the bottom, the barbarian tumbled off the steps, slid on his face across the slippery obsidian floor and slammed his head against the open bronze door, knocking it closed with an echoing *boom*.

The fiend floated down the stairs like a ghost and loomed over Thoral, who groggily got to his feet. It laughed at the swaying barbarian.

"So, Fist Wielder, we meet again," the demon rasped, bringing its flaming hammer close to light its face. The fish gasped. Necrogrond's head was attached to the giant blond ape body with iron nails and twine.

"Verily," Thoral grumbled.

"But how?" Brad asked.

"I have been given the secret of the Pudding of Immortal Life by the Bad Religion so that I might help them cleanse the elves from the land of Grome," the Necrogrond-demon roared in response. Then it leaned toward them conspiratorially. "It's actually part of a much bigger plan. There are a lot of moving parts, and the whole thing is really complicated, but the one thing I know for sure is … you're not in it!" It sprang at Thoral, and the green-burning head of its flaming hammer was the last thing the mighty warrior ever saw on Grome …

… before he rolled out of the way and didn't get killed. He sprang to his feet behind the Necrogrond-demon and gave it a ferocious spank across its hairy buttocks with the flat of his magic sword. That wasn't actually what he'd intended. He was still a little dizzy from falling down the stairs or something, but the spank was painful enough to make the monster bellow out of its mouth and both elephant trunks at the same time. The sound was frightening, and mucus splattered Thoral from head to toe.

"Run!" Brad screamed from Thoral's belt pouch.

Under normal circumstances, Thoral never ran from a fight; but his head was spinning, he was covered in mucus, he felt nauseated, and the demon's roaring was making it hard to think. So he dashed up the stairs two at a time, keeping his shoulder against the wrought-iron banister to steady himself. With his left hand, the one that wasn't holding the magic sword, he fumbled in his second pouch for the magic wand he rarely used. As his fingers found the metal rod, he considered using it, but then he decided not to. He was saving it for something really bad, and he wasn't positive that this qualified.

Up and up he raced in a tightening spiral that didn't help his queasiness, with the Necrogrond-demon huffing along behind him. Necrogrond had wasted his magic floating spell on gliding down the steps so he could look cool, but now he was regretting the choice. There were hundreds of steps. When Thoral burst from the staircase into the chamber at the top of the tower, the wheezing demon was right on his heels. The warrior was feeling even more groggy than when he first got whacked on the head. Without looking around, he raced to the far side of the room and put his back to the chamber wall. He raised *Blurmflard*'s pink, glowing blade in front of him and grimaced as two pink blades wavered before his eyes. He was seeing double now.

"What's going on?" Brad squealed, seeing how pale and shaky Thoral was.

The barbarian's only reply was a flood of vomit. He threw up all the elfish rice cookies, salted meat, and mead he'd had for brunch.

The fish could tell something was wrong. He looked around in desperation, then flung himself out of Thoral's belt pouch. He tried to clear the pool of vomit, but some got on him despite his best effort. He made a disgusted face as he flopped on the obsidian floor.

"You have defiled my inner sanctum!" Necrogrond spat as he towered over Thoral, wrinkling his nose at the barf smell.

The barbarian glared up at the monster through the tawny tangle of his singed hair and couldn't think of anything to say. He used his free hand to wipe the last of the vomit from his chin, but then regretted it because now it was all over his hand.

Necrogrond reached up to stroke his beard as he glared back at Thoral but slapped himself in the face with an elephant trunk. He was still adjusting to the new body.

"Perhaps I will make you clean this mess from my floor before I flay the skin from your very bones," Necrogrond shouted, trying to cover the awkwardness. "Perhaps I will make you lap it up like a fuzzy kitten laps up cream."

That cut it. Thoral had had enough, queasy or not. With a mighty roar, he charged the demon, his sword flashing in the flames of his opponent's burning war hammer. The weapons met with a bone-crunching clang, and Necrogrond slid backward despite his superior bulk because he was standing in the vomit and elephant-trunk mucus, and the obsidian floor was slippery to start with. Then

Thoral unleashed a flurry of fury upon his enemy. His flying blade flickered and flashed as he wove a shimmering web of magic metal, lopped the head off of the flaming hammer and plunged *Blurmflard* to its hilt in the chest of the blond gorilla body.

"Death time for you," Thoral growled, twisting the blade in the wizard's heart.

Necrogrond surprised him by laughing like crazy. "I'm totally immortal," Necrogrond tittered. "No weapon forged in this world can harm me!" He flung the useless handle of the flaming hammer aside and entwined Thoral in the crushing embrace of both of the elephant trunks, lifting him clean off the ground. Thoral kicked his feet and vomited again, but it did no good. The gorilla/elephant/immortal sorcerer combination was too much for him. He began to die—for real this time.

That's when the fish grabbed up the glowing, purple, vibrating glass vial that he had noticed sitting on a black altar on the left side of the chamber. The groggy Thoral hadn't seen it, but Brad had guessed correctly that the vial was filled with a magic pudding emitting a sickening vibration that caused Thoral's nausea. Being a fish, Brad wasn't susceptible to that kind of thing. He raised the vial aloft and, with a mighty cry, smashed it to the obsidian floor.

"Nooooo!" shouted Necrogrond's head and the two elephant trunks in slightly discordant tones that throbbed annoyingly through the air.

Thoral knew this was called tonal phase shifting or harmonic dissonance or something. He couldn't remember exactly. He wanted to ask Brad, but there was no time. The demon dropped Thoral to the floor.

Thoral shook his head to clear it, as if awakening from a fiendish nightmare into an even more fiendish reality. He got to his feet and stood in the middle of the chamber. He faced the towering demon and growled. The beast shrugged its elephant-trunk arms. Thoral raised his hand, the one that didn't already have vomit on it, and wiped a thick stream of blood from his forehead. His eyes narrowed, and violet fire seemed to kindle in their depths as he examined the blood on his knuckles.

"Right," he roared. Then he unleashed the full power of his mighty fists on Necrogrond. He tore both of the elephant trunks off the gorilla body and threw them across the room just missing the fish. The trunks splatted against the black altar and writhed around like huge worms. Thoral then leapt upon the demon and the two fell to the floor, flopping about in the combined pool of elephant-trunk mucus, vomit and glowing purple pudding. They thrashed and splashed in a frenzy of fighting, flinging gick everywhere. Although its elephant trunk arms were ripped off, the gorilla body had dexterous feet, and Necrogrond made good use of them in scratching and pinching his opponent.

But Thoral prevailed, punching and slapping with his mighty fists until the demon body was just a sloppy pile of parts and lots of thick, black blood which mixed with the other fluids. Still flailing at the pile, Thoral was surprised because, even then, Necrogrond wasn't dead. The parts wiggled and squirmed and reached for him. The whole while, Necrogrond's head shouted and screamed in a wordless fit from where it lay on the floor.

Thoral stood up and glared at the head until it shut up. Necrogrond was a mess. He had mucus and vomit and glowing purple pudding and clotty blood all over his thick black beard. The twine that had secured his head to the gorilla body was tangled in it too. He flicked his eyes to the mangled gorilla parts and then back to Thoral. The sorcerer's face contorted in rage and he seemed about to say something nasty. Instead, his head inflated and then exploded in a cloud of pink mist that sprayed in Thoral's and Brad's eyes.

The warrior and the fish stood panting and wiping at their faces. Then the whole tower melted around them like a giant black Fudgesicle until they were standing on the ground in a widening puddle of tarry liquid. Warlordhorse blinked at them from where he was grazing on some dead grass.

Just then, the elfish army rode up. They numbered a thousand and two. King Elfrod sat at their head riding bareback upon his snowy-white unicorn, Flug. His daughter was seated behind him, with her arms around his waist. Apparently, the elves never used saddles. The elfish princess slipped from the unicorn even before the beast had come to a stop. Elfrod clutched at her cloak so that she was running in place for a second, but she shrugged it off and ran to Thoral, arms wide to hug him. She didn't seem to care about the mucus, the vomit, the glowing purple pudding, the clotted black blood or the coating of pink Necrogrond head-splatter. Thoral fended her off with one sinewy arm because he didn't want to mess up her fetching riding outfit and because he hadn't had a good opportunity to check her for head lice.

"Thoral," she cried in joy, still trying to get at him.

King Elfrod nodded sagely. "Thoral," he announced, handing his daughter's cloak to one of his retainers, "you have defeated the unknown force. My people and I are deeply grateful." Then he bestowed upon Thoral a magic ring.

It was one of the great Rings of Looks that were made in the mid-elder days, back when they had that kind of skill. No one knew how to make them anymore, so it was a pretty amazing gift. It cleaned the goop off Thoral the second he donned it. Now Thoral relented and let the elfish princess hug him with her full ardor. The great Rings of Looks were proof against lice and other vermin. He breathed in the fresh smell of her recently washed hair as she snuggled him, and a slight smile touched his manly lips. Elfrod watched the snuggling with growing discomfort, as did Brad.

Thoral didn't notice, so the fish started to clamber up his leg and cleared his throat.

"It is true that we have destroyed the unknown force, which actually turned out to be this guy we killed once before," the koi declared, settling himself back in Thoral's belt pouch. "But those who gave him immortality are still at large. I speak of the Bad Religion."

"The Bad Religion?" Elfrod gasped. All around him, other elves suddenly appeared ill.

"Verily," Thoral confirmed. "Worry not. We are going to kill them."

"Thoral," the princess protested, her big emerald eyes filling with concern, "surely you cannot mean to face those evil minions of darkness and despair on your own."

"Ahem!" Brad coughed from the pouch.

"Not on my own, Princess. I will have Brad and Warlordhorse with me. We cannot turn away. Our task is not yet..." he trailed off. "What word indicates when a task has been completed?"

"Finished," Brad supplied.

"Our task is not yet finished," the warrior said.

"Then you must ride with my father's army," the princess told him.

"Ahem." King Elfrod cleared his throat. "Actually, we have some other business to which we must attend first, business of which you are well aware, Daughter. So it is fine if Thoral and his fish and his horse want to get started without us. We will catch up later."

"Then I will accompany him and aid in his battle myself," she snapped back.

"You have an appointment," Elfrod reminded her, his voice cold.

"Father!" the princess cried in distress.

"We work better on our own anyway," Brad informed her from the warrior's waist. "We're not much for ... attachments." He waved a fin at her and the gathered army.

The princess shot the fish a jealous look then glanced up at Thoral, trying to lock his startling violet eyes with her intense emerald ones.

"Oft, more can be accomplished with a small band than with a large force," the warrior grumbled, avoiding her stare.

"So you're just going to ride off then?" the princess demanded. Her expression softened. "I was hoping you would return with us to Creekenvalley so that we might discuss...an issue of significant import."

"Daughter," the king interrupted, a warning in his voice. The princess glared at him.

"Sorry, Princess," Brad reminded, "We've got people to kill. We're in kind of a hurry."

She eyed her father and the fish defiantly then shifted her focus back to Thoral. Before he realized what she was doing, she stepped in close, went up on tiptoes and kissed him.

It had been a long time since Thoral had been kissed. Not that lots of women hadn't tried. He'd rebuffed them all. Now, he froze stiff as a board. But under the gentle warmth of the princess's lips, he thawed. He closed his violet eyes. The tension went out of his massive frame. He drew her close, returning the kiss, crushing her to himself in his powerful embrace. Thoral did not notice Brad give a muffled cry of dismay as he was smooshed between their bodies. Instead, the warrior's world seemed to melt down to a single point that existed entirely between his lips and those of the princess. It was pretty nice.

"Yo! Thoral!" Brad yelled, squeezing his head out from between them. The barbarian came to his senses, breaking the kiss. He opened his eyes just as the princess was opening hers. She appeared dazed. Everyone was staring at them. Elfrod glared from the back of his unicorn. Brad glared from Thoral's belt pouch. Even one of the elves' horses was glaring.

"I needs must go," Thoral whispered to the princess. Then, before she could work her wiles on him any further, he turned, vaulted onto Warlordhorse's back and rode off into the night like a hot wind.

CHAPTER SEVEN

In the Western Wastes

Thoral and Brad rode Warlordhorse along the Crumble Road in the Western Wastes under the deadly hot sun of midday. Sand, shimmering in the heat, spread out in every direction. Thoral was half drunk on mead. He had sand in his butt crack, which he hated, and he was glistening with sweat, which he hated. Even the fish was sweaty. Brad rubbed himself on Thoral's canteen whenever the warrior wasn't paying attention. The rubbing just made the mead warmer instead of making the koi cooler. Thoral snapped at Brad every time he caught him with the canteen. They had been searching for the fortress of the Bad Religion for several weeks, but it was difficult to find, and no one they encountered wanted to talk about it for fear of getting killed—or worse. Now they were lost in the middle of the desert. Warlordhorse whinnied plaintively.

"I know, old friend," Thoral murmured, patting the horse's neck. He was always kind to that horse, even when he was crabby.

"How much longer are we going to wander these wastes?" the fish asked, pressing a damp rag to the scales at the back of his head.

"Until we find the holdfast of the Bad Religion and blot them from Grome like one blots a stain from one's carpet," Thoral grumbled. Brad grumped in silence.

Right then they came to a tumbledown sign at the side of the road. An arrow pointing off to the west was painted with the peeling word FLIGRYNGEN. Thoral stared blearily at the sign for a long time. Then he began to sing in a high, clear voice that was rather grating. He was not known for his singing, but he was half drunk.

"In the Western Waste,
Near Fligryngen,
A warrior
Was wanderin'.
The wife and babe
He left behind
Were never absent
From his mind.
From his mind were never absent they!
Sing hey ho, hey ho, diddly hey!

And a doorway in a tree was he seeking.
And a magic doorway in a magic tree was he seeking.
Always seeking.
That mysterious magic doorway in that magic walking tree he was seeking.

But as he strode
Far desert sands
An evil grode
With bloody hands
His humble home
Did sneak into
And in the gloom
Did tear in two..."

High above them, a flying squirrel wheeled on the currents of hot air and cringed at the faint sound of Thoral's song. It took in all the details of this ragtag band for its evil master, the Heartless One, as it soared on the thermal. It was just getting ready to glide away to report when it felt a sharp pain in its belly. Examining its midsection, it discovered that Thoral had shot it with his mighty yew bow, *Fwang*, and that the arrow was sticking about a foot and a half out of either side of its body.

"Jiminy!" the squirrel squeaked before plummeting like a stone to the searing sands of the Wastes. The fall, combined with the arrow, nearly killed it, but it was still a little bit alive when Thoral snatched it up from the ground by its bushy black tail and swung its broken body close to his face.

"'Tis a grasthling," said he, examining the glossy black fur and cute face. "A talking flying squirrel of Wurmf that the elves call nunghees. Oft are these rodents pressed into foul service as spies of evildoers."

"I will…tell you…nothing of my…evil master," the squirrel gasped, coughing a spray of bright blood that nearly got on Thoral.

"These squirrels taste pretty good cooked with a little lemon and butter," Brad suggested, licking his chapped lips. Thoral narrowed his eyes as he considered the broken thing. Her little pink tongue hung out of her tiny mouth, and her pretty brown eyes were half closed.

"No," he grumbled. He dismounted and pulled his special sleeping blanket from the watertight saddlebag made from sheeps' bladders, where he stored all his spare clothing and the specially made paper he used for wiping his behind. Most people of Grome used moss or sponges on sticks or hay, but Thoral was pretty particular about wiping. He spread the blanket on the sand and laid the flying squirrel upon it, spread-eagled, then returned to his saddlebags and rummaged for the incredibly sharp dagger that he usually reserved for shaving. The grasthling whimpered at the sight of the gleaming blade and made a half-hearted attempt to roll onto her belly and crawl away by dragging herself with her broken little arms, but Thoral straddled her and held her still. Warlordhorse cocked his noble head to one side in puzzlement, but the fish narrowed his eyes in suspicion.

"This will hurt mayhap," Thoral admitted. The mighty warrior cradled the squirrel's broken body and deftly cut the shaft of the protruding arrow so that he could work the two halves out of the pierced flesh without further damage. Then he took a golden pudding from his turquoise belt pouch and smeared a small dollop along the wounds. They sealed so quickly that his finger almost got stuck inside the rodent.

Now even the grasthling was puzzled. "Why do you mend me, barbarian?" the squirrel mewled in her totally cute, high-pitched voice.

"Thy broken arm bones must needs be set if thou art ever to fly again," Thoral noted, ignoring the squirrel's query. Then, before she could worry about it, he seized her by her tiny paws and pulled them quite hard in opposite directions to snap the broken bones back into alignment. The grasthling gasped in pain, her eyes rolled up in her little head, and she passed out. Thoral smeared a pea-sized amount of healing pudding onto her rough tongue and rubbed her throat until she swallowed it.

"Oh, brother. Here we go again!" Brad spat, disgusted. "That stuff costs a fortune, and those arrows aren't cheap either!"

"Mayhap this squirrel has some knowledge of the whereabouts of the fortress of the Bad Religion or will prove useful in some way we cannot yet fathom," Thoral retorted, but the fish could see that he blushed a little.

"You always do this," the koi goaded him.

"'Tis midday and high time we found some shelter from this pounding sunshine," the warrior gruffed. He stalked off toward the shade of a nearby boulder, dragging the squirrel on the blanket through the sand behind him. The fish and Warlordhorse exchanged looks. Then the horse shrugged and followed Thoral's trail.

Hours later, as the heat relented, the fish rolled over on his sleeping mat. His bloodshot eyes fell on Thoral. The barbarian was crouched over the squirrel, dabbing a cool cloth to her forehead as she muttered in unconscious delirium. Brad shook his head and tried to get back to sleep.

CHAPTER EIGHT

Into the Frying Pot

As the last rays of the sun shimmered like the heat off a hot fry pot, Thoral roused Warlordhorse and the fish. "It is cool enough to resume our search," he announced.

Brad glanced over to where the grasthling sat on the sandy ground sipping water through an improvised straw, her little arms cradled in tiny slings of fabric cut from Thoral's spare shirt. She was essentially healed, but she looked back at the fish with sad eyes.

"At least question your stupid flying squirrel," Brad demanded. Thoral frowned mightily, but even Warlordhorse was staring at him, so he squatted before the squirrel.

"We need information," he said. The squirrel dropped her gaze to her tiny little hands.

"We have ways of making you talk," the fish added ominously.

"I can't tell you anything," the squirrel protested, biting her teensy lip. "If I do, the Bad Religion will kill my husband and child."

"Yeah, right," Brad laughed and pretended to play a tiny viol (violins hadn't been invented at that time).

"Quiet, fish," Thoral barked. Brad looked startled, then stung.

"What is thy name?" Thoral asked the squirrel in a soft voice.

"Tyncie CheeChaw CheeChee WeeWaw," she quavered, unable to meet the fire of his penetrating violet gaze.

"Your kind was not always in the service of evil, Tyncie CheeChaw CheeChee WeeWaw," Thoral declared. "The elfish king, Elfrod, tells that the noble grasthlings were once friends to elf and man—and seven dwarves—but were bent to darkness against their will by the evil lords of the Bad Religion. It is for this reason only that I do not torture answers from thee, even unto thy death."

Now Tyncie gazed up at him with wonder in her eyes. "You won't kill me?" she asked.

"Nay," said Warlordhorse. It was one of his few words, and he was pretty sure it was what Thoral was planning to say.

The fish looked annoyed, but Thoral nodded. "Yes," he confirmed. "Nay. That is; No, we will not. Kill you, I mean."

"You have my gratitude, kindly warrior," Tyncie said in a teensy whisper.

"You can't let her go, Thoral," Brad objected. "She'll betray us to the Bad Religion!"

"And yet, it is my plan to let her go," Thoral admitted.

"If you can call that a plan," the fish shouted. "It will be the death of us!"

Thoral just puffed out his cheeks and raised his eyebrows in a mute signal of apparent helplessness in the face of his own seemingly dumb plan.

Two minutes later, Thoral, Warlordhorse and the fish watched the dwindling speck of Tyncie as she soared off into the shimmering heat of the Western Wastes. Brad was still pretty steamed.

"That was foolish," he scolded. He wanted to fold his fins across his chest to underscore his anger, but they weren't placed properly for that kind of thing, so he put them on his hips. Then he felt kind of effeminate, so he turned his back on the flying squirrel as she vanished from view.

"Perhaps not as foolish as you might think, fish," Thoral confided in a low voice. Brad turned to the warrior, one eyebrow raised. "Inside Tyncie's wound I secreted a magic trinket that calls out to this second magic trinket through principles of ethereal vibration." Thoral held aloft a blue orb the size of a mouse's eyeball. "She will soon lead us right to the fortress of the Bad Religion." Thoral tossed the magic trinket in the air and caught it with a flourish. He winked at Brad.

"You fox!" the fish giggled, relieved. And with that, he leapt back into Thoral's belt pouch, Thoral leapt back into Warlordhorse's saddle, and Warlordhorse leapt back into a gallop. The three of them thundered westward toward the descending orb of the sun.

CHAPTER NINE

The Rotten Teeth of Danger

Some days later, following the vibrations of the magic trinket, they had passed the edge of the desert and were hacking their way through a dead forest of withered trees when they came upon a disused path. They followed the path until it wound past an abandoned log cabin. Thoral and Warlordhorse stopped in their tracks so suddenly that Brad almost ran into them. Horse and man gaped at the ruin. Although it had once been a quaint and charming little cottage, there was a giant hole torn through the splintered timbers of one wall that had partially collapsed the thatched roof and stone chimney many years, perhaps decades ago. Thoral and Warlordhorse stood gaping at the wreck in silence for such a long time that Brad started to wonder if something was wrong. He was just about to ask, when the big barbarian started toward it. The warrior led the way, picking a path through the remains of a ruined and overgrown garden to what had once been the front door. There he stooped to pull a cracked and faded board from where it lay tangled in thorny vines. Although almost illegible, the words "Home Sweet Home" were still visible in flaked and peeling blue paint. Thoral's hands trembled as he held it, then he placed it on the remains of the shattered front door with great care. He was pale as he told the fish and the horse to wait outside while he went in to examine the place. He was gone for quite a while, during which time Warlordhorse launched into a long and rambling speech composed of nickers and whinnies and other horse noises. It was clear he was trying to say something important, but the fish didn't have a clue what he was going on about. The tiger-striped stallion finally gave up in frustration. A moment later, Thoral emerged from the cabin, wiping his eyes and sniffling.

"There is considerable dust within," he muttered and blew his nose. Warlordhorse nuzzled the barbarian, but Thoral said nothing more. Then the companions continued on through the forest.

It was spooky and Warlordhorse and the fish were on edge, but Thoral seemed the most agitated. He kept looking around and muttering to himself. Every time he did, Brad would ask, "What's that? What did you say?" But instead of taking the hint, Thoral would make no answer except to deepen his frown, his brow creased in anger or some other dark emotion. Finally, the fish couldn't take it anymore.

"What's going on?" he asked the warrior as Thoral stopped to swill some wine from a wine bag he'd bought from a traveling mercenary.

"I know this forest," Thoral offered, wiping his mouth. "It holds dark memories for me."

"Do tell," said Brad.

"They are from another life," Thoral answered, and Warlordhorse nodded as if he knew what the warrior meant.

"A literal former life or a metaphoric one?" the koi asked. You could never tell in Grome.

Thoral just grunted, leaving his companion to draw his own conclusions. The fish didn't know all that much about Thoral's life before that fateful day, years ago, when the warrior had saved the koi from drowning. In fact, as the fish thought about it, he realized that he had never met anyone who knew that much about Thoral. The tawny-haired warrior was only referred to as a barbarian because no one knew where he came from, not because he had bad table manners or poor grooming habits. And no one else the fish had met had Thoral's eye color. There wasn't even a word for that eye color in Gromish. But Thoral was not one for opening up about himself. He generally let his fists do his talking, and although they were persuasive, they were relatively inarticulate.

"So, Thoral," Brad began, and that was when Warlordhorse whinnied, rolling his eyes. It was that Brendylschmylyn danger-smelling thing again.

Thoral's nostrils flared as he sniffed the air. "Dost thou smell that?" he asked, his every muscle and sinew stiffening. The fish inhaled, and an overpowering smell of rotten flesh seasoned with anise filled his head.

"Gross. What is it?" the fish asked.

"I should recognize that foul stench even in a storm of a million other stomach-turning odors," Thoral whispered, his breath catching in his throat. "'Tis a grode." He didn't need to say more. The fish had heard tales of grodes and understood the danger they were in.

"Let's get out of here," Brad whispered. "We can just detour around its territory and avoid it." There was a strange look in Thoral's eyes that made the fish uneasy. "What's going on, Thoral?"

"Warlordhorse," the warrior breathed, "take Brad and head due north until you have cleared the grode's territory. Wait for me there. With luck, I will rejoin you in two day's span. If I do not, know that I am slain or so seriously injured as to be essentially slain."

Warlordhorse stamped a hoof and snorted in defiance.

"What *he* said," Brad seconded.

Thoral was touched. "My fine and true friends," he sighed, lifting Brad and holding him up near Warlordhorse's face so he could look the two of them in their four eyes at once, "though I am sworn to seek the fortress of the Bad Religion, I must needs fight this fiend first. We are enemies of old, and I am sworn to an older swear than the swear I swore when I swore to the elves. If my intentions prove to be untenable, you need not perish in the pursuit of the sweet and bitter comeuppance I intend to deal upon this grode."

The fish and the horse looked at each other out of the corners of their eyes. It was sometimes hard to follow the things Thoral said.

"If you mean that you're going to go fight the grode, we're going with you," Brad declared finally. Warlordhorse nodded.

Thoral closed his eyes and nodded too, keeping his lips tight. When he looked up, it was with grim resolve etched upon his features. "Then into the rotten teeth of danger we stride," he growled.

***

Not long thence, Thoral parted some gnarled tree branches and peeked between them toward a lair built of piled human bones entwined with human hair and scattered with human teeth. Flies buzzed above it in thick clouds. The stench of death hung heavy in the air as a visible fume that crawled down the sides of the bone pile and across the desolate ground like a poisonous fog.

Brad climbed onto Thoral's shoulder and peered out from beneath the tangle of Thoral's tawny hair at the edifice of death that was the grode's den. "Crap," he said under his breath, and as they watched, something large stirred within and reared its ugly head. Warlordhorse, the fish and the barbarian ducked as a giant bull grode stood, its back to them. It stretched its battle-scarred bulk, its iridescent fuchsia scales shimmering. Then it raised its piggish nose and smelled the air. Its distinctive purple-and-teal-feathered crest rose in a classic threat display.

Thoral tensed. Only one grode had a purple-and-teal crest.

A blinding rage flared in the warrior's violet eyes. As he drew *Blurmflard*, the blade glowed such a bright pink that the fish and the horse had to avert their eyes, and the bones of the hand in which Thoral clutched the hilt were silhouetted through his skin.

"Evil monster!" Thoral yelled, pushing through the tangled branches. Still on his shoulder, a surprised Brad crouched down and tried to hide in the cascade of Thoral's tawny hair while Warlordhorse watched through the trees, his eyes showing white all around. "Evil monster," Thoral continued, "long have I sought thee that I might bring about thy doom." His words boomed through the wizened and skeletal trees of that murky forest, but the beast did not seem afraid. It merely laughed in a low and throaty chuckle.

"What is this?!" the grode bellowed, spraying a thick mist of spittle that killed every fly it touched so that they fell out of the air like a blanket. "A puny human dares to challenge me?"

Thoral's affirmative reply was drowned out as the grode tilted its head to the sky and roared so loud that the rest of the flies died from shock. Brad trembled, but Thoral stood steadfast before the beast.

"I have come to claim my vengeance," Thoral spat.

"Vengeance?" the grode mused, stretching its muscles in preparation for battle. It cracked its neck and then each knuckle of its great chicken-like forefeet.

"Yes, vengeance," Thoral shouted. "Vengeance for the killing of my wife and infant son." He was still mad about that.

"Your what?" Brad hissed near the barbarian's ear. Thoral did not notice.

"Thoral Mighty Fist?" the beast growled around its mouthful of razor-sharp tusks as it peered at the warrior.

Warlordhorse pushed through the trees and came up beside the warrior.

"Ah, and you've brought your donkey as well." The grode pulled out its whip of green flames and towered over Thoral and his steed. The thing was at least nine feet tall, not counting the plume on its head which added another foot and a half. The grode started to say something else, but Thoral sprang on it, and in the frenzy of that first attack it forgot what it was going to say.

Thoral hacked at the beast, but it ducked his blow. Unfazed, Thoral did a super-high jump and kicked the evil monster in the throat with both feet at the same time. It was a trick he had learned from a talking kangaroo. That blow would have crushed the larynx of a lesser beast, but grodes don't have larynxes. Instead of dying, the grode wrapped Thoral's legs in the burning embrace of the five tails of the green-flaming whip. That stung like a swarm of hornets, but the barbarian didn't even yell as he crashed to the forest floor on his buttocks. Jarred by the impact, his sword and the fish skittered away across the scattered bones that littered the ground. Brad bumped up against a skull and lay there, stunned.

Thoral got to his feet and stood in the middle of the clearing. He faced the towering grode, who smiled and cracked his whip. Thoral raised his hand and wiped a trickle of blood from his right ear where the skin was broken. He was just about to look at the blood when the grode backhanded him so ferociously that he saw not the blood on his fingers but the trail of blood that arced behind him through the air as he flew. He crumpled to the ground, and dirt got into the cut in his ear.

"I'd tell you that I enjoyed killing your wife and child just to rub it in," the grode rasped, "I've killed so many wives and children, though, that I don't remember yours specifically." Then the grode rushed at the weaponless, wounded, weakened warrior, and at that moment it really seemed as if Thoral would lose. Seriously. He was totally defenseless.

But Warlordhorse rushed in and kicked the grode right in the chest with both back hooves. The fish, having come to his senses, tossed Thoral his glowing-pink sword. With a roar, the warrior hewed off the grode's head so that it spun through the air in slow motion and fell to the ground, severed-neck end first. Dirt mixed with blood and stuck to the neck. The head stayed alive just long enough to think about how gross this was.

Thoral stood staring at the severed head for a long time after the last light of life had faded from its beady eyes. Warlordhorse came over and nuzzled his tawny hair. Brad flopped up behind them.

"I had no idea you used to have a wife and kid," the fish stammered. "And that grode…that grode killed them?" He put a comforting fin on his friend's ankle, but the barbarian said nothing. His gaze never wavered from the bloodshot eyes of the beast.

Thoral had kind of expected that killing the grode would bring him some sort of closure or peace concerning the deaths of his wife and child. Instead, he felt hollow to the center of his being. It was like an aching emptiness right in his aorta.

Thoral raised his face to the sky and let out a strangled howl of pain and rage. Then he jumped on the grode's head with both his iron-toed boots and kicked it and stomped it and mushed it until it turned to paste. Then he kicked the paste until it was so mixed up with the torn grass and mud that it couldn't be seen anymore. He felt a little better after that, but still....

"Hey," called the fish, trying to distract Thoral, "there's some treasure and things over here...if you're interested."

Thoral walked to where Brad stood peering into the grode's lair. Sure enough, there were some gold coins and some items that were probably magical, including a telescope with glowing glyphs and a promising ball of sparkly yarn. Thoral poked through the pile with the tip of *Blurmflard* because a lot of the stuff had poop on it, and he didn't want to touch any of it until they'd had a chance to wash it. Then something caught his eye, and he gasped. It was a large silver locket on a silver chain.

Thoral would have recognized that locket anywhere because he was pretty certain it was the only one of its kind in the whole land of Grome. It was wrought in a circle, about three-and-a-half inches around, with an engraving on the cover of two dolphins leaping to kiss so that the space between their bodies made the shape of a heart. In the middle of the heart was a strange rune that was actually the letter *N* in Thoral's native tongue. Thoral had given it to his wife as a token of his love before they were married. As it turned out, she had an aversion to dolphins, but she had pretended to like the locket anyway and wore it everywhere because she didn't want to hurt his feelings. Also, there was something significant hidden inside it.

Thoral wrapped his hand in the remains of the spare shirt he'd ruined making the slings for Tyncie's broken arms and plucked the locket from the pile. He stood staring at it as it dangled from his fist. He couldn't bring himself to open it, not yet. Maybe after he'd had it cleaned. Sighing, he wrapped it in the bit of cloth and tucked it into his bag of magic items.

"We can go now," he remarked. "It is time to wipe out the Bad Religion."

CHAPTER TEN

Ominous Portents of Doom

"That darn squirrel!" Brad complained from his perch on top of Warlordhorse's noble head. Almost two weeks after the battle with the grode, the three companions were headed back to their starting point. They had halted on the high plains of Plint with the city of Reefma spread below them like a large ink stain no more than half a day's further ride. "She's leading us in circles."

"Well, *a* circle," Thoral grumped, massaging his forehead with one hand. He was nursing a hangover because he'd been drinking a lot since the encounter with the grode. Unfortunately, he'd run out of wine the day before.

"Fine then, *a* circle," the fish amended testily. "Are you sure your magic tracking thing actually works?"

"I am certain. The grasthling is in Reefma." Despite Thoral's confident tone, he shot a surreptitious glance at the tiny vibrating ball perched in its special holder on his saddle horn to make sure the glowing dot was still pointing at the city.

"Is it possible she's onto us? That she knows about the device? That she's leading us into some kind of ambush?" Brad wondered aloud.

"Mayhap," Thoral grumbled.

"Mayhap? That's all you've got to say? Mayhap?"

"I do not think Tyncie would betray us," Thoral elaborated.

"Why? Because she's cute and cuddly?" the fish exploded. He didn't literally explode because someone had cast a deadly exploding spell on him. He just said the words in an explosive way.

"No," Thoral countered. "Not because of that."

"Why then?" Brad demanded.

Thoral's lips formed a tight line.

The three of them sat there.

Glaring at his silent companion, the koi suddenly remembered that he had resolved to be more sensitive to Thoral's emotional needs because of the whole thing with his dead wife and kid. "Look, I'm sorry," Brad said more gently.

Thoral met his bulging eyes and nodded. The fish stared back, then turned and, shading his gaze from the rays of the rising sun with a fin, looked down on the sprawling city. "What's a flying squirrel doing in Reefma?" he mused, shaking his head.

Warlordhorse snorted as if to say, "What indeed?" Then he tensed, his ears twitching with alarm.

"What is it, old friend?" Thoral asked, his hand going to the hilt of his magic sword.

"Over there!" Brad pointed to their left at a group of riders approaching at a gallop. There were about a half dozen. Thoral's eagle-sharp eyes were the first to discern the nature of the riders.

"Ho and well met, elf folk and Lord Elfrod!" he called, raising his hand in salute. Then his countenance grew troubled by the cranky expressions of the elves.

"Hail, Thoral Mighty Fist," Elfrod called back as he clomped up on a delicate black stallion, reining his steed in beside Warlordhorse so that the two men were facing each other, side by side. He frowned at Thoral. So did his horse. Thoral was pretty sure it was the same horse that had glared at him earlier, when the princess kissed him.

"Something is amiss." Thoral frowned back at the king. "Where is thy unicorn, Flug?"

The elf lord's scowl deepened. "Ah and woe," he cried. "My daughter hath taken Flug and absconded. I ride now with my elite Elf Force to retrieve her." He gestured to the half-dozen, long-haired, pointy-eared warriors behind him, all of whom were female. It was well known that girl elves were the toughest, most dangerous fighters. And they weren't bad to look at either.

"Absconded? But why?" Thoral asked, his brow creasing in puzzlement.

"She left this note," the king answered, holding out a scroll of parchment to the barbarian.

Thoral took it gingerly, as if somewhat reluctant. As he unrolled the scroll, the fish slid down Warlordhorse's neck and perched upon his friend's saddle in order to peer at the document as well. The note was written in Elvish, in a fine and decisive hand:

Dear Father, Elfrod, king of the elves of Creekenvalley and keeper of the box of power,

A vision did I have within a dream this very night, that a death horn blew and there was much mourning in the Black Gem, the city that men call Reefma. All around were throngs dressed in black, and someone hurled at me a silver locket, engraved in the likeness of two dolphins leaping to kiss so that the empty space between their bodies formed the shape of a heart. Within that heart was carven a strange rune, which was actually the letter N, *which is the first letter of mine own name! The locket opened, and I glimpsed through it, as through a window, Thoral, the Fist Wielder, lying as if dead, his head hewed off. At that sight, my spirit quailed within me and I woke!*

Father! Dear Father! I must needs do something! By the time you read these words, I will have taken Flug, thy sweet unicorn steed, and left for Reefma to warn Thoral of these ominous portents of doom, for he is my special friend whom I hold dear. I know this will significantly upset our weekend plans, but I cannot participate in that joyous celebration when one for whom I truly care is in such grave danger.

Thoral frowned. He hated prophecies, premonitions and precognitions, especially the ones about his own death.

"These are foul portents," he noted.

"Indeed," agreed the king. Then he urged his horse right up beside Warlordhorse so that he was close enough for Thoral to smell that he'd had garlic in his breakfast. He fixed the barbarian with his piercing, sea-green eyes. "She hath called you her 'special friend,' Thoral."

Thoral blushed to the roots of his tawny mane. "Uhhh," he stammered. "I...um...that is to say that we have not...um...I mean..."

"He didn't even know her name began with the letter *N*," Brad interjected from the warrior's shoulder.

Now Elfrod's eyes seemed to flare with a dangerous light. "Hearken close and mind my words, Mighty Fist. You saved my fair child from that necromancer, and for that I am grateful," the elf king spoke. "But a relationship between you is problematic for a number of reasons. Although she is seventeen and three hundred years old, capable of deciding her own course, she will always be my little girl and I, her father. Since that fateful day when her mother, Blindelweegie, rode the giant white pigeon back to that land over the sea where the elves go when they're tired of humans, my daughter is all I have and the sole heir to the throne of Creekenvalley. She is enamored of you, and she's been obvious about her affections, but I'm not too clear on your position in regard to her. What are your intentions toward my daughter?"

"'Tis complicated, my friend," Thoral began, but the elf king put a hand on his forearm and cut him off right there.

Elfrod dropped his other hand to the hilt of his magic sword, *Krandarthnak*, the Fang of Light. All around them, the warrior women of the king's Elf Force drew their blades. Elfrod's horse glared at Thoral.

"For the moment, 'tis probably best that you remember that I am king of the elves and keeper of the box of power first and your friend second," Elfrod snarled, a clear note of menace in his voice. He was pinching Thoral's forearm pretty hard. "So, it is complicated, is it? Then explain it to me."

"Hey, hey!" Brad cut in. "Let's not get crazy here. If you'll allow me, your highness, I think I can clear this up." The king shifted his penetrating gaze to the fish, who swallowed audibly and then began. "When he met your daughter, Thoral wasn't looking for a romantic relationship. I mean, he had no idea she was even in that tower. I found her. See, the thing is that he was still seeking vengeance for the death of his wife and child, and without that closure, he didn't really consider himself, you know, on the market. But then, just a few days ago, he killed the grode that killed his wife, and since then he's been talking about your girl quite a bit."

"Is this true?" the king demanded.

"Uh…I …," Thoral stammered.

"Do you return her affections?"

"Well," the warrior stammered, "I…well…Yes. At least, that is to say that I was thinking that after I wiped out the Bad Religion, perhaps she and I…Well, I thought…Of course, with your permission…But also, I intended…That is to say that I was thinking…because we kissed, you see…But not if she was not of a like mind…And certainly, not before the destruction of the Bad Religion…" He trailed off, looking helpless despite his massive strength.

The elf king considered him for a long moment, his piercing eyes locked on Thoral's violet ones. The barbarian struggled not to blink. Elfrod released Thoral's arm, leaving a red mark that was going to turn into a bruise.

"I am satisfied for the moment," the king announced finally. He slapped the warrior on his thickly muscled back and forced a somewhat awkward laugh, as if the whole thing had been a joke. Brad sagged in relief. Thoral forced a laugh of his own while the Elf Force ladies sheathed their weapons in perfect unison except for the two youngest ones, who sheathed theirs too, but their timing was off, and one of the older ladies shot them a withering look.

"So what now?" Elfrod asked.

"I suggest we ride into the city and find your daughter," Brad began, "so that you can take her back to the safety of Windendale, your hidden home—"

"Creekenvalley," Elfrod interrupted. "We elves call it Creekenvalley. We have our own names for everything."

"Yes," Brad allowed. "You can take your daughter back to … Creekenvalley … before we find the flying squirrel we're searching for so we can finish tracking the Bad Religion to their lair and slaughter them," the fish replied. "First, perhaps you might tell us the fair princess's name?"

"She is called Nalweegie, the Evening Snack," Elfrod revealed, "because to look on her in twilight quells the hunger of one's heart without making one feel overfull, as can happen with a more substantial meal."

"Nalweegie," Thoral murmured. The king nodded sagely. Brad rolled his eyes.

CHAPTER ELEVEN

Bankruptcy

Around lunchtime, the companions and the elves rode up to the western gate of Reefma, called the Broken Gate. Even the elves called it that because it *was* broken. They were all hungry because they hadn't had time to eat, and Thoral was getting a little shaky from lack of alcohol. Two tired city guards in dirty black armor and brown-plumed helmets blocked their way with crossed halberds. One was eating a baked yam on a stick.

"Halt," demanded the guy on the right.

"Yeah," said the guy on the left. He was the one with the yam.

"We seek entry into the city," the captain of the Elf Force, Nimrodingle, told them with a courteous bow. She was tall and golden haired, attractive in a stern and butt-kicking kind of way. She appeared to be in her late thirties, but she was actually seventeen hundred and four.

"This is the Broken Gate. You have to pay one copper coin as a fee to enter here so we can get the gate fixed," the guy with the yam explained around a mouthful. "Each. It's on account of the city bankruptcy."

Nimrodingle raised her eyebrows and shot a look at Elfrod, her storm-cloud-gray eyes flashing.

"Bankruptcy is a terrible thing and often no one's fault," the elf king noted sagely. He nodded to his captain, and she reached into her coin bag to dig out eight copper coins, one for each of the riders.

"None of these horses are talking horses, are they?" the guard inquired casting a suspicious eye on the animals. "They're a coin apiece, too."

Nimrodingle shot another surreptitious look at Elfrod. The elf king gave an almost imperceptible shake of his head, so the captain didn't say anything about the king's steed. The delicate black stallion dropped its gaze to the ground.

"We seek an elfish princess riding a unicorn," Thoral informed them, coming to the front as the guard with the yam was counting the money.

"Oh, hey, Thoral," the guard without the yam greeted, waving to the barbarian as he recognized him. "Black hair, green eyes? That the one?"

"Well met, Trenton," Thoral waved back to the guard without the yam. "Verily. Did she pass this gate?"

"Yeah, we let her in just after dawn," Trenton answered.

"She did not happen to say where she was going, by any chance?" Thoral asked.

"Well," confided the yam-eating guard, "she was acting pretty melodramatic, kind of lost and weepy, and she was hard to understand, what with the heavy Elvish accent, but she said something about searching for a tremendously precious treasure to complete her heart. I thought she was probably speaking metaphorically, but Trenton told her that her best bet was the Bazaar on Strange Street. You can get almost anything there."

"Oh, great," Brad piped in, poking his head up out of Thoral's belt pouch. "That place is full of smugglers, con men, and thieves."

"Oh, hey, Brad," Trenton waved to the fish.

"Hey, Trenton," the koi waved back.

"Do we need to charge an extra coin for the fish?" Trenton asked his fellow guard.

"No, talking animals are free if they can be carried or ride on a lap," the yam-eater advised.

The transaction complete, the party filed through the Broken Gate, but as Thoral was passing by, Trenton motioned him closer.

"There was a strange fellow asking about you," the guard confided in an undertone, "dressed in black robes and with a hood pulled low over his face so I couldn't see who he was. At first, I thought he might be one of those dark riders, the Glurpgronders, but his breath wasn't foul enough, and he didn't have a skeletal horse."

"Hmmmm," said Thoral, rubbing his chin as he thought. "And you let this stranger in?"

"He was already in," Trenton replied. "He came up from behind us. I suppose we could have let him out if he'd wanted to go, but he didn't ask about that."

"What did his voice sound like?" Brad asked.

"Hard to tell," Trenton replied. "It was just a raspy whisper, like the fellow had a bad sore throat. I offered him a cup of water, but he was not thirsty."

"Hmmmm," Thoral considered. His head was pounding. Trenton put a hand on Thoral's leg and leaned in closer, not noticing the warrior's wince. Thoral didn't like people touching him.

"The fellow gave me a silver coin, Thoral," the guard said in a concerned whisper. "Said he'd have more for me if I provided any useful information about you. He wanted to know about your comings and goings and any secret things you might be up to. So I asked him how I would know secret things that you were up to if they were secret? He said that maybe it would be something you would tell me in confidence because you and I are friends, but I said that we were more acquaintances really, although we'd been out drinking together a few times. I mentioned that I thought our relationship might develop into friendship, but it would be presumptuous to start calling us friends at this point."

"I thank you for this information, Trenton," Thoral declared, slipping Trenton a gold coin before urging Warlordhorse forward to catch up with the elves, who were waiting impatiently on the other side of the gate.

"What's this for?" Trenton called after him.

CHAPTER TWELVE

The Strange Bazaar

The Strange Bazaar was aptly named because it was on Strange Street. No one could remember if people had decided to hold the bazaar on Strange Street because that would make for a cool-sounding name or if the street came to be called Strange Street because the bazaar was there and offered some pretty strange stuff. In the end, it didn't matter. But the merchants of the bazaar always argued about it with the people who lived on the street.

The Strange Bazaar was a sprawling thing. It ran down Strange Street for blocks and blocks, and people had set up all kinds of brightly colored tents and carts and stands to sell all kinds of things. Most of the things were boring, like carpets and fry pots, but there was a lot of weird stuff, too. The street was too choked with activity to ride along, so the companions had to leave their steeds at the edge of the market. They paid a filthy peasant boy a few coppers to groom the horses and watch over them, although Thoral took one look at him and told him not to touch Warlordhorse. Warlordhorse was not pleased with having to stay behind, but Thoral told him to keep an eye peeled for Flug, the unicorn. That seemed to mollify the last lord of the Brendylschmylyn. Also, there was a pretty girl horse there, and Warlordhorse was into that.

The bazaar was a riot of bad smells and annoying sounds: the shouts of vendors hawking their wares; the unpleasant odors of dubious street foods sizzling over makeshift grills; the jingling of little bells on the pierced nipples of bare-chested male belly dancers; the pungent aromas of exotic spices, incenses and rare oils; and the braying, squawking, grunting and occasional farting of animals being traded or sold. Thoral bought a skin of wine and chugged half of it as he and the elves walked.

"Help!" a little piglet wept, poking a pink foreleg toward Thoral from between the bars of a hanging cage. "I am a free creature being illegally imprisoned."

"Me too!" shouted six other piglets from the tightly packed cage. Their cruel-looking dwarf captor slapped the bars with a leather flail, and they all cowered.

"Talking peegs, sir?" the dwarf hawked in the thick accent of the slavers of Fubar as he blocked Thoral's path. "Zey make goot pets, or you can eat zem."

"Hie thee hence or I will annihilate thee," the barbarian snarled down at him. The dwarf narrowed his pink eyes but faded back out of Thoral's way. "It is terrible that they do that to talking animals," the warrior grumbled to lord Elfrod, who wrinkled his nose in disgust.

"Talking animals always get the short end of the stick on Grome," Brad noted from Thoral's belt pouch. "I mean, I hate to play the talking-animal card, but you wouldn't see them do that to—" He stopped midsentence as they passed a cage full of nontalking piglets right next to a cage full of human children, both labeled PETS OR MEAT. That kind of shut him up.

Thoral nodded at the fish glumly. "Injustice," the warrior said. It wasn't clear if that was all he was going to say or if he was beginning some longer observation, but then the elf king spoke.

"Thoral," he pronounced, turning to the barbarian, "methinks we might improve our odds of finding my fair daughter, Nalweegie, if we split up. What thinkest thou?"

"Mayhap," Thoral allowed. "What if Brad and I take the section where they sell magical items? You and a portion of your Elf Force take the section where they sell musical instruments, fruit and items made of wood. Another pair can investigate the section where they sell weapons, boots and religious items, and the remaining two can wander about."

The elf king contemplated this suggestion for a long moment then nodded. "This is a plan fat with wisdom," he conceded sagely. "Let it be done."

"Verily," said Thoral. "Let us meet here again when the Great Bell in the ancient Astronomer's Tower of the Prophets' Guild next rings."

With that, the companions separated, none of them realizing that the bell was out for repairs.

***

The section of the Strange Street Bazaar with the magic stuff was, by far, the most interesting. That's why Thoral had picked it. As the warrior and the fish entered the area, the chaotic bustle of the market faded. It was both quieter and more mysterious than the other areas. Bearded wizards in conical hats, green-faced witches in black gowns, and hooded priests of various mystic religions eyed them appraisingly from half-moon-festooned tents and pentacle-painted stalls. A raven croaked at them from the shoulder of a Chufuian enchantress in a gauzy gown who clearly wasn't wearing any underclothes. A sorcerer in a turban that marked him as a man of the cliff city of Wellins held a sign that read Magic Puddings, Half Off.

Thoral drifted over to a table spread with glittering, finger-sized crystals as he polished off the last of the wine.

"Can you tell me if this is a Walking-Door Tree Compass?" he asked the gnomish magicmonger standing behind the counter in a theatrical purple crushed-velvet robe with silver spangles. The warrior held out the compass he had found after killing Necrogrond the first time, and the gnome took it in his tiny, chubby hands. Thoral found the big compass in the little hands very cute, but he'd learned over time not to call gnomes cute. The magicmonger fitted a magnifying lens to one bright blue eye and peered at it.

"It's a misplacement compass," he responded, his voice a grumbly bass. "It always points unerringly to an assigned item so you can't lose it, unless you lose the compass. This one looks like an elfish model.

It's engraved with the initials *L.E.* on the back. Possibly the maker's mark, although I've never seen that one before. Probably worthless, but I'd give you ten silvers for it."

Thoral was considering the offer when the magicmonger surprised him with another.

"Eleven silvers then. That's a good deal," the gnome pressed him.

"No, thank you. I will hang on to it," the barbarian replied, sensing that he might have something more valuable than the merchant wanted to let on.

"Look, this is a pretty old compass," the gnome noted. "There's no telling whether whatever it was supposed to point to even exists anymore, or if it's just focused on somebody's house keys or something."

"Thank you, no," Thoral said firmly. Then, putting the compass away, he indicated the crystals on the table. "Do any of these have… um…energy?"

"Energy?" the gnome repeated, stroking his thick white beard with a puzzled expression, his one eye still ridiculously magnified by the lens.

"Do any of them make sparks or produce a tingling sensation when touched to the tongue?" Thoral tried to clarify.

"They are not for licking." The gnome frowned.

"I do not wish to lick them," Thoral growled, a note of frustration in his voice as he struggled to frame his question in a way the gnome would understand. "Do any of them…shoot small bits of lightning or make flashes of light accompanied by a snapping noise?"

Recognition dawned across the gnome's face. "Are you looking for a Narthkrykryn? A zapping crystal?"

"Narthkrykryn!" Thoral smiled in relief. "I always forget what they are called."

"The elves. They've got a weird name for everything," the gnome complained, shaking his head in disgust.

"The elves." Thoral rolled his eyes. "So, do you have any Narthkrykryn?"

"I only have empty ones," the gnome shrugged. "Sorry."

"Don't get distracted," Brad interrupted, climbing onto Thoral's shoulder. "We're not here to buy stuff."

"Verily," Thoral replied, stalking away from the table.

"I've got some nice vibrating crystals," the gnome called after him. "I could let you have a full set in exchange for that Misplacement Compass." Thoral just shook his head.

"Can I ask you a personal question?" Brad asked as the two walked through the tangle of vendors.

"Do you mean *another* one?" Thoral still had a headache.

"Are you really interested in Nalweegie, or what?" The fish ignored his jibe.

Thoral's grin faded and he pursed his lips, thinking.

"I mean, I jumped in with that thing about you talking about her after killing the grode, but that was just because Elfrod seemed kind of mad that you didn't even know her name," Brad pressed on. "You know, given that you kissed her and all."

"I thank thee for thy intervention, fish," Thoral declared, ducking his head to pass under a bunch of shrunken heads hanging from a line. "In truth, my feelings are mixed. The princess is fair of face and form—"

"She's smoking hot," Brad interjected with a wicked smile.

"—but I had not thought to find love again after the deaths of my wife and child," Thoral finished in such a downbeat way that the fish was embarrassed to have made a flippant comment.

"Yeah, about that," Brad frowned. "How come you never mentioned any of that before? We've been adventuring together for years now, and that seems like the kind of thing you might tell a guy. What other secrets are you keeping?"

Thoral came to an abrupt stop and turned his head to meet the fish's gaze. "I suppose it is time that I tell thee of my past," the warrior said slowly. "No one now living knows this tale, but—"

"Thoral!" A totally cute, but desperate-sounding little voice interrupted as a talking flying squirrel glided down out of the sky and landed on the warrior's muscled forearm.

"Tyncie?" Thoral asked, breaking into a disbelieving grin.

"Yes," she confirmed. "I have been seeking thee to warn thee."

"What are you talking about?" Brad demanded. "We're the ones who've been seeking you. How did you even know we were in Reefma?"

"The evil brothers of the Bad Religion are all abuzz that you have entered the city," the little squirrel panted. "And my vile master, the Heartless One, especially! A death team of deadly Pooja Assassins has been dispatched to dispatch you!"

"Assassins!" the fish gasped.

"And they are closing in even as we speak," the squirrel quavered, her little eyes round with fear. "I was following them secretly from the air as they quested for you when I happened to spot you just ahead of them. They cannot now be far behind."

"Tyncie CheeChaw CheeChee WeeWaw, this is a brave deed," Thoral praised, his eyes soft with admiration. "Are you not, though, risking your life and the lives of your husband and child to warn us?"

"Yes," Tyncie affirmed, "but I had to. In all of my wretched life, thou art the only human to show this grasthling true kindness." Then she snuggled Thoral with her tiny little arms, rubbing her cute little head against his powerfully muscled side. He stroked her beneath the chin and rubbed her belly. Then, violet eyes sparkling a bit more than usual, he bade her go.

"Thou hast shared thy warning, sweetling," Thoral warned, his voice grave. "Now go, quickly, before thy role is discovered."

It was clear that the squirrel did not want to leave the warrior's side, but with an effort, she tore herself away. "Don't get dead!" she cried, then leapt into the air and soared away.

"I told thee so," Thoral gloated to Brad as he watched the grasthling go. The fish remained silent.

Tyncie's passage had attracted some attention to the warrior and the fish. Flying squirrels were rarely seen in Reefma. All around their immediate vicinity, merchants and customers alike turned to see what the commotion was about.

That's how Nalweegie noticed them.

"Thoral!" the elfish princess cried, excitement and relief comingling prettily in her dulcet voice. She raced to Thoral's side from where she had been haggling with a rainbow-robed fairy mage over a magic wand at a table not ten feet away and threw her arms around the warrior's neck. "Oh! Well met!" she cried, standing on tippy toes to lay her ivory cheek against his bronzed chest. "Well met, my sweet and special friend. Thou art still alive. I rejoice that I am not too late to warn thee, Thoral Mighty Fist."

"Thoral Mighty Fist?" another voice hissed. This voice made everybody's blood run cold and the hairs stand up on the backs of their necks.

"Who wants to know?" Nalweegie retorted, her cheeks flushing, her eyes narrowing with wrath. Thoral followed the princess's dangerous gaze to the beady red eyes of the leader of a black-clad and heavily armed death team of Pooja Assassins.

CHAPTER THIRTEEN

The Pooja Assassins

"Thoral!" Princess Nalweegie cried, stepping in front of the warrior to shield him, her emerald eyes burning as she stared down the advancing circle of half-lizard assassins. "Pooja Assassins!"

There were indeed six Poojas, each with six arms, each arm armed with a wickedly curved scimitar. Each Pooja also had a prehensile tail, each tail clutching a scimitar as well. They flicked out their long, snaky tongues in unison, tasting the air for any advantage, and swung their blades in swooshy arcs. All around the Poojas and their prey, merchants and customers scattered and ducked.

"Run princess," Brad whispered. "Get out of here and start screaming for your dad. He's with his Elf Force somewhere in the bazaar."

"Poojas!" Nalweegie shouted at the half lizards, revulsion mixing with contempt in her voice. Elves and Poojas pretty much hated each other's guts–It's a long story. Thoral stepped in front of the princess to shield her, but she immediately stepped back in front of him. When he tried to step in front of her a second time, she grabbed his arm and wouldn't allow it.

"No!" she cried. "This seems connected to a dream I had of you. Let me fight. These assassins may be planning to kill you."

"We *are* planning to kill him," the leader of the Poojas hissed, surprised. "That's our plan exactly. How…how did you know?"

"You shall not pass!" Nalweegie cried, her voice fierce. "I will not let you!"

"Really, Princess," Brad said urgently, "Thoral might be able to hold these guys off for a few minutes, but your dad and his Elf Force would be really handy right now, and it would be really useful if you would get them. You should run and scream. Really."

"I am the Elfish Princess of Creekenvalley, daughter of Blindelweegie, daughter of Tindelweegie who came out of a clam. I do not run screaming from danger," the princess snarled. "I run screaming *toward* danger. I will not leave my special friend's side while he is in peril." With that, she drew her bright, thin sword, Whisper, from its sheath at her belt.

Thoral raised his eyebrows. He and the fish exchanged a surreptitious look behind Nalweegie's back.

"OK," the leader of the Poojas hissed. "We don't normally do freebies, but I guess we can kill you too."

At that, Thoral growled and loosed his magic sword, *Blurmflard*, that his wizard mentor, Yiz, had lent him. As always in the presence of evil lizard spawn, its ancient blade flared deep purple.

"Careful, he's got a magic sword," the leader of the Poojas cautioned his death team. "It looks pretty sharp."

"It *is* pretty sharp," Thoral roared, flinging himself at the half lizards preemptively so as to protect Nalweegie.

"AAAUUUGGGHHH!" Brad shrieked as the air turned into a tornado of whirling blades. Thoral was quick as a cat fired out of a catapult, but the six Poojas had forty-two blades between them, and Thoral had only *Blurmflard*. Ten scimitars flashed in at the fearless fighter, but he met them all, his blade ringing like a bell. Then ten more blades flashed in at him. He ducked those. But then ten more blades flashed in at him. The warrior did a backflip and kicked those with his iron-toed boots. But then ten more blades flashed in at him. He knocked those aside with the heavy brass bucklers on his forearms, which haven't been mentioned previously but were there the whole time. But then the last two blades flashed in at him. The barbarian was now out of tricks, so he could only watch as they sliced toward his well-muscled neck. The last thought to flit through his mind was that he should have used the metal magic wand that he rarely used. Now he'd never get to use it.

"No!" Nalweegie shouted, flashing *Whisper* between Thoral's neck and the offending scimitars so that they were deflected. Sparks showered everywhere. A third of the half-lizard death team then turned their full focus on the princess, hissing as they came. She was driven back by the ferocity of their fourteen-bladed onslaught. Thoral saw what was happening and strove to fight his way to her side. The four remaining Poojas blocked him.

"Run and scream, Princess," Brad bellowed in an effort to be heard over the deafening whistle of the swords. "Run and scream!" But even if she had been willing to run—which she wasn't—escape was now impossible for Nalweegie.

"Protect thy neck, Thoral," Nalweegie grunted, fending off the vicious attacks of the Poojas. "I dreamed that thou wert dead and thy head hewn off."

"Look to thine own sweet neck," Thoral roared as he chopped two arms off one Pooja. He did pull his chin down a little though. The wounded Pooja hissed in rage and spat venom in Thoral's face, but Thoral deflected it back into the Pooja's eye with *Blurmflard*. The assassin screeked in agony, and its eyeball swelled up and popped like a popcorn kernel.

"Dost thou think my neck sweet?" Nalweegie shouted, doing a spectacular flip over the head of one of her attackers and stabbing it in the back as she landed.

"I do," Thoral yelled, punching the exploded-eye Pooja in its ichor-dripping eye socket so that gick splattered everywhere.

"And I find thee...very...enticing," the princess panted, tugging at her pinioned blade.

"Where's this headed?" Brad screamed, leaping to avoid the razor edge of a sweeping scimitar.

"I find thee enticing as well," Thoral yelled back to the princess, ignoring the fish.

"In fact, my dearest special friend," Nalweegie shouted, "I think that, with all my heart, I may—" Her words were cut off as she tried to yank her blade free of the Pooja's back, but the half lizard spun toward her, wrenching Whisper from her delicate grasp instead.

"You may what?" Thoral called, too embroiled to notice Nalweegie's predicament as he tore his Pooja's brain out through its eye hole while hacking the legs out from under another and defending himself from the other two. Brad didn't notice either. He was biting the Pooja leader's face.

"I may…love thee," Nalweegie declared as she backed away, bringing her empty hands up before her to ward off the fourteen blades poised to strike her down. She bumped up against a vendor's wagon and was trapped. Her emerald eyes went wide.

As the word *love* registered, Thoral felt his heart leap like a startled bunny. He didn't have time to think about the implications or what his reaction should be, but hearing her confession of love, he felt strangely buoyed by a feeling he had not experienced in many years. What was that sensation? Joy? Terror? Either way, a raw energy surged through him, and he chopped his two remaining attackers completely in half at their waists with a single blow so that their top halves fell to the ground and their bottom halves staggered and sat down on top of the top halves. Their butts were sitting on their own faces.

Thoral spun toward the princess, his emotions all a jumble. He was just in time to see her fall beneath her two Pooja Assassins.

"The irony!" Brad yelled, spitting out a mouthful of Pooja face.

"NOOOOOOOOOO!" Thoral thundered, a searing agony flooding his heart and drowning the newborn joy—or rabbit or whatever it was—therein. He raced toward Nalweegie, a red haze blurring his vision.

He was too late. The Poojas lay atop her, writhing in transports of slaughter.

CHAPTER FOURTEEN

Pledges Unpledged

"Hey, wait a second!" Brad shouted as Thoral prepared to leap on the Poojas atop the princess. "There are arrows sticking out of them."

It was true. Each of the Poojas had ten or fifteen elfish arrows sticking out of its back. Apparently, they weren't writhing in transports of slaughter but twitching in agonized death throes. Thoral's brow creased in puzzlement as he seized a Pooja in each of his mighty fists and hurled them away from the fallen princess. They both crashed into vending carts and broke all their bones. Then he knelt beside the fallen elf maiden.

"Nalweegie," Thoral whispered, sitting down beside her and cradling her perfect head in his muscular lap. "Nalweegie. Lost to me." Brad looked on, shaking his head at the tragedy. Thoral was always very emotional and melodramatic when his friends were killed. The fish put a comforting fin on the warrior's back.

"She's gone, Thoral. I'm so sorry."

"I…I…," Thoral stammered, weeping now. His hot tears splashed upon the princess's snowy cheeks. She seemed dead. It was convincing. "I…I loved thee too, Nalweegie."

Her emerald eyes fluttered open.

"Repeat that," she breathed.

He did not, but she didn't seem to notice as he pulled her lips to his and smothered her with noisy kisses. Brad's mouth hung open.

"Ahem," a voice announced from behind the three. Thoral and Nalweegie broke off their ardent lip lock. There stood Elfrod with his Elf Force, their slender long bows at the ready, all of them smiling enigmatic elf smiles except for the king, whose expression wasn't particularly enigmatic.

***

"And I also love thee," Nalweegie breathed. She was talking to Thoral's scars as she kissed each one of them in a cramped sleeping room at the Inn of the Gruesomely Gashed Gnome. The fish had rented the room under the false name Mr. Underlake after the fight at the bazaar, and the companions had sneaked in by ones and twos over the next few hours until they were all gathered. They'd brought the dead Poojas with them disguised as friends who had passed out from drinking too much so that the assassins' evil masters wouldn't know what had happened. This had been particularly tricky with the ones who were chopped in half. The hope was to buy a little time while Thoral, Brad, and Elfrod came up with a solid plan. Unfortunately, that wasn't how things worked out.

Thoral and Nalweegie were the first to arrive at the room, and by the time the others filtered in, the two were lost in a deep conversation about the nature of their feelings for each other. Nalweegie seemed to have been fishing for another declaration of love from Thoral, but the cagey barbarian had pretended he didn't realize that's what she was after. The conversation had somehow devolved into kissing, only stopped by Elfrod's entrance.

Thoral now lay facedown on his sleeping blanket with his eyes closed, while the princess sat on the floor beside him and showered his old wounds with affection. She'd already been at the scar-kissing thing for half an hour, and it was getting on everyone's nerves, except maybe Thoral's. Brad and Elfrod were particularly bothered.

"How many scars dost thou have left to kiss?" the elfish king demanded.

His daughter glanced up at her father from a two-inch scar at the back of Thoral's neck, a scar from a wound he'd sustained trying to climb over a fence when he was twelve. "I know not," she answered brazenly, "but I shall persist until I have kissed each and every one of them. They are precious to me." She glared at her father, and he glared back. The Elf Force ladies stared at their feet and pretended to be interested in other stuff, except the youngest two, who grinned and nudged each other in the ribs. Age was always difficult to determine with elves, but they seemed to be teenagers.

"Hey, Thoral." Brad broke the tense silence, speaking from the low wooden table where he'd been eating peanuts for the last half hour. "Aren't there some bad guys you've sworn to slaughter? We still need to locate them."

Thoral leapt to his feet so fast that Nalweegie fell over backward and everyone else was alarmed. "I had forgotten about that," the warrior exclaimed. "We must needs find the Bad Religion and wipe them out." He drew *Blurmflard* and tried to raise the blade heroically, but it stuck in a wooden beam in the low ceiling.

"But, Thoral, true love of my heart," Nalweegie protested, struggling back to a sitting position as Thoral fought to free his sword. "I simply cannot allow it." There was steel under her sweet voice.

Everyone turned to look at the princess.

"Come again?" Thoral said, pulling the sword free and causing a little shower of splinters to rain down on his head.

Nalweegie gave an indulgent smile as she stood and put an arm around him. "I cannot allow you to pursue this quest to find the Bad Religion," she stated, brushing splinters from his hair. "Not here in Reefma, leastwise."

"But I am sworn to do it."

"And yet you cannot do it," she insisted. "I have other plans for you." She smiled at the warrior's frown and traced the crease of his brow with a delicate finger. "You see, my foolish fearless one, I am afraid that you will be reckless and get thyself beheaded in this very city, as you were in my dream." She stood on tippy toe to kiss his sensual lips, but the warrior pulled back, holding her at arm's length.

"Princess," said he, "I have sworn the swear that I have sworn, and I am as good as my word. Further, I do not intend to be beheaded."

"But in my dream I did see thy headless body sprawled upon the black-tiled floor of a dim-lit feasting hall at the foot of a tall figure all cloaked and hooded in black," Nalweegie countered, her cheeks flushing as she stamped her perfect little foot for emphasis. Then she went for him again, lips puckered.

"It was but a dream, my love," Thoral grumbled, still holding her at arm's length.

"I am Nalweegie, the Evening Snack, whose dreams are oft as not prophetic visions of a future that may yet come to pass," the princess huffed. "Tell him, Father! Sing him that song that was sung by the Brindlehound at my birth that foretold that I would have the second sight. The song of a hundred verses. The one with the tedious chorus. Or better, tell him of that time two weeks ago when I dreamed it would rain and rain it did, despite starting off clear. Or of that time two years ago when I dreamed we would have baked eel for luncheon, and baked eel we had indeed."

Thoral, Brad and the Elf Force warriors all turned to see how Elfrod would respond to this, hoping he would not sing the song of the Brindlehound. The king wore a pained expression. "Sweet daughter," he began, "these things are accurate but hardly conclusive. Think of all of the dreams thou hast had that did not come true. Like that one from just a week ago in which thou didst welcome one and all to the great feast we should *even now* be attending back in Creekenvalley. The dream in which thou wert embarrassed to find thyself wearing naught but thy short clothes. Remember that? And yet here we are rather than there. Despite your obligation to attend. Despite the importance of that feast to the elves of Creekenvalley. That dream did not come to pass." He glared at her quite pointedly.

"In your face," Brad said to the princess. "And what's this feast you're missing?"

"Ah, dear father," Nalweegie threw back, ignoring the fish, green fire in her emerald eyes. "What of that time, three hundred and seven years past, when on my tenth birthday I dreamt those extra lines of the Goomy Prophecy of Doom?"

"That prophecy has not come to pass," Elfrod reminded her.

"Fine!" the princess cried. "Then what of the very next night, when I dreamt a dream of a dreamy man from a foreign land with tawny hair and eyes of purple who traveled with a talking fish and did save me from the clutches of a vile necromancer with a beard?" Everybody looked startled, except the king.

"Verily," he conceded. "I had forgotten that one."

With a relieved smile, Nalweegie pushed in toward Thoral, lips puckering once more. But her triumph was short lived. The mighty warrior rebuffed her yet again.

"Alas, this matters not," Thoral sighed, "for I am Thoral Mighty Fist."

Everyone gasped. The princess sagged, defeated. Once Thoral noted that he was Thoral, there was no point in arguing further. Everyone knew it. That's just how it was.

Nalweegie wept. "How am I to bear losing you whom I have so recently found?" she cried, and the mighty warrior relented and let her get in close beside him. She sniffled, her perfect little nose pressed against his gleaming chest, where the gap in his skimpy leather vest revealed it.

"There is always a possibility that your dream was just a dream," Thoral whispered, stroking her raven hair, "but if not, one thing I have learned in my wanderings of the land of Grome is that trying to prevent a prophecy from coming to pass almost always makes it come to pass in a way that it would not have come to pass if there had been no effort to prevent it from coming to pass. It is horribly…"

"Ironic," Brad supplied.

"It is horribly ironic," the warrior concluded.

"Surely," Nalweegie whispered, her lips warm against his skin, a tear slipping down her snowy cheek, "you are not saying that we must simply surrender to fate. Please tell me you are not just going to knowingly march into the teeth of certain death."

"That's pretty much what he's saying," Brad interjected, not the most helpful thing he'd ever said. Nalweegie stifled a sob, and Thoral shot daggers at the fish from his eyes. Not literal daggers, like those shot by some evil wizards. Shooting daggers from his eyes was metaphoric for Thoral, not one of his actual powers.

"Cease thy weeping," Thoral murmured to his princess. Then, raising his voice to a snarl, he continued. "Thoral Mighty Fist does not surrender. Not to any foe, nor even to fate if fate be foolish enough to make itself the foe of Thoral Mighty Fist. NO! Thoral Mighty Fist does not march into the teeth of certain death; he punches certain death in the teeth, shattering some whilst knocking others right out of the gums. That is the variety of thing that Thoral Mighty Fist does." He flushed a little, embarrassed by his clumsy syntax. "Generally."

"Fine then," Nalweegie whispered. She pulled away from Thoral, snuffling as she struggled to compose herself. She pretended to wipe just the tears off her face with her sleeve, but she also wiped her nose. Thoral noticed because hardly anything got past him. He was a formally trained noticer. "I should like to…discuss a few things with you before you punch death in the teeth, my love," the princess sniffled, shooting him a meaningful look.

"Elfrod," Thoral said, turning toward the elf king both to avoid having to watch more nose wiping and to change the subject, "I…" He searched his mind, desperate for anything unrelated to bring up. "I… have a quick question for you. Hast thou ever seen one of these before?" He dug in his belt pouch and produced the misplacement compass he had gotten the first time he killed Necrogrond. "I was told this was probably of elfish make." He held the compass out to the elf lord, who squinted at it for a moment before his fine-featured face registered shocked recognition.

"I believe that is my old misplacement compass!" the king exclaimed. "Long have I wondered where I misplaced it. May I?" Thoral passed it to him and Elfrod examined it with growing excitement.

"Yes! It is mine. See, here? This engraving, *L.E.*, stands for Lord Elfrod." He gave a broad smile. "This was tuned to some keys I lost many ages ago, unfortunately at the same time I lost the compass. You didn't happen to also find a key ring with a green rabbit's foot on it, did you?"

"I did not," Thoral answered. "No key ring."

The king's face, which had been glowing with pleasure, fell. His regal shoulders sagged. "Ah," he sighed. "That would have been lucky indeed. May I ask, where on Grome you came by this?"

"I found the compass in the stronghold of the necromancer who kidnapped Nalweegie," Thoral replied. "And I am honored to be able to return it to you."

"With the necromancer?" the king mused, frowning. "How strange. How very strange indeed." Then his face brightened. "I thank you, Mighty Fist, for this second precious item you have returned to me. With it, I can now locate my keys. I am indebted to you more than you know."

"Whatever the debt, you can repay it in full by taking your precious daughter and leaving the dangers of Reefma posthaste for thy secret kingdom, Windendale—"

"Creekenvalley," Elfrod corrected.

"Creekenvalley," Thoral continued, "where you may secure the safety of princess Nalweegie, fair Evening Snack—"

"And newfound love of your heart," the princess interjected with an odd note of desperation in her voice.

Thoral paused. The princess couldn't see the barbarian's expression cloud because he was still facing her father.

"And newfound love of your heart," the princess repeated, biting her lip.

Thoral hesitated. The elf king's eyes bored into the warrior's, his own expression stern and searching. From the table, Brad tried to catch Thoral's eye, drawing a fin across his throat to forestall him, but the barbarian did not look away from Elfrod. Thoral took a deep breath. "And … and newfound love of my heart," he stammered.

At that, Elfrod turned to his daughter. They stared at each other for a silent moment. The Elf Force held its collective breath. The king dropped his eyes to the compass in his hands. He turned it over and over, his brows knit in deep thought. Finally, he sighed in resignation.

"I release thee from thy obligation, Nalweegie," the king pronounced. A smile lit Nalweegie's face, and she ran to her father and embraced him. Thoral gazed on the pair in some confusion.

"OK, what the heck is going on?!" Brad demanded.

"My daughter was pledged to wed a wealthy foreign prince," Elfrod explained as Nalweegie squeezed him. "It was a political arrangement. She and I had an agreement that she would not be forced to go through with the ceremony if she found true love before the event."

"And I have," Nalweegie cooed. She pulled away from her father and beamed at Thoral.

He wore the expression of a man who had just been slapped across the back of the head with a stout walking staff.

"Wait. What?" Brad asked.

"But I am still taking thee back to Creekenvalley," Elfrod cautioned her. "Methinks Thoral's counsel is right on this count."

"It would be if I were the one in danger," his daughter grumped, but she allowed Elfrod to steer her toward the door, an arm around her shoulders. As they reached the exit, she paused for a moment at the threshold and looked back at Thoral. He opened his mouth as if to speak, but then closed it again. The princess suddenly raced back, threw her arms around his neck and smashed her lips against his. They made out in a tangled frenzy for what seemed like forever while everyone else stood blushing and uncomfortable.

Out of breath, flushed and disheveled, Nalweegie pulled back. She cupped the warrior's face in her delicate hands. "Don't get your head chopped off," she told him solemnly. Then she left, the rest of the elves filing out behind her while nodding or doing little goodbye waves to Thoral and Brad. Elfrod was the last through the door.

"Thoral Mighty Fist, we will await thy return to the hidden happy halls of Creekenvalley," he announced. "You too, Brad. There will be much rejoicing then."

"I can't wait," the fish responded.

"I cannot, too," said Thoral.

"Do be careful," Elfrod warned. "Maybe get some neck armor."

"I will," Thoral agreed.

"Just a bit of *fatherly* advice," the elf king said, not only putting extra emphasis on the word *fatherly* but also winking and nudging Thoral in his well-muscled ribs. "Or should I say father-in-law-erly?" He strode from the room and was gone.

"That's kind of charging before the war horn, don't you think?" Brad asked as soon as he was sure Elfrod was out of earshot. "I mean, it's not like we're going to give up adventuring and settle down just so you can marry some elfish princess," the fish scoffed. "You're Thoral Mighty Fist, for God's sake. Am I right?"

"Mayhap."

"Again with the mayhap," Brad complained, kicking his big pile of peanut shells off the table in disgust. "You don't really love her. You just got your blood heated up when she kissed you, and then you got carried away and said you loved her because you thought she was dead, and now you feel guilty because she believed you."

"Mayhap," Thoral said again.

"Think about who you're mayhapping here, buddy," Brad scolded. "I know you better than you know yourself, and you are definitely not in love with little Princess Perfect. She's not even your type."

"We must needs talk of this later," Thoral growled. "Right now, we have slaughtering to do."

CHAPTER FIFTEEN

The Dull Bit

Thoral did buy some neck armor. Not because he was scared but because he had told Elfrod he would, and he always did things he said he was going to do. That was the only reason. He wound up getting a thick iron collar even though Brad told him it made him look like an escaped slave.

"It's just kind of stupid looking is all I'm saying," the koi observed, running one flipper along the collar as he perched on Thoral's massive shoulder inside his voluminous hood.

It was evening now. Dinnertime, basically. The big barbarian didn't dignify Brad's comment with a response as he strode away from the armor section of the Strange Bazaar, his black-hooded cloak fluttering behind him. The cloak was for disguise, just in case the Bad Religion hadn't figured out what had happened with the Poojas yet. It was all part of Thoral's plan.

"Walk me through this plan one more time," Brad suggested.

"One: Put on a cloak for disguise. Accomplished," Thoral recited. "Two: Purchase some neck armor. Accomplished. Three: Find the hideout of the Bad Religion and slaughter them to a man. In progress."

"It's a solid plan," the fish conceded, "but that last point seems like it could use some elaboration. Again, how are we going to find the hideout of the Bad Religion?"

"Methinks we will get Warlordhorse, put a black, hooded horse blanket on him for disguise and then ride around the city seeking likely places and asking people on street corners," Thoral replied. "It is not that large a city. Methinks we can check the whole thing in less than a month."

The fish was silent.

"Dost thou have a better idea?" Thoral grumbled.

"Well, I'm a little concerned that if we start riding around the city all hooded and cloaked, we're going to draw a lot of attention to ourselves," Brad mused. "I mean, I wouldn't even be surprised if people mistook you for one of the Glurpgronders, the nine-and-a-half Black Riders of the Dark Lord, Mauron. Those guys are still searching for his missing Great Pudding of Power so that Mauron can bind everyone in darkness and rule all of Grome, and they always travel hooded and cloaked so that no one can see that they're really ghosts or skeletons or something. People hate those guys, and they wouldn't talk to you if they thought you were one of them."

"I thought Mauron was killed a thousand and two years ago," Thoral objected.

"Yeah, but he recently got halfway reincarnated or something," Brad answered. "You know how these things go. Apparently, his soul was hidden in an envelope or a bag or a box, and some kid accidentally let it out. Now, if the Glurpgronders can just bring Mauron his missing pudding, he'll eat it and come fully back to life, and then he'll don his magic Bracelet of Evil and be unstoppable, and his forces will wash across the land like a big dark spill. There's a prophecy about it and everything."

"I hate prophecies," Thoral complained. "And puddings."

"Yeah," Brad nodded. "Even if people don't mistake you for a Glurpgronder, if you spend a month walking around in a big hooded cloak asking everybody if they know where to find the secret hideout of the Bad Religion, it's going to get back to them."

"True," Thoral conceded. The two of them continued on in silent contemplation, Thoral's footsteps echoing off the crumbling cobblestones of Strange Street.

"What if I used a better disguise?" Thoral asked finally, toying with the Ring of Looks Elfrod had given him.

"You have a better disguise?"

"I have an idea for something," Thoral affirmed.

"Nah," Brad frowned. "No matter what the disguise, asking about the Bad Religion for a month is still likely to raise some flags."

"True," Thoral conceded again. They turned off of Strange Street onto Murder Street, heading back toward the Inn of the Gruesomely Gashed Gnome.

"I hate this part of adventuring," Brad sighed.

"The dull bit," Thoral said gloomily.

"The dull bit," the fish agreed.

They walked all the way back to the inn, arriving well after dark, without coming up with a single decent idea. They checked in on Warlordhorse to make sure he was happy and fed, then grabbed a quick bite to eat in the common room. Thoral had mutton and Brad had some kind of meat pie. The horribly disfigured innkeeper walked up to their table as they were being served.

"How goes it, Mighty Fist?" the gnome croaked, winking with his one good eye. Or maybe he was just blinking. There was no way to know for sure.

"Acceptable," the warrior replied.

"Up to anything interesting, my friend? Any new adventures?" the gnome asked, his torn and puckered face twisting in what was probably meant to be a smile.

"Nope," Brad interjected. "Taking a bit of a break, actually. Just relaxing and trying to get a little peace and quiet." He glared at the innkeeper, fins crossed over his chest.

"I'll let you eat then," the gnome croaked.

"That guy gives me the creeps," the fish whispered as the little man hobbled away from the table.

"He has always been kindly to me," Thoral grumbled. "Are you sure you are not merely put off by his hideous disfigurements?"

"Like I'd be that shallow," Brad huffed.

"What other reasons do you have then?" the warrior demanded. The fish was silent for a long time.

"Just because I can't articulate a reason doesn't mean there isn't one."

***

"Dost thou have any ideas?" Thoral asked as they lay in the darkness of their small room, in their small bed, trying to get to sleep. The barbarian was having a hard time getting comfortable.

"Here's a thought," Brad offered. "Try sleeping without your sword in the bed. I hate when you do that when we have to share."

"*Blurmflard* gives me comfort," Thoral grumbled, shifting the blade from between them to his side of the bed.

"Because it's so hard and poky?" the fish demanded. "Or because it sometimes glows for no reason and wakes us both up?"

"It is a memento of my wizard mentor, Yiz," Thoral replied. "He gave it to me in happier days."

"Yeah, yeah, I'm well aware. Didn't he give you anything else that would be better to sleep with though? Maybe something smaller or less razor sharp?"

"Dost thou have any ideas or not?" the warrior gruffed.

"No," Brad said. "You?"

"I have the niggling feeling that I have forgotten something that might be useful," Thoral growled, "but other than that, I have nothing."

"Yeah," the fish sighed.

"You know," Brad said after a moment in a gentler voice, "I was proud of you for not getting drunk after dinner tonight." Thoral was silent, so the fish continued. "I mean, generally speaking, you drink a lot when you're bored or frustrated, and you were both tonight, so … you know … nice." When the barbarian did not reply, Brad suspected that he had fallen asleep.

"Too long have I tried to drown my sorrows in warm ale," Thoral finally grumbled. "And I don't even like ale. Especially when it is warm."

"Does this 'new you' have anything to do with the princess?" Brad asked suspiciously.

"Good night," Thoral grumbled and rolled over, pulling most of the blanket off the fish.

***

Since they still didn't have any ideas the next morning, they stayed in their room and played cards all day. Brad wanted to discuss plans Thoral might have for a future with Nalweegie, but the barbarian had a headache and was pretty cranky, so they didn't. By evening, the bodies of the Pooja Assassins were attracting a lot of flies. Brad rented another room under a different false name. They moved into the new room and put a DO NOT DISTURB sign up on the door of the first room. As the fish was sitting on the table in their new room counting their remaining supply of money, something occurred to Thoral.

"Bradfast," the warrior said, pinching the fish's dorsal fin between forefinger and thumb.

"You know I hate when you do that," Brad snapped.

"Sorry," Thoral said, releasing the fish, "I have an idea."

"Did you think of whatever it was you forgot?"

"No. I thought of something else. What if we go back to my acquaintance Trenton at the Broken Gate and tell him to arrange a secret meeting between himself and the mysterious stranger who asked him for information about me," Thoral suggested. "Then we overpower the stranger and demand to know if he is a brother of the Bad Religion. If he is, we make him lead us to their fortress."

Brad nodded appreciatively. "That just might work," he said.

CHAPTER SIXTEEN

The Worst-Laid Plans of Fish and Men

"So you want me to tell the mysterious stranger that you're going to jump him?" Trenton asked twenty minutes later as he stood watch at the Broken Gate. They couldn't close the gate because it was broken, so the guards just put sawhorses across it at night and took turns standing there telling people they couldn't come in.

"No," Brad said evenly.

"But that's what you keep saying," Trenton argued, holding his little brass lantern closer to the opening in Thoral's hood so he could see the koi better.

"Not at all," the fish explained from Thoral's shoulder. "That part is secret."

"If it's such a secret, how come I know it?" Trenton asked, shifting his eyes from the fish to Thoral and then back again. A bunch of other guards, who'd been leaning in to catch the conversation, nodded at the logic.

"Secret from the mysterious guy," Brad clarified. "And this is a private conversation," he huffed, shooting a meaningful glare at the other guards. Looking affronted, they pretended to go back to their various duties.

"It won't be secret from him if I tell him," Trenton pointed out.

"We don't want you to tell him," Brad replied.

"OK, now you've lost me," Trenton said, mystified. "I thought you were *asking* me to tell him."

"See, we are asking you to tell him that you have information, but the part where we jump him is actually a trick," the fish explained, trying to keep his voice level.

"So you're only going to pretend to jump him? It's just a trick?"

"No, we're really going to jump him, but we need you to lure him by saying you'll give him information about Thoral," Brad answered.

"What kind of information?" Trenton furrowed his brows.

"Information about my secret plans," Thoral said, frustration coloring his voice.

"I would never do that!" Trenton objected. "You're my friend, Thoral. Well ... you're more of an acquaintance, but I think there's the possibility that a friendship could develop over time. I mean, I like you, and you're cool to hang out with. You're the legendary Fish Wielder, for God's sake!"

"The what?" Brad barked.

"The Fish Wielder," Trenton answered, but there was a tentative note in his voice now.

Brad gaped at him.

"I am the *Fist* Wielder," Thoral grumbled.

"Oh," Trenton said, his brow creased with puzzlement. "I thought ... you know, because you and Brad are always together—" The other guards, who had forgotten they were not supposed to be listening, had drifted into a little knot behind Trenton again.

"No," Brad said flatly. "It's *Fist* Wielder because he has such abnormally prodigious hand strength." There was an awkward moment of silence.

"Have you ever thought of changing it?" Trenton asked, the other guards nodding approval.

"No. He hasn't," the fish snapped. "Now, can we get back to what you should tell the mysterious stranger? And would the rest of you please *bug off*?!"

"Sure, sure. Sorry," Trenton apologized as the others made a half-hearted show of returning to their work.

"Great. Tell the stranger that you will give him information about Thoral's secret plans."

"But I would never reveal secrets entrusted to me by the *Fist* Wielder," Trenton protested, overenunciating the word *fist*.

"Tis all right in this instance because I want you to tell him in order to lure him," Thoral growled.

"I don't see why he would show up if I tell him your secret plan is to jump him," Trenton sighed, exasperated. "How's that going to lure him?"

"Yeah, how's that going to lure him?" one of the other guards seconded, the rest crowding in behind him.

"Mayhap this was not my finest idea," Thoral huffed.

***

Three hours later, however, as a wan and gibbous moon was rising over the basalt walls of Reefma, Thoral and Brad lurked in the concealing darkness of Thoral's hooded cloak. They stood in the shadow of a pile of boxes in an alley just off Dark Street in the Thieving District, waiting for the mysterious stranger to arrive. He was already an hour late.

"How much do you want to bet that Trenton screwed up the plan?" Brad whispered near Thoral's ear. He was again standing on his companion's shoulder within the depths of the warrior's voluminous hood.

"A considerable sum," Thoral whispered back, his breath misting in the chilly air. "If only we could find someone to take that bet, we would be rich." He flexed the fingers of his right hand, cramped from an hour and a half spent holding the weighted gladiator's net he intended to throw over the mysterious stranger. The mighty barbarian hadn't had any alcohol in a couple of days now, and the tedious tension of waiting was reminding him of why he liked to be drunk.

"You want to play Guess What Number I'm Thinking one more time?" the fish asked in a low voice.

"No."

"You want to talk about what's going to happen with Nalweegie when we finally wipe out the Bad Religion?" Brad whispered.

"No."

"We have to talk about it sometime," the koi complained. "Have you told Warlordhorse anything yet?"

"He would not understand," Thoral sighed.

"You've been adventuring with him even longer than with me," Brad hissed. "Don't you think he deserves to know that you might be retiring to spend time with your princess? He's your horse, after all."

"He is not my horse," Thoral said softly, his violet eyes boring through the darkness to somewhere else entirely. "He was only lent to me by my wizard mentor, Yiz…" His voice cracked. "…just like the magic sword, *Blurmflard*."

Brad looked up at him, surprised by the sudden change in his friend's demeanor. "You want to tell me about it?" the fish whispered.

Thoral closed his eyes and was silent for a long moment before he took a deep breath and began. "I was not always as you know me now," he whispered. "No one now living knows this tale, but—"

He was interrupted by the sound of a patent-leather boot scuffing the cobblestones of the alley. Thoral went silent. He and Brad leaned forward and peered out from the concealment of the shadow of the big pile of boxes. A mysterious figure, cloaked and hooded in black, had entered the alley, his form edged with a sliver of silver light from the sliver of silvery moon.

"Wait for it," Brad breathed right in Thoral's ear.

The massive muscles of the warrior's forearms bunched as he tensed to throw the heavy net over their quarry. A few steps closer and the mysterious stranger would be their captive.

"Wait for it," the fish whispered.

The cloaked figure peered around the dark alley. "Trenton?" the stranger hissed, creeping closer to the ambush.

"One more step," Brad whispered.

The figure started to take that final step. "Trenton?" he hissed again.

"Now!" Brad breathed.

Thoral started forward, hefting the weighted net.

Just then, Trenton stepped into the alley with his lamp from the Broken Gate. "Hey, mysterious stranger," Trenton greeted the cloaked figure, startling him enough that he drew a long thin sword from its sheath at his belt.

Thoral scrambled back into the shadows, narrowly avoiding being revealed by the yellow glow of the lamp.

"What the—" Brad gasped.

"Ah, Trenton," the stranger hissed, dipping the point of his sword. "You are late."

"I stopped to buy a yam," Trenton explained. "A baked yam on a stick. It took a little longer than I figured because the yam vendor had just sold his last one right before I got there and I had to wait for one of the ones in his cart to finish baking. They take a long time. I guess I could have gone to another vendor, but this particular guy does his yams with all the fixings and even puts a little cheese—"

"OK, I get it. No problem," the stranger hissed, resheathing his blade. "Look, I'm a busy man. You said you had some secret information for me about what the Fist Wielder is up to."

"Yes," Trenton said, "I do."

Thoral and Brad exchanged worried looks.

"Excellent," the hooded figure hissed.

"Hey," Trenton said suspiciously. "You're not a Pooja Assassin, are you?"

"What do you know of Pooja Assassins?" the stranger hissed, pulling his sword again and drawing himself up so that he loomed over the guard.

"They hiss a lot," Trenton noted, cringing a little. "And so do you. That's all."

"Oh. OK. I thought maybe you were specifically referencing them in an I'm-playing-with-you-in-a-kind-of-cat-and-mouse way because you knew what happened to the squad of them that went missing a couple of days ago and you were trying to get a rise out of me to see if I was connected with that," the stranger said in a much more normal voice, relaxing back to his regular height.

"No," Trenton disclaimed. "I was really just wondering because of the hissing. You hiss a lot."

"Yeah, it's kind of an affectation," the stranger nodded, resheathing his blade. "You know, so people won't recognize my voice. You don't seem like a cat-and-mouse-games kind of person anyway."

"I'm not," Trenton confirmed. "I don't even like cats."

"Good," the stranger said, "because if I thought for a single second that you were trying to trick me into admitting that I'm a Dark Brother of the Bad Religion and that I helped arrange for that death squad to try to kill Thoral Mighty Fist, I'd have to kill you, too."

In the shadows, Thoral's eyebrows went up. Brad's would have, but fish don't have eyebrows.

"I'm definitely not trying to trick you into *that*," Trenton said, putting way too much emphasis on the word *that*. Everybody noticed it. The fish buried his face in his flippers.

"But you are trying to trick me into something?" the mysterious stranger hissed. He was back to hissing, just like that.

"Awww crap!" Trenton said, shaking his head. "You already know this is a trap? I told Thoral and Brad that their secret plan wasn't much of a secret if even I knew about it."

"A trap?" the stranger hissed, drawing his long, thin sword again. He crouched into a fighting stance and looked warily about the alley.

"Yeah," Trenton admitted. "I lured you here so that Thoral could jump you and torture you for information or something. He's trying to figure out who you are and some other stuff, I guess."

"So you've betrayed me? The Fist Wielder is here right now?" The stranger peered around into the darkness, his sword at the ready. Trenton looked around too. He held his lamp out at shoulder height and moved its beam in a slow half circle.

"Thoral?" he called into the darkness. "Brad?"

Thoral and Brad, holding their breath, crouched further back into the shadows behind the pile of boxes.

"I'm starting to doubt they're here, though," Trenton sighed. "I'm pretty sure that if they were here, they would have jumped you a long time ago, back when you weren't expecting it. You know, before you pulled your sword. I mean it would be pretty stupid of them to have waited while I accidentally revealed the whole trap. No, I guess I must have screwed up the plan somehow. I probably got the wrong night."

The stranger hissed a sigh of relief and lowered his sword.

Thoral sprang.

CHAPTER SEVENTEEN

Chasings in the Dark

The problem was that Trenton got in Thoral's way. The gate guard saw the blur of motion from the shadows and panicked, thinking that a bogey monster was attacking. There were a lot of bogey monsters in the land of Grome, so it wasn't a totally crazy fear. He screamed and tried to dodge out of the way, flinging his lantern into the wall of the alley where it clanged and went out. Miscalculating his escape path, Trenton jumped right into the mysterious stranger, knocking him out of the way so that Thoral landed on Trenton instead of his actual quarry. The two of them crashed to the ground in a big heap entangled in the gladiator's net with which Thoral had intended to snare the stranger. Brad was caught too because he was still on Thoral's shoulder.

"Bogey monster! Bogey Monster!" Trenton screamed.

While the three of them thrashed around, trying to escape, the stranger leapt to his feet. Noting his attackers' predicament, he made a show of calm by peeling off one of his black leather gloves and ostentatiously slapping the dust off his cloak with it. When he was done, he cleared his throat to attract attention, languidly putting his glove back on. Trenton finally figured out that it was Thoral and Brad in the net with him rather than a bogey monster and managed to calm himself. They all stopped thrashing and from the confinement of the net, peered up at the mysterious cloaked figure.

"So," the stranger gloated, pointing at them with the tip of his sword, "you must be the mighty Thoral Mighty Fist! Oh, how the mighty have fallen!" He started an evil laugh, but was cut off.

"Actually, my name is Trenton," Trenton corrected him. "The other guy is Thoral. Not the fish. The fish is named Brad."

"I was talking to the other guy," the stranger snapped.

"Oh, that makes sense," Trenton conceded.

"You have us at a disadvantage, sir," Brad interrupted, trying to sound cool with the fact that they were trapped in the net. "You know our names, but we do not know yours."

"That is not your only disadvantage," the stranger gloated. "In addition to not knowing my name, you are also at my mercy." He recommenced his evil laughter, but Trenton cut him off once more.

"Are you choking?" Trenton asked in alarm. "Do you need help?"

Although no one could see the stranger's eyes because of the hood, his body language suggested that he was glaring at the guard. "I do believe I will take almost as much pleasure in killing you Trenton as I will in dispatching Thoral Mighty Fist." The stranger sneered. He raised his sword, preparatory to stabbing them with it. Thoral growled in helpless rage.

"Wait!" Brad shouted.

The stranger stayed his hand. "What?" he asked.

"Aren't you going to gloatingly tell us your evil plan before you kill us?" the koi asked.

"No," the stranger hissed, drawing back his hand again to start delivering killing blows.

"Wait!" Brad shouted once more so that the stranger stayed his hand.

"What now?" the stranger spat, sounding kind of aggravated.

"You seemed to enjoy that little bit of gloating you did when we first got tangled in the net. I bet it would be even more satisfying to gloatingly tell us your whole plan. It would be like rubbing it in," Brad argued. "I mean, think about it from our point of view. We're helpless, at your mercy, about to die. The only thing that could make it worse for us and consequently sweeter for you would be if you gloatingly made us listen to all the bad stuff you're going to be up to once we're dead. Think about it."

"No," the stranger hissed for the third time. And with that, he stabbed Trenton through the chest.

"Hey, ouch!" Trenton complained. Those were his last words.

"That *was* satisfying!" the stranger gloated. He realized that Brad was right. He did enjoy gloating.

His gloat was short lived.

With the stranger's sword lodged in Trenton, Thoral threw the full force of his massive sinews into action and flung himself toward his opponent, snapping the blade under his weight as he rolled up the sword as if on a ramp and bowled into the stranger's shins. The figure in the black cloak let out a surprised squeal as he went flying backward and sprawled on the cobblestones. The leather-clad barbarian leapt to his feet, flinging the net away as he spun to face his opponent.

A hail of finger-length war darts coated in poison pudding greeted him so that he had to dodge acrobatically to avoid being skewered by the flying projectiles. One dart came so close to his right eye that it actually severed one of his tawny eyelashes as he blinked them closed. He tucked and rolled, drawing *Blurmflard* in one seamless motion as he sprang to his feet right in front of the stranger. He had practiced that move a lot because it was so cool looking and never failed to surprise his enemies.

But the stranger wasn't there.

"Drat!" Thoral roared. He spun toward the mouth of the alley just in time to see the tails of the black cloak disappearing around the corner.

"Go get him!" Brad yelled as he knelt on the cobblestones beside Trenton. He was too small to cradle the guard's head in his lap, and he didn't have a lap anyway because he didn't have any legs, but that's what he would have been doing if he could have. Technically, he wasn't even kneeling because he didn't have any knees. He was tailing, but the overall effect was roughly equivalent to kneeling.

Thoral ran over and crouched beside the fish. "Trenton," he whispered, his voice catching in his throat. "Trenton, my dear acquaintance."

Brad grimaced. There wasn't time for one of Thoral's dramatic death speeches. He always got so emotional when people died. "There's nothing you can do here," Brad scolded the warrior. "Get after the bad guy." He reached his fin up and gently closed Trenton's eyelids.

With a look of rage and sadness mixed with a small amount of embarrassment, Thoral leapt up and took off after the stranger. As he ran, he tried to sort out his feelings. He didn't know Trenton all that well and the guard was dim-witted and annoying, but Thoral felt responsible for his death. If he hadn't come up with the plan to put Trenton in danger, the guard would still be alive. It never sat well with Thoral when innocent people died, especially if it was his fault. Guilt and anger seared his heart and he thirsted for vengeance. Then he remembered how poorly the whole vengeance thing had worked out with the grode. It hadn't even felt good in the moment and it didn't fix anything. Besides, he needed to keep the stranger alive for information. And yet he was itching to punch the guy's head off. He was conflicted.

Thoral howled like a wolf as he ran beneath the wan light of the gibbous moon. All around town, people shivered in their sleep because of the fell quality of his dread ululation. Some people who were awake shivered, too, including the mysterious stranger. He was so wide awake he felt in danger of hyperventilating. He fled through the dark streets of the Thieves' District like the shadow of a snake, knowing there was no way he could survive a fair fight with the likes of Thoral Mighty Fist.

The stranger was fast. His running ability had been augmented through dark magic and pudding alchemy so that he could run as fast as a giraffe, which is about five miles per hour faster than the fastest human. He always experienced a sore lower back and buttocks the next morning, but that was a small price to pay in exchange for survival. He raced around a corner and down the crumbling cobblestones of Crumbling Cobblestone Street, past the long-deserted temple of the hideous tentacle-faced god of the foreign sailors. Nobody worshiped that god anymore because he was a jerk and his name was so hard to pronounce, even by Gromish standards. Even so, the mysterious stranger made the sign of the holy box as if to ward off evil. The dark windows of the abandoned edifice watched his passage like soulless black eyes. Not eyes that had been punched, not bruised eyes– but eyes that had black irises, or at least irises that were so dark brown that they appeared black. The building watched him with that kind of windows.

The mysterious stranger slowed to a walk and cast a backward glance over his shoulder for any sign of pursuit. Nothing. Had he evaded the legendary Fist Wielder so easily? After everything he'd been told about how dangerous the barbarian was and how no Dark Brother could risk leading the warrior back to their secret hideout? He came to a complete stop and scanned the length of the street to make sure no one was watching. In the dark depths of his black hood, he indulged in the luxury of a gloating smile.

Of course, that's when Thoral dashed around the corner from Dark Street with his sweat-glistening muscles and mane of tawny locks edged in silver moonlight. The stranger gasped. How could Thoral have covered the distance so fast? He hoped for a moment that his cloak would hide him from the pursuing warrior, but then Thoral pointed right at him and let out another of those blood-chilling howls. The stranger's bowels gurgled with anxiety. Why hadn't he killed Thoral first? Stupid! Now he would have to alter his plans. He sprang back to full speed, raced up the road and made a sudden turn from Crumbling Cobblestone Street onto Turny Lane, hoping to lose Thoral along its many impractical curves.

About a half mile behind the stranger, Thoral smiled. Turning onto Turny Lane was a significant tactical error. Thoral had realized, back in the alley, that the stranger was running way faster than a normal human. The tawny-haired warrior had miscalculated a bit, judging that the guy was running about as fast as a mule deer, or three miles per hour faster than the fastest giraffe, so he had begun to run as fast as a whippet, or about a half mile an hour faster than a mule deer and consequently three and a half miles an hour faster than the stranger or a fast giraffe. At that rate, on a straightaway, it would have taken him at least another three minutes to overcome the stranger's lead. Three minutes of opportunity for the stranger to lose Thoral. But on a curving course—and given the stranger's giraffe-like gait—the guy would have to slow down by more than a half mile an hour, reducing the catch-up time to something less. If Thoral had been good at math, he might have been able to calculate how much less, but he was more smashing-things oriented.

Thoral shot a look at the defunct temple of the tentacle-faced god as he raced past it. The tentacle-faced god kind of freaked him out, too. It was more than deeply weird that the tentacle-faced god was known in Reefma. This fact made Thoral wonder about things he didn't like to think about–things like the nature of the universe and reality. He forced down his creepy sense of foreboding and concentrated on the task at hand. Three minutes. What avenues of escape would his quarry pass in that time? Where could the stranger get in three minutes?

Only two-fifths of a mile ahead, but out of sight because of the curves, the stranger felt a cramp. He knew he could run through it, but it hurt like the dickens and he worried that he might not make it to safety before the barbarian caught him. If his sword wasn't broken and if he hadn't used up all his poisoned war darts, he might have considered hiding in an alley until the warrior ran past and then ambushing him, but there was no way he was going to try that now. He had just a small hatchet left, and he'd been warned about Thoral Mighty Fist: That you shouldn't attack him unless there was no chance at all that he could fight back was common knowledge.

No, he'd just have to keep up his speed and hope he could make it to his destination before the warrior caught up with him.

The stranger raced on, realizing that the sharp twists and turns of the road were forcing him to slow his pace a little. If he weren't careful, he'd soon be running only as fast as a warthog or a common house cat. He cursed his lack of foresight. And then he arrived at the intersection with Treacherous Precipice Street. He smiled and took a left.

One minute and twelve seconds after the stranger, Thoral arrived at the intersection and noted the signs of his quarry's passage. He was unfamiliar with Treacherous Precipice Street, but its name didn't bode well. Almost as soon as he turned down the dark lane, it began a steep incline. It must, he thought, be climbing toward Reefma's old city center from when Reefma was just a small stronghold overlooking the mighty River Spink on a high hill called the Teat. The Black Gem had long ago spilled over the walls of the old hold and grown a thousand and thirteen fold and ten in the intervening centuries, but the ruins of the ancient keep were still a popular attraction for tourists drawn by the breathtaking views of the city. Thoral had been there once, ages ago, with both his wife and his wizard mentor, Yiz. Warlordhorse had such a problem with his inner ear that he had been overcome by dizziness the first time they looked over the cliff at the edge of the river. Disoriented, he keeled over and fell off the cliff. Thoral had to catch him by his tail and pull him back up. The incident embarrassed the great tiger-striped stallion so much it ruined the whole outing. They left before they could walk across the swaying rope bridge to the abandoned watchtower on the far side of the river, even though the brochure claimed that it was "enchantingly romantic" and that the bridge was the oldest, longest and highest such structure in all of Reefma. Yiz was really disappointed.

Thoral worked hard to make sure he didn't decrease his speed on the steep hillside. It would be too easy to slow to the speed of a reindeer or a white-tailed deer, and he couldn't afford that. He was hopeful that heading up was another tactical error on the part of the mysterious stranger, but now he wondered where his black-cloaked quarry was leading him and why.

Despite the view and the tourism, the neighborhoods that clung to the sides of the Teat were not heavily populated. This was partly out of a superstitious fear that the ruins at the top were haunted by the ghosts of the garrison of soldiers killed when a large portion of the old Teat guard tower plunged down the eroding side of the cliff and into the icy waters of the mighty Spink. But it was also out of a more well-grounded fear that the rest of the hill was unstable and likely to fall into the river one of these days despite repeated attempts to shore it up. A handful of people died every year in such collapses, and the governors of the city were happy to line their pockets through expensive engineering boondoggles to support the sagging Teat. The net effect was that the higher you went, the more the buildings lining Treacherous Precipice Street were going to be deserted and the streetlamps unlit.

As Thoral neared the top of the Teat, dark clouds scuttled in front of the gibbous moon, murking its already wan light. Thoral drew *Blurmflard*, and said the magic word to make it glow. He held the incandescent pink blade aloft as he ran so as not to miss any signs of his quarry's passage or any sudden chasms where the road might have collapsed, unaware that the sword's garish light was drawing unwanted and portentous attention.

picking his way around cyclopean blocks of tumbled masonry and the foundations of long-since-fallen walls. Soon he stood at the foot of the perilous rope bridge that spanned the chasm above the mighty Spink and led to the abandoned watchtower on the far side. It was here that Warlordhorse had fallen. He inhaled again. Yes, the stranger had come this way. The creaking bridge swayed before him into the gloom where it was swallowed by a dense and creeping bank of fog that roiled like a ghost under the moonlight.

Thoral frowned. The span was hundreds of feet long and barely two feet wide. If the stranger was waiting for him in the darkness somewhere on the slippery, fog-shrouded expanse, *Blurmflard* would be useless. He daren't swing the mighty blade with support ropes stretched taut all around. If Brad were with him now, the fish would caution him against walking out on that treacherous path. But the fish was not with him. Thoral sheathed his magic sword and clenched his fists until his knuckles cracked like exploding stones. The sound echoed off the cliff walls, preternaturally loud in the stillness of the night. Somewhere far below, the mighty Spink murmured to itself on its way to the Briny Sea, as if put out by the startling noise. Thoral stretched his shoulders, limbered up his arms and strode out onto the bridge. It swayed nauseatingly under his weight.

"Mysterious stranger," Thoral rumbled into the night air as he marched along the expanse, "if thou thinkest thou wilt gain some advantage in unarmed, close-quarter fighting, then thou art mistaken. Destroying thee will be easy, so show thyself now whilst I am still predisposed to grant thee mercy."

Thoral's words were a bluff. Destroying his opponent *would* be easy. It was keeping him alive so that he could be questioned about the location of the hideout of the Bad Religion that would be tricky. Not killing the stranger while still winning the fight on this swaying, fog-slickened bridge would take some doing.

Thoral slowed as he approached what he judged to be the middle of the span. The fog was so dense it virtually blinded him. He sniffed the air again, hoping the intensity of the sweaty smell would give him some indication of how near his opponent was, but the foggy air was oddly free of taint. The warrior inhaled more deeply. Nothing. He frowned, puzzled. Then his eyes widened in realization. He placed a hand on one of the support ropes, it thrummed beneath his calloused palm.

Thoral whirled about, his feet skidding on the mossy planks. He freed *Blurmflard* from its sheath as he tore back along the bridge, faster than even the fastest cheetah, while the support ropes jerked and thrummed under the blows of the stranger's hatchet. He raced out from the edge of the fog bank forty feet from the cliff face and spotted the villain hacking away at the knot where all the key ropes came together–It was a poor design. The stranger squealed in fright at the sight of the onrushing warrior and gave one last, frenzied chop. The severed ropes whistled and snapped through the cold air. Thoral's stomach gave a sickening lurch as the bridge fell away under his feet and he plunged into the dizzying abyss.

CHAPTER TWENTY

Tofu

"Fool," the mysterious stranger gloated as he peered over the side of the cliff into the foggy darkness. There was a satisfying clang—probably the barbarian's body bouncing off the sheer rock wall—and then silence. The stranger was flushed and panting from the exertion of cutting the ropes and the surge of fear at seeing Thoral almost make it back. But his plan had worked! He sagged to the cold ground, his hatchet dropping from his nerveless fingers, and he skootched a few feet away from the edge of the precipice. He put his back to the massive anchor post of the suspension bridge and allowed himself a shiver of glee as the fog rose around him.

He'd done it! He had killed the mighty Fist Wielder. His evil master, the Heartless One, would be very pleased, even though he hadn't followed his master's orders to the letter. Technically, he was supposed to kill Thoral and bring his head back to the hideout of the Bad Religion for questioning. Everybody figured that the head would be much less dangerous if not attached to that mighty body. Even dead, no one was quite certain what Thoral might do if his body was intact. A small worry rose in the stranger's heart and gnawed on the leg of his self-satisfaction. Would he be punished for killing Thoral without getting the head? He chewed his lip, thinking.

The Heartless One was not called the Heartless One because of an overly forgiving nature. Although he had never spoken with the Grand Master of the Bad Religion, he had seen the left nipples of fellow brothers torn off for smaller deviations from orders. And people still whispered about that one guy who was grated to death with a cheese grater for some error or other. Was it too late to get Thoral's head? The warrior must have landed somewhere. If his body had tumbled onto the jagged rocks beneath the precipice, going down to get it might not be such a big deal. Sure, it would be messy work, and the head might be a little mushy from the impact, but his orders didn't specify anything about its condition, just that he was to bring it. He supposed that as long as even the tiniest scrap of brain had not been bashed from the skull, his evil colleagues would be able to reanimate the head enough to interrogate it. Yes, the only real problem would be if the barbarian had landed in the mighty River Spink. If so, his body might be halfway to the Briny Sea by now.

Agitated, the stranger leapt to his feet in the swirling fog but immediately crashed into a support beam from the bridge that had been right over his head. He spun sideways and staggered to the very brink of the precipice, where he teetered, waving his arms and clutching at the dark air trying to regain his balance. It was no good. He let out a piercing shriek and tumbled over the edge without appreciating the irony.

But he did not fall to his death. Instead, he hung suspended in the air, his flailing feet kicking at the river fog. After a moment, when his terror subsided just a touch, he turned his head and tried to look over his shoulder, but he could only see the inside of his own hood. He raised a trembling hand to pull the fabric back from his eye to see by what miracle he had been saved.

"Hello," said Thoral Mighty Fist. The warrior had him by the back of his thick black cloak.

"How?" the mysterious stranger barked in disbelief, all pretense of hissing gone. "You went down with the bridge."

"I will satisfy thy curiosity," Thoral allowed. "When the span gave way, I leapt to the face of the cliff just below the fog line and clung there. Then I climbed up."

"That's ridiculous," the stranger scoffed. "Given your body weight, the slipperiness of the rocks and the angle of the cliff face, there's no way you could have found a handhold."

"I did not," Thoral countered. "I drove my magic sword, *Blurmflard*, lent to me by my wizard mentor, Yiz, into the cliff face as if the stone were but butter that had been sitting at room temperature for some time."

"Curses!" the stranger huffed.

"Indeed," Thoral said with just the faintest hint of his own gloating. "Now I think it is time you satisfied my curiosity. Let us start with the revealment of thy concealed identity."

"Revealment isn't even a word," the stranger protested, but Thoral ignored him and grabbed the edge of the stranger's hood with his free hand. The guy clutched at the fabric with both hands trying to prevent him, but Thoral ripped it right off the cloak and dropped it over the edge of the cliff so that it fluttered down into the fog. After watching it disappear, the warrior turned his startling violet gaze upon the pallid face of the mysterious stranger.

"Your eyes are a peculiar color," the stranger said.

Thoral frowned. The stranger had a soft, chubby face, reddish hair, watery blue eyes and a weak mouth. He appeared to be in his early twenties. The barbarian didn't recognize him.

"I had developed a strong expectation that thou might be the evil necromancer I did kill twice already," Thoral said. "But unless I am sorely mistaken, we have never met."

"No," the stranger said, dejected. "I mean, yes. That is, you're right, we've never met."

"So why then did thou conceal thy face and mask thy voice?" Thoral asked.

"It's supposed to be ominous," the stranger conceded, sounding a little sheepish. "All the evil brothers of the Bad Religion do it."

"Fair enough. Now tell me who you are, why you were trying to kill me and where lieth the hideout of the Bad Religion."

"My name is Tofu," the stranger sighed, but Thoral burst into laughter before the stranger could say more.

"What?" Tofu demanded.

"That is funny. Thy name is Tofu."

"What's funny about it? Lots of people are named Tofu."

"Verily, I beg thy pardon," Thoral said, trying to control his mirth.

"That's just rude," Tofu snarled. "You've got me dangling over the edge of a thousand-foot drop, totally at your mercy, and you're mocking my name?"

"Chastise me not," Thoral countered. "Thou hast killed my friend Trenton and tried to kill me. Do not lecture me about rudeness."

"Point taken," Tofu sighed. "So I suppose you're going to drop me in the gorge if I don't answer your questions?"

"Verily."

"Well…I guess you'd better drop me then."

"Careful," Thoral warned. "I am not bluffing."

"I know," Tofu said, his lower lip trembling. "We were warned that you were pretty merciless. The thing is, the Bad Religion will do worse than kill me if I tell you. They'll know the second I start to reveal anything, and their retribution will be horrific. There's really no point in me giving you information to save myself a quick death given the slow, excruciating death that lies in store for me if I cross the Heartless One."

"The Heartless One?" Thoral repeated. "Who is that?"

"Our Grand Master," Tofu answered.

"Hark!" Thoral said, frowning. "I would rather not have to drop thee into this gorge to thy certain death. I will feel bad about it in the morning, and you seem to have information of great value to me."

"Oh, I could tell you stuff that would turn your hair white," Tofu confided.

"So perhaps we could work out an arrangement, thee and me."

"What kind of arrangement?"

"What if you were to join my force and I were to place thee under mine own protection?" Thoral offered.

"Seriously?" Tofu asked, sounding kind of hopeful for the first time since dangling over the edge. "Even though I killed your friend?"

"He was in reality, more of an acquaintance," Thoral returned.

"Can I think about it for a minute?" Tofu asked.

"Mine arm is mighty, but it grows tired," Thoral grumbled.

"Fine! Done! Yes!" Tofu caved. "I'll tell you everything. But you have to swear to protect me from the Bad Religion."

"I will do more than that," Thoral told him, "for I am sworn to slaughter that Dark Brotherhood to a man. After you tell me where to find them, there will be no Bad Religion to exact vengeance upon thee." And with that, he heaved Tofu back over the edge and set the turncoat on solid ground.

The ex-evildoer was somewhat stunned by this turn of events, but he smiled at the mighty warrior through the fog. "You know, you're not nearly as bad as the bad guys make out," he said. "So what do you want to know?"

"Let us start with the location of the hideout of the Bad Religion and progress to the details of their plot against the elves," Thoral suggested.

"Well, that's the funny thing," Tofu started, but he was interrupted by the sudden clatter of hooves on stone. "Oh, crap!" he shrieked. "They're coming for me!"

"I am as good as my word," Thoral growled. "Grab up thine hatchet and get thee behind me." Tofu hastened to obey, snatching his weapon from the slippery ground and raising it defensively as he moved behind Thoral.

"He's right behind you with a hatchet. Duck, Thoral!" Bradfast the fish roared as he raced forward on Warlordhorse. Thoral dodged and the tiger-striped stallion planted his front hooves and spun, delivering a perfectly executed flying-double-back-legged kick to Tofu's chest so that the hapless Dark Brother sailed backward into the void and vanished into the gorge with a shriek.

"Got him!" the koi shouted in triumph.

Thoral stood gaping as the shriek stretched and then cut off.

"Dang it, Brad!" Thoral roared.

CHAPTER TWENTY-ONE

Coins of Blood

"Honestly, he looked like he was about to hit you with that hatchet," Brad said, shaking his head as the companions sat eating breakfast in the common room of the Inn of the Gruesomely Gashed Gnome some hours later. "We thought we were rescuing you."

"Well, I guess it was an honest mistake," Thoral grumbled into his oatmeal. "I am sorry I was not more appreciative of your effort."

"No apology necessary. Although, you might want to smooth things over with Warlordhorse a bit. He used his Brendylschmylyn danger-sense to smell out where you were, and then it took everything he had to go out on that cliff face, given his issue with heights."

"He is a true friend," Thoral acknowledged. "And so art thou, Bradfast, although thy timing could not have been worse."

"The guy was really just about to tell you where the hideout of the Bad Religion is?"

"Verily," Thoral grumped.

"Wow!" The fish shook his head again. "So I guess we're back to square one."

"Mayhap."

The two of them ate for a moment in silence. The gruesomely gashed gnomish innkeeper came by their table to see if they needed any more bread, his one eye glittering merrily, but they waved him off.

"So as long as we're apologizing for things," Brad said, trying to cheer his friend, "I suppose I should admit that you were right about that stupid flying squirrel."

"WHAT?!" Thoral roared, spraying the fish with oatmeal.

"Geeze," Brad complained, wiping gruel out of his eyes. "What's the big deal?"

"That is it, Brad! That is what I forgot," Thoral exclaimed, his eyes alight with excitement.

"Come again?" the fish said, puzzled.

"The tracking trinket! I secreted a tracking trinket in Tyncie CheeChaw CheeChee WeeWaw," Thoral cried with a grin. "We can simply follow its ethereal vibrations straight to the hideout of the Bad Religion." He fumbled in his belt pouch and produced the other trinket, holding the blue, mouse-eyeball-sized crystal between thumb and forefinger. Its dot was glowing bright.

"Duh!" Brad said, striking his forehead with a fin. "It sure would have saved an awful lot of time if you'd remembered that sooner."

Thoral's smile faded. "And the lives of Trenton and Tofu," the warrior groaned.

"Oh..." Brad fumbled for something to say. "Thoral...I... wow...Look, I forgot about the tracking trinket, too. It wasn't your fault." But the damage was done. The mighty warrior stared into his oatmeal.

"So often the price of my mistakes is paid in coins of blood," he said morosely, laying the tracking trinket on the tabletop. "'Twas even so with mine wife and child."

"Thoral—" the koi started.

"'Tis true," the warrior sighed. "They were happy, my wife and son, dwelling in the humble house of my wizard mentor, Yiz. But I was not. A quest I had set myself– to find a Walking-Door Tree–and from that task I would not be dissuaded."

"What's a Walking-Door Tree again?" Brad interrupted.

"A tree that walks around with a door in it," Thoral explained. The fish nodded, making a mental note to ask more about that later.

"The child was but newly born when a traveling gypsy told me the whereabouts of the object of my search," Thoral continued. "And so I left my love and my child in the care of Yiz, and he lent to me his mighty steed, his magic blade and one of his two puny crystal-ball marbles that I might contact him when I had found the tree." The barbarian paused, staring into the dregs of his gruel as if watching the memory unfolding therein.

"And did you find it?" Brad prompted.

"Aye. After many days. But as I took out the crystal-ball marble to share my triumph, already my wife was using it to reach me. She cried out that they were under attack. The grode had come. He tore his way through the back wall of Yiz's cabin to get at them."

"No way." Brad's eyes were wide.

"Way," said Thoral. "My wizard mentor had been playing with the baby and was caught without his wand of power. Yiz was struck down trying to protect my child. I saw him ripped apart, and his blood splattered the crystal-ball marble as he fell. Yet, alas, cruel fate did not allow his crimson life-fluid to obscure my view of the horror to come. The foul beast went for my screaming infant. Crazed with mother fury, my wife moved to protect him, thus dropping the gore-slicked crystal-ball marble, which lodged in the floorboards at her feet. It was from that vantage that I helplessly watched her throw herself upon the grode. The beast merely laughed at her valor as it slapped her down. In that instant, the monster's visage was permanently inked upon my brain in horror, much as a tattoo is permanently inked upon one's skin in ink. Then the beast trod on the crystal-ball marble and it went black. The screams and sounds of mayhem continued for a few moments before even they went silent."

"Holy crap!" the fish exclaimed. "That's horrific!"

"Yes," Thoral whispered.

"What did you do?"

"I raced back to the cabin," the warrior continued. "Even with Warlordhorse running full out, it took days. I could have used *Blurmflard* to teleport back in the blink of an eye, but I had forgotten the magic word to trigger the spell. I still cannot remember it. When we finally arrived at the cabin, all was eerily silent. The house was abandoned and reeked of death. Inside, all was wreckage and blood and filth. There were torn clothes, my son's smashed crib and one breast upon the rough floor. My wife's. The left one. I recognized it instantly."

"Wait, what?" Brad interrupted.

"It was all that was left of my beloved," Thoral said, his voice catching. "A last forgotten bit of flesh overlooked, no doubt, in the foul feeding frenzy in which the grode consumed my family and my mentor."

The fish was speechless.

"I buried her breast and began my quest. A quest for vengeance," Thoral sighed. "Far and wide I searched for that grode, though ever he eluded me. Years I searched. And then, by chance it seemed, I found him. He fled and I chased him down. Fast he ran, about the speed of a pronghorn antelope. Warlordhorse was faster. At last, the grode stopped and I raged at him about my murdered love so that he might know who was about to kill him and why. As it turned out, the grode was cleverer than I. It was not by chance I had found him, but by his own wicked design. He had tricked me with a sly ruse and lured me into a trap. He caused boulders to roll upon us and Warlordhorse and I were hurled over a cliff to our deaths."

"YOU DIED?!" Brad gasped.

"Well, certainly it seemed as if we must die. I mean, it seriously appeared that way," Thoral backpedaled.

"You didn't literally die, though," Brad clarified.

"No. It appeared as if we must, but instead we fell into a river and were washed miles and miles downstream. I slipped into unconsciousness and would have drowned except that Warlordhorse pulled me from the water and breathed life back into my lungs. That was the first time my mighty friend saved my life."

"Whoa. That's eerily similar to that time you saved my life when I almost drowned," Brad observed.

"It is odd that you cannot swim," Thoral noted. The fish nodded. Thoral pushed on. "I was alive, though I had sustained serious injuries, as had Warlordhorse. By the time we returned to the scene of our encounter with the grode, he had vanished without a trace. I had been outsmarted." The warrior stared at his mighty hands then balled them into even mightier fists. "For a time, I lost my will to live. We wandered aimlessly, eventually taking on random adventures in order to fund alcoholic binges through which I attempted to drown my sorrows. That was how we found our way to Reefma, Warlordhorse and I. It was on one such bender that I stumbled across you, drowning in that fountain, and breathed life back into your lungs."

"So that's why your breath smelled like vomit and mead!" the fish exclaimed.

"Aye," Thoral conceded. The two of them sat in silence for a long moment.

"Well, wow!" Brad said. "That explains a lot."

"Verily," Thoral sighed.

"That was some bad stuff that happened to you," the fish said. "It's good that you've told me. You've always been so guarded about your past; I'm glad you were able to open up and tell me the full story."

The barbarian winced.

"Actually, that is not the full story," he admitted.

The fish frowned up at the warrior. "Do tell."

"I was not always as you know me now," Thoral began, leaning in conspiratorially toward the fish. "No one now living knows this tale, but—"

And, of course, he was interrupted as the tracking trinket began to vibrate, making a buzzing sound on the rough wooden table.

"Tyncie is on the move!" Thoral exclaimed. The companions leapt to their feet, upsetting a jar of strawberry preserves that Thoral had been using to flavor his oatmeal. It fell to its side on the table as the heroes raced from the room and the last of its contents spilled to the floor, pooling in sticky puddles shaped portentously like coins of blood.

CHAPTER TWENTY-TWO

The Bad Religion

An old, decrepit woman in a tattered shawl as gray as her care-lined face limped through the night gloom and ground-scuttling fog on the crumbling cobblestones of Crumbling Cobblestone Street. She leaned on an ancient walking staff, sighing with every step. Her hairy chin trembled as she mumbled to herself. A drunken gnome, who was stumbling home after a late night of carousing, bumped into her. The old woman squawked in outraged surprise.

"Excuse me, mother," the gnome apologized. The old woman wasn't his mother because he was a gnome and she was a human. It was just considered respectful to call old women *mother* on Grome.

The toothless crone clutched her threadbare shawl tighter and shook her staff at him, glaring, but said nothing as he staggered off. She watched him suspiciously with her bloodshot gray eyes until the darkness swallowed him, then she started to hobble down the road again.

The dark, dilapidated temple of the hideous tentacle-faced god of the foreign sailors crouched in the wan light of the gibbous moon like a hungry ghoul. The black windows of the abandoned edifice watched the dark street like the empty black eyes of a shark. From one of those apparently empty black eyes, eight actual evil eyes peeped out in all directions like the hideous tentacles of some weird octopus whose tentacles happened to be made out of the sightlines of evil people's eyes.

Four black-cloaked and hooded priests of the Bad Religion stood just inside the window, guarding the entrance to their secret hideout.

They were on high alert since the deaths of their first hit squad, the loss of their Pooja Assassins and the mysterious disappearance of their brother Tofu the night before. Tofu wasn't literally their brother; that's just how the priests referred to each other. They didn't even know him personally. Well, one of the four knew him a little and had watched him run past the night before and make the secret hand signal that indicated that there was trouble and that no one should come out. And a good thing too, because Thoral Mighty Fist had come racing along right behind Tofu, and everyone had been warned about the kind of damage the Fist Wielder could do.

The brother who had watched Tofu run past and three other priests were standing in the darkness when they saw the old woman hobble into view out of the fog. The men tensed as taut as bowstrings as they squinted at her. They had all ingested puddings for night vision and sharp hearing at the beginning of their watch and so saw the old crone as if she walked in broad daylight and heard her as if she were speaking with her lips to their ears.

"It is just an old woman," the leader of the watch whispered. He wasn't whispering just for secrecy's sake. It would have been deafening to the others if he'd spoken in a normal voice, what with their sharp hearing.

"She poses no danger," the lowest guy in the watch assessed, also in a whisper. He was, incidentally, the guy who'd watched Tofu run past. He had been the *leader* of the watch until Tofu didn't come back. He was demoted for not sending out a kill team to follow the barbarian and was still kind of chafing about that. Also, one of his nipples had been torn off as punishment, and he was definitely chafing about that.

"It is for me to assess the danger level," the newly minted leader hissed. He'd read a scroll on leadership qualities that morning and was trying to demonstrate his dominance. He was a bit loud and everybody winced.

"Fine," the lowest guy whispered sourly. "What is your assessment of the danger?"

The four priests watched the old lady working her way laboriously along the uneven cobbles, panting with the effort, her bony hand trembling as she clutched her staff. The clacking of the grimy stick and the shuffling of her sandaled feet echoed thunderously in the empty darkness as a backdrop for her mumbled complaints.

"Gnomes," she blared to herself in a raspy whisper. "Drunken layabouts! Do zey care about a poor, old, helpless voman viz barely zee strengz to make her vay home? Zee injustice!"

"She seems harmless," the senior priest judged. "Racist, but harmless."

"No racist is truly harmless," the guy with the torn-off nipple suggested.

"Oh, shut your trap," the newly minted leader snapped. "I meant she's harmless in this context."

The men relaxed again. Even as they did, the old woman's step faltered, and she seemed to stumble. But, no, she did not fall. She sprang forward, transforming as she moved. A golden-maned giant leapt from her decrepit old body as if shedding a cloak of vapor that dissipated as he emerged from it. The crone's staff was revealed as a great yew bow, razor-tipped arrows already whistling from its string.

"Fwang," the bow sang, whispering death at its intended victims. "Fwang, fwang, fwang."

The four priests fell without even a single strangled cry, arrows buried to their feathers in the brothers' throats.

"Show-off," Brad whispered in Thoral's ear from his perch on the barbarian's shoulder.

Ignoring the jibe, the warrior sped forward and vaulted catlike through the dark opening of the window. He crouched beside the bodies for a moment, ensuring they were dead, then retrieved the arrows as Brad leapt from his shoulder to check the pockets of their robes for anything useful. He found only black lint. Thoral had a little difficulty because one of his arrows was stuck in the demoted guy's neck bones. The warrior had to snap that guy's head off, but the shaft was undamaged. Thoral was relieved because he had his arrows specially made to his own design, and they were pretty expensive.

After wiping the arrows clean on one of the brothers' cloaks and tucking them back in his quiver, Thoral raised his right hand to his lips. On his ring finger, the Ring of Looks that Elfrod had given him scintillated with elfish magic. Thoral breathed across the golden band and a sudden cloud of vapor coalesced out of the air around him, completely obscuring him. The mist congealed around the warrior's form then sucked tight to his body, transforming him into an exact likeness of the leader of the priests. Magic disguise was one of the four powers of the great Ring of Looks.

"Really?" Brad said, disapprovingly.

"Is something bothering you?" Thoral asked, surprised by his tone.

"You couldn't just put on one of these guy's robes like we used to do before Elfrod gave you that fancy ring?" the fish demanded.

Thoral frowned at him. "What is the word for that attitude you are projecting right now?" The barbarian asked. "You know, that word that encapsulates the idea of sour grapes?"

The fish narrowed his eyes at the warrior in tight-lipped silence. Brad knew what word. Thoral always had a problem remembering it. They stared at each other over the dead bodies of the evil brothers.

"Jealousy," the koi spat finally.

"Jealousy is unbecoming, Brad," Thoral noted.

"Not everyone can wear magic rings," the fish sulked.

"And this bothers you because...?"

"Because I helped kill that sorcerer guy *both times*, and yet Elfrod gives *you* a gift I can't possibly use," the fish grumped. "I hadn't really thought about it before you transformed into that old woman. I just thought it was a pretty ring, but now that I know how cool it is, it's kinda bugging me."

"What if you took a turn wearing it on a chain around thy neck?" Thoral offered. The fish considered this.

"Does its magic work if you don't wear it on your finger?"

"No," Thoral admitted. "You have to wear it on your finger."

"So empty gesture then," Brad pointed out.

"Well, I would be giving up its use whilst you wore it," the warrior countered. "Surely that is worth something."

"I'll think about it," the fish answered. "In the meantime, you don't have to go using it all over the place. That's like rubbing salt in the wound."

***

Not far away and not long after, in the cavernous and dim-lit Great Feasting Hall of the Bad Religion, a tall, sable-cloaked priest paced the obsidian flagstones in a dark mood, his face obscured by the inky shadows of his hood. He cupped an onyx chalice in his hands from which he sipped at blood-black wine. The hall was crowded with hundreds of robed and hooded brothers having a late-night snack. Some were seated at the dozens of long mahogany feasting tables; others walked among them, refreshing drinks and handing out toasted bagels, dark with poppy seeds. All were listening to the tall one hold forth.

"Thoral Mighty Fist has twice slain the excellent, extraordinary and formidable Necrogrond," the tall one hissed as he stalked along the head table. There was a general grumble of anger from the gathered horde.

"Yes," said his chief henchman, Frobo, standing near the front of the group.

"And he poisoned the three brothers sent to poison him," the priest roared.

"Yes again," Frobo nodded, encouraging the crowd to boo and hiss their displeasure with a hand gesture.

"And he has most likely wiped out the death squad of deadly Pooja Assassins sent to wipe him out," the tall one spat.

"Yes," Frobo agreed. The crowd made outraged noises.

"And now! Brother Tofu has vanished without a trace after he was seen being chased by the barbarian!" the tall one raged, pacing in his fury.

"Yes," affirmed Frobo.

"I know in my aorta that the Fist Wielder has killed him," the tall one barked.

"Yes," Frobo agreed again. The gathered acolytes booed, shaking their hooded heads.

"Our brothers scour Reefma for some word of him or his accursed fish companion, yet no scrap of information comes to light," the tall one roared.

"Yes," Frobo sympathized while everyone else hissed.

"The Heartless One grows ever more affronted," the tall one bellowed, coming to a dramatic stop. "If we do not kill this barbarian soon, our very nipples will be forfeit." He drained his wine chalice and thrust out the goblet for a refill as a kind of visual punctuation.

"Yes," Frobo nodded. He was pretty much a yes man. He shuddered at the memory of last night's de-nippling as another brother brushed past him to refill the tall one's wine from an ebony pitcher.

"WE MUST FIND THORAL MIGHTY FIST!" the tall one screamed maniacally. "A THOUSAND GOLD COINS TO THE MAN WHO CAN FIND THIS BARBARIAN!!"

That's when Thoral threw off his drink-server disguise. "I will claim that prize," he laughed, his unnaturally white teeth and startling violet eyes sparkling in the gloomy room. The tall priest was so startled that he let out a high-pitched shriek and almost jumped out of his robe. He crashed right into Frobo, and the two of them fell into the throng of their gathered subordinates, knocking them down like dominos.

Then Thoral drew his great yew bow, *Fwang*.

"Fwang, fwang, fwang, fwang, fwang, fwang," *Fwang* sang as Thoral fired into the crowd. Six more priests fell without a single strangled cry escaping them, arrows buried so far in their throats that it was impossible to tell which direction they had come from. The rest of the brothers scrambled in screaming panic as Thoral leapt up onto one of the feasting tables. "Fwang, fwang, fwang, fwang, fwang, fwang, fwang, fwang, fwang, fwang, fwang, fwang." Thoral's great yew bow sang again and again. Although they were expensive, he had a lot of arrows.

The black-robed brothers of the Bad Religion tripped over their fallen comrades in their frenzy to get away from the crazed barbarian. There were more fwangs, and more brothers fell, arrows buried to the feathers in their Adam's apples, mouths, noses, eye sockets, ears and skulls. Thoral was pretty much a neck-and-head shooter.

"Blast it!" the tall priest roared from the floor as a Dark Brother sprawled across him with an arrow sticking in one side of his head and out the other. He shoved the dead man aside in fury and struggled to his feet, enraged by the chaos Thoral was causing. As he recovered his footing in the stampeding crowd, he saw something that changed his mood to exaltation.

"HE IS OUT OF ARROWS!" the priest bellowed, his voice booming through the hall with the aid of a magical amplifying spell. "HE IS OUT OF ARROWS!"

The announcement silenced and stilled the panicked brothers. One hundred and seventy-one pairs of eyes went first to the tall priest then shifted to the golden-maned warrior where he stood astride a feasting table. His bow was silent, his quiver empty. He shrugged, grinning.

To a man, the horde rushed him.

"TO THE DEATH!" Thoral cried, leaping down from the table and into the nearly two hundred men swarming him. He dove into their midst without the slightest hesitation, wielding his great yew bow like a cudgel. But there were too many. They knocked him down and surged over him until he was obscured from sight, like some big noble ant covered in smaller evil ants. It looked as if Thoral would lose. It completely looked that way. Seriously.

And he did.

A great cry of triumph went up, and a knot of priests dragged the golden-haired warrior out of the throng, insensible, blood streaming from his forehead. The tall priest, noting that Thoral appeared unconscious, rushed in and grabbed the warrior by his golden locks, yanking his head up so savagely that Thoral was bound to have a sore neck the next morning if he survived. Of course, if you knew Thoral, you'd know that this was exactly the kind of ruse he would pull, pretending to be unconscious to lure the chief bad guy in close enough to kill him. Classic Thoral.

Not this time. This time, he appeared to be unconscious for real. The tall priest pulled out a wickedly curved scimitar and lined it up with the back of Thoral's neck, just below his neck armor, while other priests held the barbarian steady. The tall priest raised the blade and lowered it to the back of Thoral's neck to make sure his aim was true. Normally, he would just have gone for it, but the neck armor made it a little trickier. He raised and lowered the blade one more time. It would be totally embarrassing to mess up in front of such a big crowd. The unconscious warrior's eyelids fluttered. The priest raised his vile blade in a two-handed grip above his head, his arms trembling as he prepared to chop. It seemed as if Thoral was doomed. For real this time.

The tall priest swung his blade in a great, glittering arc, striking just below the metal collar, chopping right through Thoral's massively muscled neck and lopping off the brave barbarian's handsome head, which fell to the floor with a wet thud.

"Thus ends the Saga of Thoral Mighty Fist!" the tall priest exulted, grabbing Thoral's severed head and raising it aloft by its shaggy golden locks, gore streaming to the floor as the gathered brothers roared their approval. Thoral's neck armor slipped off and fell to the ground with a clang, then rolled away into the crowd as if ashamed of its poor performance. The priest threw his head back as he cackled a black-hearted laugh of maniacal joy to the vaulted ceiling. His hood slipped off, revealing the black-bearded countenance of Necrogrond.

CHAPTER TWENTY-THREE

The Pudding Thickens

OK, so Thoral wasn't really dead. With the great Ring of Look's fourth power, magic copying, he had made a double of himself and then projected the double into the feasting hall. The real Thoral was standing on a balcony at the back of the room from which, disguised as a brother of the Bad Religion, he'd been shooting everyone.

"I don't get it," Brad whispered to him. "How could Necrogrond behead your magic double and hold the head up and everything? That was super convincing."

"After the double was pulled down by the crowd, I projected it onto one of the Dark Brothers," Thoral explained. Thoral didn't know it, but that guy had been Frobo.

"Wow!" Brad whispered. "Raw deal for that guy."

Thoral's brow creased in sadness. "I know," he said. "And who can say whether that man deserved the doom that befell him or if he—" The Fist Wielder cut off, raising a finger to his lips.

"Now that Thoral is dead," Necrogrond was shouting to his evil fellows, "I can finally tell you the details of our evil plan."

Thoral pricked up his ears and shot a look at Brad. The fish would have pricked up his ears too, if he had any. He was even more steamed at Thoral about the whole ring issue now that he knew the full extent of its power, but that discussion would have to wait.

"Many of you have asked about the large, glowing purple gem that we installed in the throne chamber last month," Necrogrond said. "Well, now I can reveal that it is actually … the Goomy Crystal!"

A sudden buzz of whispered chatter was audible among the brothers. Apparently, many of them knew what the Goomy Crystal was. Thoral and Brad had never heard of it, and they frowned in consternation. Necrogrond held up his hands to shush his followers.

"For those of you who do not know what the Goomy Crystal is," the sorcerer continued, "it is the last of the ancient Voodoo Stones of the Dark Lord Mauron, used in the forging of the Bracelet of Evil. It is a massive reservoir of unpleasant vibratory energy. And so *no one* must touch it." He paused for a moment, stroking his black beard and staring at his audience. There was an uncomfortable silence. The gathered brothers all knew that he was referring to the recent unfortunate incident in which a junior acolyte had fallen under the sway of the crystal and had been instantly cremated when he licked it.

"We have acquired the Goomy Crystal because it alone can point the way to the last resting place of the Great Pudding of Power," Necrogrond shouted, flecks of spit spraying from his mouth with the frenzy of his passion. The room erupted in a babble of voices.

"The pudding was destroyed," one guy said indignantly.

"Elfrod was said to have washed it down a drain," another guy scoffed.

"Surely, it would have gone bad by now," a third guy complained.

"The pudding is just a fairy tale that people with poor parenting skills use to threaten their children into behaving," a fourth guy asserted.

"NO!" Necrogrond roared. "The pudding is real. It is out there, and it is still as potent as the day Lord Mauron cooked it up." Then his countenance darkened, and he recited the vile "Poem of the Pudding" in the uncouth language of Splerph, where the pudding had been cooked on the black stove of Mount Grundle. An actual cloud formed over the sorcerer's head as he spoke, and it seemed to suck the light and warmth from the room. That's how uncouth Splerphish is.

"Nerglock pudding barfgick bloog,
Nerglock pudding turdlog toogg,
Nerglock pudding snotchunk Grome
Guglug buglug slugbug glome
Ratfart chub ta slimerug gloop
Lardblock taga maga poop!"

"For those of you who don't speak Splerphish, that means,
One pudding to rule them all
One pudding so sweet
One pudding to own the world
Such a tasty treat
Then you can survive the Bracelet
And everyone else's defeat!"

Necrogrond finished and paused for a moment to let the cloud dissipate and to let the lighting in the room return to normal, although the temperature remained uncomfortably cool. When it was bright enough to see again, he continued. "Once we have the pudding, the Heartless One will consume it, gain protection against the Bracelet of Evil, put on the bracelet and summon the power of the tentacle-faced god to dominate the world of Grome as its ruthless overlord."

Most of the gathered priests raised their eyebrows and murmured their satisfaction at the scope of this convoluted plan, although there were some who got the shivers or felt the need to pee out of fright.

"Of course," Necrogrond added, almost as an afterthought, "the first thing we will do is destroy Lord Elfrod and the elves. They're the only ones who still know how to counteract the pudding or unmake the bracelet."

There were more nods of appreciation and assent from the crowd, but Thoral's blood ran cold. "Oh," Thoral whispered, "I cannot have that. We had better kill all these evildoers right now." He moved to draw *Blurmflard*, but Brad stayed his hand with a fin.

"I'm concerned about their numbers," the fish cautioned. "There must be about a hundred and seventy-one of them, not to mention that Necrogrond is immortal or whatever. And you're all out of arrows. I don't like those odds. I think we'd do better to find this Goomy Crystal while everyone is distracted and destroy it. That will spoil their plan, and then we can just burn the whole place down with everyone inside and pick off anyone who manages to escape. Maybe fire will kill that sorcerer guy. He's proving as tough to get rid of as a weed."

"There is much wisdom in your words," Thoral nodded. "Although I am certain I would prevail if it came to a pitched battle."

"Sure you would." Brad rolled his eyes. The two of them slipped out of the room to begin their search for the Goomy Crystal.

Of course, just after they walked out, Necrogrond continued his speech.

"Oh, hey, everyone!" the sorcerer said. "I nearly forgot to mention that our plan is already underway. Just a few hours ago our agents captured Elfrod's daughter, Nalweegie, as she attempted to sneak into our hideout. She's refusing to tell us what she was up to, but the Heartless One will be here shortly to kill her."

CHAPTER TWENTY-FOUR

The Goomy Crystal

Thoral stood outside a fancy gilded door in a dark corridor of the ancient temple with Brad crouching on his shoulder.

"It's in there," Brad confirmed in a whisper. He'd used his koi whiskers to hone in on the unpleasant vibratory energy the crystal was throwing off.

Thoral tried the door. It was unlocked. Stealthy as a cat trained as a sneak thief, the barbarian sneaked through.

The room behind the door was as ostentatious as it was vast. It was well lit for all its size, by the evil purple glow that throbbed nauseatingly from a princess-cut, bowling-ball-sized gemstone that sat atop a soapstone altar at the far end of the chamber. The altar was carved to look like the tentacle-faced god, and the walls of the room were done up with lurid frescoes, bas-reliefs and architectural flourishes that featured tentacles and guys with octopi for heads. The sculptures weren't especially good from an artistic standpoint, although the pulsating light of the purple gem made them look as if they were undulating in a serpentine way that was pretty creepy.

"Do you suppose that's the Goomy Crystal?" Brad asked sarcastically, gesturing toward the big glowing gem.

"Mayhap," Thoral answered with a hint of a smile.

"It's a shame we have to smash it," the fish whispered. "I bet we could get a small fortune for it on Strange Street."

Thoral's sharp eyes searched the room for any sign of traps or defenses, but it was hard to tell if there was anything amiss given the undulating quality of the walls and ceiling. He sighed in resignation then crossed the vast expanse on tippytoe until he stood before the crystal. It rested on a cushion of purple crushed velvet beside a small box containing several finger-sized, glimmering cylindrical crystals. Thoral raised his brow at this but then turned his attention back to the Goomy Crystal. He waited a moment, bathed in the pulsating light, to see if anything was going to spring out at him. When nothing did, he relaxed and turned his head to address the fish.

"This seems too easy by half," the warrior gruffed.

"Or maybe it was just an excellent plan," the koi countered.

"Mayhap," the barbarian conceded. Then he raised a mighty fist to smash the gem.

That's when the giant snake that guarded the crystal dropped from the rafters of the throne room onto Thoral and smushed him to the black marble floor, sending Brad flying. It was a jet-black snake, about thirty feet long and as thick around as two fat men hugging. Its bright red skull-and-crossbones-shaped markings, in combination with the sizzling venom dripping from its gleaming two-inch fangs, suggested to Thoral that it might also be poisonous.

"Snake!" Brad screamed, flopping away on his belly as the snake encircled Thoral in its undulating coils. Man and snake rolled across the marble tiles, locked in a deadly wrestling match. The snake struck at Thoral lightning fast, but the barbarian still had one arm free and blocked its bite with the heavy brass buckler on his forearm. He rolled over on its head, trying to crush it. Its skull was too thick. The snake wriggled under the warrior's buckler for a moment, pumping out great gouts of stinking venom that corroded the metal and left nasty stains where it pooled on the floor. Then it managed to get its head free. It reared back and struck at Thoral's throat. Its teeth clanked off Thoral's neck armor, and it hissed in outrage. It pulled back for another strike, simultaneously squeezing Thoral with bone-crushing force. Brad danced in on his tail fins and slapped at the cold-blooded beast with his pectoral fins, distracting the snake just long enough to prevent it from striking. Thoral was in sad shape. The snake held him so tightly that he couldn't inhale, and he started turning blue from lack of oxygen. His ribs cracked, at the point of breaking. His vision darkened and it seemed as if he was finally really going to be killed. This wasn't some magically projected double the snake was squeezing. It was really Thoral, and he was really dying. Seriously.

But then Thoral flexed every muscle in his body at once. With a sound like a massive whip cracking, the snake tore in half, like a stack of jelly-filled donuts ripped apart from inside the shaft formed by their holes. Ragged half-coils of snake flopped everywhere, and Thoral was bathed in a cascade of slimy snake innards.

"Gross!" Brad gagged, impressed, as he struggled out of a sticky pool of gore.

"Verily," Thoral returned. Raising the Ring of Looks to his lips, he breathed across it and was all spiffy clean again. Brad narrowed his eyes at the warrior as snake goop dripped down his scales.

"Those of us who weren't given magic rings could use a towel," the fish grumped.

Thoral produced his towel from one of his belt pouches and tossed it to the koi. Then he squared his shoulders and approached the Goomy Crystal once more. He balled his mighty fist and focused his penetrating violet gaze on the innards of the great gem like an expert jeweler, examining it for any internal flaw that might render one point more susceptible to fracture than another.

The gem was perfect. Actually, it was more than perfect. It seemed alive. The purple light danced within the depths of its purple facets like purple fire. Thoral felt as if his spirit were being sucked out of his purple eyes and into its purple interior like curling purple smoke sucked out of a weed pipe and into the lungs of some evil purple smoker. He stood before the gem, transfixed.

CHAPTER TWENTY-FIVE

The Peril of Nalweegie

Back in the cavernous and dim-lit Great Feasting Hall of the Bad Religion, Princess Nalweegie was dragged before Necrogrond and forced to the floor at his feet in chains and little else. He had ordered his minions to dress her in the skimpy underclothes that he always carried around with him in case a woman fell under his power.

"Ah, fair Evening Snack," Necrogrond gloated. "We meet again."

The princess glared up at him through the tangled locks of her disheveled raven hair, her ivory breasts heaving, her emerald eyes alive with the fierce green fire of her chartreuse hatred. "You!" She spat the word and then literally spat spit on the hem of his black robe.

"So you remember me. I am pleased," the sorcerer chortled. Truth be told, he was kind of into being spat on. He stroked his black beard but then realized he was doing it again and stopped.

"How is it I find you whole?" Nalweegie asked. "Twice now, Thoral Mighty Fist, the love and light of my life, has mangled thee even unto thy death."

"I have consumed a pudding of immortality, my dear," Necrogrond giggled. "No weapon forged, crafted or assembled on the world of Grome can bring about my doom. Neither fleshy appendage, nor shard of bone, nor bit of rock, nor rigid limb of plant, nor fibrous rope, nor suffocating cloth, nor pinching fingers, nor drowning liquid, nor stompy boot, nor tooth or claw of monster or beast, nor flame, nor ice, nor lack of any vital substance like air or food or blood, nor heatstroke, nor hypothermia, nor infectious disease, nor poison, nor tainted food, nor parasitic attack, nor any fall, nor accidental or intentional crushing or mangling, nor allergic reaction, nor garroting wire, nor any magic conjured or created in this universe, nor old age, nor lack of sleep or exercise, nor even overconsumption of undercooked meats or fatty snacks can do me in. I simply come back to life whenever I feel like it."

"Wow!" Nalweegie said, her eyes wide. "That's pretty thorough."

"It's just *thorough*," Necrogrond corrected her. "If something is thorough, it's thorough. You can't be partially thorough, so it's stupid to say that something is *pretty* thorough. It doesn't make any sense. It's as bad as saying something is completely complete."

"Well, despite how thorough your protection is, I'm pretty sure Thoral will still figure out some way to kill you once he learns you have captured me," the princess countered.

"Oh, really?" Necrogrond asked, doing a pretty good job of faking actual concern. "Maybe we should check with him."

"What?" Nalweegie said, caught off guard.

"Yes, we should ask him," Necrogrond continued, unable to contain a gleeful smile. He reached behind him as the princess watched in pretty confusion. "Hey, Thoral," Necrogrond called, "what are you going to do now that I've captured Nalweegie?" And with that, he pulled out the gore-dripping head, still a perfect copy of Thoral's, and swung it at Nalweegie so that congealing neck blood spattered her fair skin.

"No!" she screamed, trying to scramble back in horror and despair, her own head spinning as Necrogrond stepped aside to reveal the headless, leather-clad, muscle-bound body sprawled in a pool of blood behind him. "Noooo!"

"Yessssssss," the sorcerer sighed, drinking in her pain like a rich and steamy hot chocolate with clotted cream.

CHAPTER TWENTY-SIX

Mind War

"Hey, Thoral," Brad said for the fifth time, snapping his pectoral fin as a human might snap his fingers. Thoral stood swaying, his startling violet eyes fixed, unblinking, on the Goomy Crystal.

"THORAL!" the fish yelled. "THORAL!"

The barbarian was lost in the purple depths of the crystal, its evil voodoo power wrestling for control of his mind.

"Being," the crystal whispered, its voice caressing the wrinkly surface of Thoral's brain.

"Yes?" Thoral answered out loud.

"Ah, great! You're back," Brad said, relieved. Thoral didn't hear him.

"Being," the crystal repeated. "Lick me."

"No," the warrior grunted.

"Just one lick."

"No."

"Fine. Then join me. Together we can rule this world."

"No," the barbarian repeated.

"I heard you the first time," Brad said. "What's going on?" Thoral didn't acknowledge him in any way.

"I can sense an unusual force in you that I have sensed in only one other being in all the history of this world. Give yourself to me, and I will teach you to forge a toe ring that will shake the very pillars at the foundation of Grome," the crystal whispered.

"I am not sure I want that kind of toe ring," Thoral growled.

Brad stood at the warrior's feet and frowned up at him. "Are you talking to me?" the fish asked, looking around to make sure no one else was in the room with them.

Thoral ignored him. He was distracted because the Goomy Crystal was bending the full force of its unpleasant vibratory energy on him. A lesser man would have licked the crystal already.

"Come on, everybody wants that kind of toe ring," the crystal cajoled. "With that kind of toe ring you could bend the whole universe to your bidding."

"Verily?" Thoral asked. "Could I travel to different dimensions?"

"Hey, Thoral," Brad said, a bit alarmed now, "you're starting to freak me out. What are you talking about?"

"Certainly. Different dimensions, other worlds, parallel universes. I am the Voodoo Stone that taught Lord Mauron everything he knew," the crystal said silkily. "I'm the one who showed foul Glurpgrond how to forge the magic Bracelet of Evil. I could do the same for you, teach you how to forge an evil toe ring, earring, headband, choker or anklet. Together we would be gods."

Thoral was quiet for a long moment, considering. Turmoil seethed within the violet depths of his eyes as longing struggled with righteousness egged on by regret. He knew he should refuse the crystal, knew that it was evil. He opened his mouth to speak, but no words came. He swayed drunkenly, staggered back a half step.

"Can I have a moment to consider?" Thoral finally asked.

Brad was done trying to talk to his friend. Something weird was going on. He started to scramble up the warrior's leg to slap him in the face.

"You disappoint me, being," the crystal sighed. "I offer you the universe, and you need time to think about it? If you will not join me, I will devour your soul, possess your mind and cremate your body. DECIDE!"

"Then let us battle!" Thoral roared. He hated being rushed. With that, he threw the full force of his will at the psychic essence of the Goomy Crystal, and the two of them had a mind war.

Although outwardly Thoral was just standing there, eyes fixed on the crystal, inwardly he was locked in deadly combat with the stone's essence in the form of a hairless purple giant. That's how mind wars work. The warrior's consciousness punched the crystal's essence right in the gut and then grabbed it around its midsection and tried to throw it to the ground. Unfortunately, the crystal's massively muscled psyche burst free and delivered a stunning, double open-handed slap to Thoral's mental ears so that his psychic eardrums popped and threw off his spiritual equilibrium. The warrior's soul staggered backward, and the crystal kicked his consciousness hard in the psychic testicles. Thoral's spirit doubled over, ethereal eyes watering, and the crystal closed on him, chuckling. It grabbed his being by his astral golden locks and drove its ghost knee into the barbarian's phantasmagoric chin, then smote him upon the top of his insubstantial head with both psychic fists so that the warrior's essence crumpled to the ground, dazed. Thoral struggled back to his transcendental hands and knees, but the crystal smashed a psychic chair across Thoral's incorporeal back. He went down, his subconscious on the verge of unconsciousness.

The Goomy Crystal's essence stood over the beaten warrior's astral projection and fished around in its spirit pocket for a straw with which to suck out Thoral's soul. The warrior tried to find his ethereal feet but could not. The crystal took its time tearing the end off of the ghostly paper wrapper containing the straw and then blew through the straw so that the wrapper shot Thoral in the ghost-face. It didn't hurt the warrior psychically, it was just very mean-spirited on a symbolic level.

The crystal yanked Thoral's mental projection toward itself by the lapels of his insubstantial leather vest and inserted the tip of the straw so deep into Thoral's psychic solar plexus that it punctured his soul. Then, with a wink, it started slurping up his essence.

Thoral's physical body showed immediate signs of distress. It started to shake, sweat broke out on his real forehead, his actual skin went gray, the light went out of his physical violet eyes, and his corporeal lips started to chap. Then his whole concrete-self began to wither.

"Thoral!" Brad shouted, now on his friend's shoulder. "What's happening to you? Snap out of it!" But the warrior paid him no heed and continued to desiccate before the horrified koi's very eyes.

The Goomy Crystal pulsated and chortled and made psychic lip-smacking sounds as it continued to drink down Thoral's life essence. "Yum," it sighed, delighted. The warrior made only a slight choking noise as his soul deserted him and he gave up the ghost.

"THORAL!" Brad shouted again, and he slapped his companion so hard across the face that the warrior's head turned just enough to break his eye contact with the Goomy Crystal.

Thoral blinked, as one awakening from an unsatisfying mid-morning nap. His body was so dried up that it was starting to smoke. He could barely move, but his hand found its way to the hilt of *Blurmflard*, the magic sword lent to him by his wizard mentor, Yiz.

The crystal shrieked and focused all of its unpleasant vibratory energy on trying to suck down the last little frothy bits of Thoral's soul, but the warrior staggered forward and slammed *Blurmflard* down on the stone with all of his remaining energy.

There was a brilliant purple flash and a cataclysmic—but silent—explosion. The last of Lord Mauron's Voodoo Stones exploded into a billion shards of whirling crystal with such force that Thoral and Brad were hurled across the room. They banged up against one of the ostentatiously carven walls and crumpled to the floor. All was silence and jet-black darkness.

"Thoral?" Brad called into the murk, his voice rasping from having inhaled a bunch of purple crystal powder. It had an overpowering grape flavor. "Thoral?" No answer came. The fish stifled a sob and felt around in the darkness for his fallen comrade. His questing fins found only cold marble. Defeated, he gave up and sagged to the floor, tears welling in his big bulging eyes. How long he lay there weeping he did not know, but it was about thirty seconds.

And then a pink glow brightened the cavernous throne room, glinting off the coating of shimmering crystal dust that blanketed Brad.

"I thank you, fish," a voice rasped in the growing light. And Thoral was revealed, *Blurmflard* clutched in one mighty fist, a trickle of blood at the corner of his manly smile. "But your slap is weak like a pixie's." The two hugged as brothers. Well, as brothers if one were a human and the other a fish.

"And now," Brad said, "let's go kick Necrogrond to paste."

"Agreed," Thoral answered. "Hold a moment, though. Methinks I saw something of interest beside the Goomy Crystal. Necrogrond will keep a few moments longer." The companions got to their feet and approached the powder-covered alter again.

CHAPTER TWENTY-SEVEN

Princess of Despair

Back in the cavernous and dim-lit Great Feasting Hall, Necrogrond stared at Princess Nalweegie with a leering, icky look on his face as she lay weeping on the floor beside what she believed to be Thoral's severed head. She looked pretty good in the skimpy underclothes and chains.

"My beloved idiot," the princess whispered through her tears, "I came back for you because somehow I knew you would not heed my warning, even though I think it would have been hard to have been more specific about what was going to happen to you. Alas, I am too late, for here lies your severed head, just as I saw it in my dream. And now that you are lost, I cannot face the thought of having to marry another."

Unable to hear her, the sorcerer chose this unfortunate moment to lean down and whisper in her ear, "I might be able to talk the Heartless One out of killing you if you agree to marry me. You have to decide right now, though. There isn't much time. Our leader will be arriving any moment."

The princess sat up, sniffling and wiping the tears from her cheeks. "Really?" she asked. "You would spare me? Last time you captured me, you said you were going to eat me."

Necrogrond cocked an eyebrow at her. "That was last time," he said. "I can be merciful to those who serve me. Especially if I'm not hungry."

The princess gave him a long and searching look. "You do have a fairly attractive beard," she admitted, casting her eyes down demurely.

Necrogrond stroked his thick black beard and tried not to smile.

"Can I touch it?" the elfish princess whispered, her cheeks flushing.

Necrogrond shot a secret glance around the crowded hall to see if anyone was watching the exchange. "You should say 'may I touch it,' but I suppose you may," he answered. "You must hurry though. The Heartless One will be here any second." He leaned in close to her, thrusting his chin out to give her better access.

In a flash, Nalweegie had him by the beard and was on her feet. She tossed a loop of her chain around the sorcerer's neck, twisting it tight with surprising strength for one so delicate.

"Everyone back!" she roared to the assembled brothers, yanking Necrogrond off his chair and onto the ground in front of her. "If anyone moves, I will twist his head right off. I swear it."

"Gak," Necrogrond spluttered, clawing at the chain. He was trying to remind the rest of his order that he was immortal and that they shouldn't hold back on his account, but the princess was constricting his windpipe so that he could only make weird noises. Nalweegie gathered the chain into one hand and drew Necrogrond's wickedly curved scimitar from his belt sheath with the other. She brandished the blade at the gathered Dark Brothers.

"Clear a path to the door," she shouted, gesturing toward the main entryway of the feasting hall.

"Grrglrrrr," Necrogrond gurgled, trying to pry the chain away from his throat just enough to tell the brothers not to listen to her. Her grip was like iron, and he couldn't get a breath. The Dark Brothers looked at one another in fear and confusion, many of their eyes going to the piles of their dead brethren still heaped about, with Thoral's arrows sticking out of their heads and throats. The survivors stepped out of Nalweegie's path to the door.

The elfish princess brandished the scimitar, yanked the chain tighter still and pulled Necrogrond around, his butt squeaking on the polished floor. He wasn't wearing underpants. He never did.

Then she dragged the struggling sorcerer backward toward the door, his feet kicking to no effect, his fingers still clawing at the chain as the assembled brothers watched in eerie silence.

Nalweegie made it to the door and was trying to figure out how to turn the handle without releasing either the scimitar or the chain when the portal swung wide, as if of its own accord. A scarlet-robed figure loomed in the opening, its face concealed by a voluminous hood.

"The Heartless One!" the gathered brothers gasped. They dropped to their knees, heads bowed.

Princess Nalweegie's emerald eyes went wide. "Rats," she whispered.

CHAPTER TWENTY-EIGHT

Narthrykryn

"Zapping crystals," Thoral said as he stared down at the finger-sized crystals in the box on the altar.

"Narthrykryn?" Brad asked from the warrior's shoulder.

"Yes," the barbarian confirmed, a tentative smile touching his lips. "I can never remember what they are called." He reached toward them but hesitated, his hand hovering in the air just above the stones. "I wonder if any hold a charge. It has been years since I have seen a charged one."

"No idea. Can you tell just by looking?" the fish questioned.

The warrior shook his head. He stared down a moment longer then plucked one from the box and brought it to his lips. He poked the tip of his tongue at it, wincing in the event that—

ZAAAAP!

A blue spark arced from the tip of the crystal to the tip of the barbarian's tongue. He almost dropped the stone in the jolt of the initial shock but used his faster-than-a-cat reflexes to recover. A huge grin spread across his face.

"Is that good?" Brad asked, puzzled.

"That is good," Thoral confirmed.

"Can we use these to fight the Bad Religion or something?" the koi wondered.

Thoral was no longer listening. He was digging through his bag of magic stuff that held his dearest possessions, including the coil of what appeared to be white string, the metal wand he very rarely used and the thin, black, rectangular box that hadn't worked in years.

As the fish watched, brow furrowed in puzzlement, the warrior removed the thin, black, rectangular box and brought the tip of the crystal to touch its oddly perforated bottom. There was a crackling sound, and the face of the box changed from dead black to a kind of glowing black. A small, white semicircular symbol blinked on in the center of the rectangle. The fish peered at it from Thoral's shoulder. It appeared to be the silhouette of an apple with a bite out of it.

"What magic is this, Thoral?" Brad asked. The warrior didn't seem to hear him. His handsome face bore a look of intense joy the fish had rarely seen, and he was fumbling in the pouch again, his hands shaking as he took out the coil of what looked like white string. He plugged one end of the string into the box and separated the other end into two strands that terminated in white blobs. These blobs he inserted in his ears. And then the whole face of the box lit up, revealing a picture of a sunset behind mountains so lifelike that it took Brad's breath away. Strange runes in no language the fish had ever seen also appeared. Thoral swiped a trembling finger across the bottom of the screen, and many little square shapes of various colors converged across the picture of the sunset. Thoral touched one of these and swiped his finger across the screen several more times. Brad heard a buzzing, throbbing sound, coming from the blobs in Thoral's ears.

"*Grvlxrzp*," Thoral sighed, tears welling in his eyes. "*Rxlrgp zrgrlrinxt*!"

"What?" Brad demanded. "What did you say?"

"Sorry," Thoral said, his voice too loud, his face beaming. "I was overcome. Listen."

As the fish frowned, the warrior touched the box again and the sound was silenced. He pulled the blobs from his ears, disconnected the string from the bottom of the box and then touched its face again.

There was a rhythmic clicking sound, like two sticks clacking together, and then music unlike any Brad had ever heard blasted from the box, stirring the fish's soul with its raw power and ferocity. As a rough, high-pitched voice started screaming lyrics in an incomprehensible language, Thoral started to thrash his head to the sound, his tawny mane flying. It was "Back in Black" by AC/DC.

CHAPTER TWENTY-NINE

Meanwhile...

Nalweegie swung the scimitar at the Heartless One with everything she had. The red-robed figure sidestepped the blade and lashed out at the elfish princess with a scarlet-shrouded arm. Nalweegie dodged back, putting Necrogrond between her and her opponent.

"No closer or he dies," she warned, putting the scimitar to his throat. The Heartless One surprised her by delivering a flying kick to the sorcerer that broke her hold on him and sent him tumbling across the floor as if he'd been kicked by an elephant. He crunched into the far wall, screaming in pain as a large number of his bones exploded from the impact. The Heartless One took no notice. The silent, crimson-cloaked figure advanced on Nalweegie.

The princess cast about with her eyes, desperate for an avenue of escape, but the Dark Brothers had begun to close in on her like the deadly drawstring at the waist of a pair of very dangerous drawstring pants. Nalweegie ran the calculation in her head. Her best chance was still the door behind the Heartless One; decisiveness would be her best ally. Without a moment's further hesitation, she launched herself at the carmine-caped commander of the Bad Religion, swinging her scimitar with considerable ferocity and expertise.

Unfortunately, she was no match for the surprising speed of her foe, who again sidestepped her blow, but this time, struck back. The Heartless One slapped the elfish maiden's forearm with such force that both her radius and ulna were shattered. Before Nalweegie's emerald eyes even had time to register her shock, before her delicate pointed ears even heard the clang of her weapon on the black floor, the Heartless One had seized her by the throat and lifted her one-handed off the ground.

The princess's dainty feet thrashed the air, and she clawed at the Heartless One's hand with the hand of her unbroken arm. Her opponent's grip was like grumburger, a metal the dwarves mine deep below the surface of Grome that is harder than steel and consequently super pricy. The blade of *Blurmflard* was forged of pure grumburger. Nalweegie gasped for breath, her milky-white complexion reddening to the color of a strawberry milkshake and her emerald eyes bulging. She fought with everything she had, to no avail. As the Dark Brothers watched, she continued to slap ineffectually at the Heartless One's hand while the russet-robed figure stood silent and implacable. After a moment, her struggles grew weaker.

CHAPTER THIRTY

Ciphers Deciphered

"So...what the heck?" Brad asked after the last notes of the song had shivered off into silence.

Thoral eyed his friend long and hard. He sighed. "I was not always as you know me now," he began. "No one now living knows this tale, but—" He stopped, and both man and fish glanced around expectantly for something to interrupt him. When nothing did, he continued. "I come from another world," the warrior concluded.

The fish did a double take. "Another world?" Brad asked.

"Or a different universe or dimension," Thoral hedged. "I am not certain."

"This explains so much!" Brad exclaimed. "The odd accent, the preposterously fast reflexes, the strange hygiene practices. Are everyone's eyes that weird color in your dimension?"

"No, my eyes changed color after I arrived here. I do not know why," Thoral mused. "They used to be blue. My home planet is called Earth, and I came to Grome by accident some thirty-odd years ago when I was but a boy of thirteen."

"Holy crap!" Brad exclaimed. "You're forty-three? You look much younger."

"It is an estimate," Thoral answered. "There was a long section after my wife was killed when I was drunk and lost track."

"Did she come from Ears too?" the fish asked.

"Earth," Thoral corrected. "And, yes, she did. Nancy and I came through together."

"Nancy?" Brad asked. "What an outlandish name."

"Would you care to see a picture of her?" Thoral asked. He reached down inside his leather vest and produced the silver locket with the leaping dolphins that he'd been wearing ever since he'd scrubbed the grode poop off it and sterilized it with alcohol. The fish leaned down to take a closer look as Thoral pried open the cover of the locket. Inside one of the oval halves was a photograph of a pretty, sweet-faced, auburn-haired girl in a bikini, but Brad barely glanced at it, instead focusing on the photo in the other half, of a scrawny, blond-haired boy in short pants. The fish knew immediately it was Thoral.

"Where are your huge muscles?" Brad demanded. "You look totally wimpy."

"I was just a normal boy on my world, but my gigantic muscles and fantastic athleticism began developing shortly after I arrived on Grome."

"Nice. I wonder if I would turn into some kind of super fish on your planet."

"There are no talking fish who can breathe air on Earth," Thoral told him. "So you would already be fairly amazing."

"How do they make these pictures so realistic? Magic?" the koi questioned.

"They are called photographs," Thoral said. "They are made with science." He closed the locket and tucked it back into his vest so that it nestled in the golden chest hair over his heart.

"Science? What's that?" Brad asked.

"That is complicated to explain," the warrior noted. "It's the same thing that makes my iPhone work." He indicated the black rectangle that had played the music.

"You brought that with you, I assume."

"Yes. And a few other things," Thoral answered. "I should tell you the full story later, after we have slaughtered the brothers of the Bad Religion and burned this vile temple to the ground with Necrogrond inside it."

"Oh, yeah," Brad said, shrugging. "That." They left the throne chamber.

CHAPTER THIRTY-ONE

Meanwhile Some More

Nalweegie's limp body hung in the Heartless One's hand. The leader of the Bad Religion pulled the princess close to examine her, then dropped her body to the floor like a rag doll. Necrogrond came limping up, snapping some of his bones back into place, his head still partly caved in. He crouched down beside Nalweegie and put his fingers to her purpling throat. There was a faint pulse.

"She's not dead?" he rasped in surprise through his damaged larynx. Of course she wasn't dead. The Heartless One made no answer but stared at him in eerie silence as his head began reinflating to its normal shape.

Necrogrond concealed a sigh of exasperation. This was standard operating procedure. The Heartless One rarely spoke, as if far too important to bother with words. Yes, it was spooky, but it was also kind of annoying.

"So you spared her to use her to bait a trap for her father," the sorcerer guessed confidently.

The red-robed figure shook its head.

"No, not that," Necrogrond said, shaking his own head. He was much more tentative about his next statement, this time making sure to frame it as a question. "Okay, so did you spare her to torture her for information about how to find the secret valley of the elves?"

Again, the Heartless One indicated a negative.

"Hmmm," Necrogrond said, trying to buy some time while his mind raced. It was always dangerous guessing wrong more than twice before the leader of the Bad Religion. He'd seen the left nipples of other brothers torn right off for three bad guesses in a row.

"Uhhhhh…" he stalled, sweat popping out on his brow. A drop of it also slithered down his spine and went between his butt cheeks. "Did you spare her life so that we could…uhhh…" The rest of the gathered brothers watched, wincing on his behalf, holding their collective breath.

"So that we could…um…sacrifice her to Great Cthulhu?"

"Bless you," the Dark Brothers said in unison.

"No, Great Cthulhu, the tentacle-faced god," Necrogrond clarified. Then he squinted up at the Heartless One, bracing himself for denippling if the guess proved wrong. He knew his nipple would grow back; he just wasn't eager for it.

The crimson-cloaked leader nodded. Everybody sighed in relief except the Heartless One and Nalweegie, who was too unconscious to sigh.

"Can I be the one who kills her?" Necrogrond wheedled. His master nodded. "Excellent," the sorcerer gloated, clapping his hands together and rubbing them vigorously. He stooped and stroked Nalweegie's unconscious cheek, then tweaked the tip of her nose. The Heartless One clucked in disapproval.

"Do we have to wait for the stars to be right or something, or can we kill her right away?" Necrogrond asked.

The Heartless One nodded. The sorcerer wasn't completely positive that this meant Yes, kill her right away because the nod could just as easily have meant Yes, we have to wait for the stars to be right. He decided to go with the kill-her-right-away option because that was his preference, and the Heartless One would have to speak to correct him if he was wrong. "So I'll just kill her right away then." He shot his boss a sidelong glance and saw no sign of objection, so he snapped his fingers to summon some Dark Brothers to help him.

In no time, the unconscious princess was bound spread-eagle to one of the mahogany dining tables, and Necrogrond was looming over her with a sacrificial dagger in his hands. The gathered assembly of Dark Brothers and the Heartless One watched with hungry eyes. Necrogrond was waiting for her to wake up so that she'd be aware when he plunged the dagger into her spleen, payback for her pretense of liking him in order to get close enough to choke him. Unfortunately, she showed no signs of reviving.

"Hey," Necrogrond said to the Heartless One, stalling, "did I mention that I beheaded Thoral Mighty Fist a little while before you got here?" His boss was silent.

"It's true," the sorcerer bragged. He snapped his fingers at one of his Dark Brothers, who fetched the barbarian's apparent head from where it lay on the floor. "Chopped his head right off." He brandished it at the Heartless One, who came forward, took the head from him and stared at it intently. Necrogrond was about to launch into a detailed account of Thoral's demise, but just then, Nalweegie moaned. The sorcerer hurried over to her side, paying such rapt attention to her fluttering eyelids that he didn't see the Heartless One pry open the head's unmoving eyelids and bring it even closer to stare into the violet eyes.

"Good morning, fair Evening Snack," Necrogrond tittered at the princess as her emerald eyes finally opened.

For a moment, her eyes were clouded by pain and confusion, then her memory flooded back. She thrashed against her bonds with such vigor that the closest of the Dark Brothers took a step away. "Release me!" the princess commanded. Necrogrond only laughed in her pretty face and held his ugly sacrificial dagger over her attractive belly button, making sure that the knife caught the torchlight so that she clearly saw the hideous blade.

"I'm about to plunge this sacrificial dagger into your spleen and sacrifice your soul to the tentacle-faced god," Necrogrond taunted her. He raised the blade above his head, aiming right for the princess's spleen, his hands trembling with anticipation. "With your permission, Heartless One," he said, shooting a glance to his master for approval.

The Heartless One was walking away, still carrying Thoral's head. Necrogrond frowned in consternation. "Your pardon, Heartless

One." Necrogrond raised his voice a bit. "Can we finish this before you do … whatever you're doing?" The Heartless one ignored him, opened a small side door into a private chamber and began walking through with Thoral's head.

"Well, do I have your permission to continue without you then?" the sorcerer demanded peevishly. The Heartless One waved a hand at him dismissively then vanished into the room. Necrogrond was about to call out a clarification question, when the door closed with a solid thunk, cutting him off.

There was a long and awkward silence in the dim-lit feasting hall. The gathered Dark Brothers all looked from Necrogrond to the closed door then back again. Even princess Nalweegie was kind of puzzled despite her terror and the pain from her broken arm bones.

"I'm going to take that as a *yes*," Necrogrond noted to the assembly. He shook his head as if shaking off the interruption and then refocused on his helpless victim. "Sorry, where were we?"

"You were just about to release me," Nalweegie supplied, forcing a smile despite her pain.

The sorcerer snorted. "Nice try," he sneered. "I was in fact, just about to stab you in the spleen as a sacrifice to Cthulhu."

Nalweegie's composure broke. Cthulhu, the tentacle-faced god, was the second-most disgusting and evil god in the whole canon of the gods of Grome. There was a pretty good chance that if she were sacrificed to him, he would slobber all over her soul before slurping it down like a tasty snack cake and she would be doomed to an eternity of anguish in his gurgling, constipated bowels.

Necrogrond noted the effect his pronouncement had upon the elf and smiled in triumph. "Struggle all you want," he gloated. "Scream to whatever elfish gods normally protect you, but know that there is no one who can save you from this fate."

Nalweegie surprised him by taking his advice. She screamed so suddenly and piercingly that a bunch of the Dark Brothers actually got the hiccups.

CHAPTER THIRTY-TWO

The Sound of Distant Screaming

Sneaking down one of the poorly lit hallways of the ancient temple discussing options for setting the place ablaze in a way that would burn up the largest number of people, Thoral and Brad froze in their tracks at the sound of distant screaming.

"Nalweegie!" Thoral cried and sprinted in the direction from which the shrieks rang.

CHAPTER THIRTY-THREE

Third Time's the Charm

Nalweegie screamed and screamed, but Necrogrond only laughed harder as he held the dagger above her.

"I didn't really think you would scream," the sorcerer smirked when she had to stop to take a breath. "I thought you were going to do one of those things where you are bravely silent but your eyes brim and maybe one tear rolls down your fair cheek. That's always poignant, although this was way more satisfying."

The princess narrowed her emerald eyes at him in fury. "Why do you not just keep quiet and kill me already?" she said through clenched teeth.

"Fine, spoilsport," Necrogrond retorted. "My arms were getting tired anyway." He jerked the blade up a fraction and then slammed it downward to permanently silence her beautiful, sensual, yet surprisingly-loud-scream-emitting lips.

However, a massive, reverberating boom made him flinch just short of delivering the killing blow, and he stabbed the sacrificial dagger into the tabletop. The door to the dim-lit Great Feasting Hall had been kicked open with such massive force that it swung all the way round, hit the wall to which it was hinged, bounced back and slammed closed again.

"Did anybody see who did that?" Necrogrond barked as he struggled to free the dagger tip from the table. The assembly of Dark Brothers looked around at each other. They shrugged nervously. This had been a stressful night for them already. Necrogrond pulled the dagger free and raised it to strike again as fast as he could, but just as he did, the door opened once more, with less force this time.

The sorcerer blanched. "You!" he choked.

"YES, ME!" Thoral Mighty Fist bellowed.

"But...but I killed you," Necrogrond objected, flabbergasted.

"And I you," Thoral pointed out. "Twice."

Strapped to the table and unable to see the door from her angle, Nalweegie struggled to lift her head and see what was going on. "Is that Thoral?" she cried, thrashing against her bonds. "My love?"

Necrogrond glanced down at her, up to the dagger in his own hands and then back to Thoral. He noted the barbarian's empty arrow quiver. The sorcerer's eyes went all crafty, then all gleeful. "It's actually good that you're still alive," he said. "Because this way you'll be able to helplessly witness me sacrificing your girlfriend to the tentacle-faced god, which will be satisfying *and* funny."

"I will kill you first," the warrior growled.

"He will," Nalweegie confirmed.

"Actually," Necrogrond corrected them, "I don't think so. You see, I've already got my sacrificial dagger poised over Nalweegie's spleen ready to strike, while you are two hundred yards away, out of arrows and blocked by nearly two hundred of my dark brethren. Each one is willing to throw away his own life to delay you the few precious seconds it will take me to finish my hideous work." He leered at Thoral in a self-satisfied way that made the barbarian clench his fists and grind his teeth in anger.

"If thou dost harm her," Thoral whispered in one of those chillingly dangerous whispers that can carry across a whole room, "I will tear thee limb from limb."

"I'll help him," Brad seconded from Thoral's shoulder.

"I'm so scared." Necrogrond pretended to quake in his boots, then brightened. "Oh, wait! You already tore me limb from limb once, didn't you, Thoral? But guess what? Here I am, about to stab your girlfriend. So, empty threat. I think I may have mentioned before that I'm essentially immortal?"

Thoral glared at him.

"Got you there, didn't I?" Necrogrond tittered. He raised the sacrificial blade high above the princess again. "Any other threats you want to try?"

Thoral stared at the sorcerer, his brain working furiously. He wasn't sure, but it appeared as if the sorcerer were clutching a spleenfang, a type of sacrificial dagger specifically forged for sucking people's souls out through their spleens. Even at the speed of a cheetah and with the full force of his massive sinews, the warrior knew he wouldn't be able to win through the crowd to Nalweegie before Necrogrond stabbed his love. *Fwang*, his mighty yew bow, was useless without arrows. *Blurmflard*, the magic blade lent to him by his wizard mentor, was also useless at this range. Even if he flung the blade, its velocity would be low enough by the time it had crossed the room that Necrogrond would be able to sidestep it. Thoral even considered throwing Brad at the sorcerer, but there were just too many things that might go wrong.

"The look on your face is priceless," the sorcerer gloated. "However, I tire of this game, and I'm eager to see your expression… when I do this!" And with that, he plunged the blade down, two-handed, toward the quivering midsection of the helpless elf maiden.

There was an obnoxiously loud bang that made almost everybody jump. Necrogrond and the rest of his Dark Brothers didn't know that the deafening crack was a gunshot because guns hadn't been invented on Grome, but the sorcerer was aware that something had gone seriously wrong with his own midsection. He froze, mid-stab, and stared down at the gaping hole in his chest. Puzzled, he looked back up at Thoral.

The warrior had assumed a shooter's stance and was squinting down the barrel of the metal wand he rarely used. It was a Smith and Wesson .357 Magnum, and he had just put his last remaining bullet into Necrogrond's heart. There had been no other choice.

The spleenfang sacrificial dagger fell from Necrogrond's nerveless fingers as he stood gasping, his lifeblood spurting out of his body from both the front and back. He concentrated on regenerating himself, but the familiar itchy, tingling sensation did not begin. Something was wrong.

"How?" he managed to whisper as he sagged against the wall behind him.

"You once told me that you could not be harmed by any weapon forged on Grome," Thoral told him. "Figure it out."

Necrogrond struggled to utter one last memorable line. Given that he had truly thought himself immortal, he hadn't prepared anything in advance. Under the circumstances, he couldn't come up with something appropriate. He keeled over, crumpling to the floor in a pool of his own blood. As he breathed his last, he was further aggravated to see the door to the private room swing open and the Heartless One step through. Then he expired.

All eyes turned from the dead sorcerer to the red-robed leader of the Bad Religion. Thoral dropped his gun and swept *Blurmflard* from its sheath, tensing to spring to Nalweegie's aid. Brad knotted a fin in the warrior's thick blond hair so that he wouldn't fall off when Thoral leapt into action. The princess held her breath, really stressed out by all of the last-minute stopping and starting of her deadly peril but still kind of glad to be at another stopping point. The Dark Brothers steeled themselves for the inevitable order to throw themselves on the warrior, despite some serious misgivings about how things were going to turn out for most of them. The tension in the room was so thick you could frost a cake with it. But no one was prepared for what happened next.

"Teddy?" the Heartless One breathed, pulling back her hood, her soft, feminine voice catching with emotion as her auburn hair tumbled around her pale, haunted face. "Teddy, is that you?" She was talking to Thoral.

CHAPTER THIRTY-FOUR

The Heart of the Heartless One

"Nancy?" Thoral whispered, stunned. Brad's jaw dropped.

"No way!" the fish breathed in total disbelief. It was the girl from the photo, her previous prettiness refined to a severe, almost painful beauty.

"Oh my God, Teddy!" the Heartless One beamed at Thoral from across the room, tears falling from her striking mauve eyes. Her accent was just like Thoral's. "When I saw your severed head…" She trailed off, overcome by emotion. She took a step toward him.

"I…I… " Thoral stuttered, thunderstruck. "The grode…I…I thought…" he trailed off too, stepping toward her.

"I thought I had you killed." Nancy wept, taking another step toward him. "I had no idea you were Thoral Mighty Fist. If I had even suspected he might be you, I never would have ordered him killed. I thought you must have used the Walking-Door Tree to go back home all those years ago, but then they handed me your head, and it all seemed so obvious."

"Oh, Nancy…When I found your breast in Yiz's cabin, I thought…I thought the grode had eaten the rest of you," Thoral said in a rush, crying now too, taking another hesitant step in her direction.

"My left breast *was* torn off. I've got a huge scar there." Nancy laughed through her tears. "That is why they call me the Heartless One. These idiots know hardly anything about anatomy." She gestured at the assembled horde of Dark Brothers, who all frowned and looked a little put out.

"If you survived," Thoral asked, his voice catching, "what of the baby? What of Yiz?"

Nancy closed her eyes and fresh tears trickled down her cheeks. "The grode slaughtered them," she answered, her own voice cracking.

Thoral let out of a sob of anguish but then shook his head and forced himself to focus on Nancy. "You are alive," he sniffled, holding out his arms toward her as he approached. "I thought I had lost you forever, and yet you are alive."

"I have never loved another since we parted," Nancy sobbed, opening her own arms to him as she closed the distance between them.

As these words hung in the air, Nalweegie cleared her throat. She was still tied to the table, slathered in Necrogrond blood and struggling to keep her head up so she could see her man. "Um, Thoral my dearest love, what is going on here?" she asked, a hint of steel in her voice. The Dark Brothers all nodded as she said this, then turned to see how Thoral would reply. He froze in his tracks.

Nancy stopped and contemplated Nalweegie, her brow furrowing. "'Thoral *my dearest love*?" she repeated. She turned her mauve gaze back on him.

"Awkward," Brad hissed under his breath. Thoral looked back and forth between the two women, stricken.

"Uh…" he started. "Uh…"

"Why did you just call my husband your dearest love?" Nancy demanded, turning on Nalweegie, her mauve eyes burning.

"Why did you just call my dearest love your husband?" Nalweegie returned, fire in her emerald eyes.

"Someone kill this elf!" Nancy ordered her men icily. "Finish the sacrifice!"

"NO!" Thoral cried in a strangled voice.

Nancy, pretty ticked off, turned back toward her golden-maned husband, but at the sight of him, her expression softened.

"Teddy," she whispered, walking toward him again, "tell me this girl means nothing to you, and come to me. You will not believe the incredible endeavor I am engaged in. I'm going to eat the Pudding of Power and don the Bracelet of Evil."

"About that," Thoral said sheepishly. "I am afraid I destroyed your Goomy Crystal, and you cannot use it to find the pudding. It is just dust now."

"That's OK," Nancy smiled. "I already used the crystal, and I know where the pudding is."

"You already used it?"

"Yes, a few hours ago," Nancy beamed at him. "So it does not matter that you destroyed the crystal. I forgive you. We can get the pudding and master the power of the bracelet—together. We just have to kill Nalweegie first."

Thoral gaped. "She…" he stammered.

"Must die," Nancy coaxed, taking another step toward him. "It is part of my plan."

"She…" Thoral groaned.

"Means nothing," Nancy breathed. "She is not real. None of these creatures are real. None of this world is real. Only I—and maybe you. It took me so long to realize, but it is the only explanation. This world is my nightmare, or maybe our nightmare, although I am not really sure how something like that could be, exactly. We can figure it out together. Either way, it is all just a dream, and I'm pretty sure that all I need do to finally wake from it is to totally destroy Grome. I know that sounds harsh," she said, her brow creasing, "although since everything is just in my head, it means I can do whatever I like with it or to it, or to anyone who lives here, except maybe you. Because you are real. Maybe. Do you not see?"

Thoral stood transfixed, a stupid look on his face.

"Is she crazy?" Nalweegie asked, still struggling both to keep her head up and to avoid passing out from the pain of her shattered arm bones.

"I am not crazy, *you* are pretend," Nancy snapped at the elfish princess.

"I'm pretty sure she's crazy," Brad said from Thoral's shoulder.

"Because a talking fish is a real thing?" Nancy growled.

"I'm real, and so is my love for you, Thoral," Nalweegie cried.

"Someone kill that elf," Nancy ordered her men. Several of the more decisive brothers started toward the princess, pulling daggers, while a few of the brothers who had been paying the closest attention were starting to question their allegiances.

"Thoral!" Nalweegie said, squirming on the table, panic in her voice.

"Thoral!" Brad said, alarmed.

"Thoral!" Nancy said, disgusted. "What a stupid name! I should have figured it out the first time I heard it. Theodore Henry Oral. T. H. Oral. Now it is time to be my Teddy again, eat that pudding, put on that bracelet and destroy this world so we can wake up. Then none of this will have happened. And the first step is killing this silly girl. It is the only way. You see that, do you not?"

There was a long silence. Even the brothers who had been moving in to kill Nalweegie hesitated, waiting on the barbarian's reply.

"I see," Thoral said softly.

"No!" Nalweegie sobbed.

"No!" Brad gasped.

"Yes!" Nancy beamed, her eyes alight with triumph. "I knew you would see!" The Dark Brothers started toward Nalweegie once more, raising their blades.

"I see that you must be stopped," Thoral sighed, his heart as heavy as fifteen or sixteen pounds of lead. The brothers hesitated again.

"What?" Nancy asked, her smile fading.

"You have become crazy and evil. You are no longer my Nancy. You are the Heartless One, leader of the Bad Religion, which I am sworn to destroy."

Nancy's face went through several rapid expression changes. Shock to anger, anger to sadness, sadness to horror, horror back to sadness. It would have been kind of funny if it weren't so heartbreaking. The Dark Brothers, daggers in hand, watched her to see if they were still supposed to go through with the murder of Nalweegie. It was hard to tell.

"Please," she pleaded, tears welling in her eyes again. "Do not do this, Teddy. I lost you once and it destroyed me, but now we can be together again." The brothers turned to Thoral for his reaction.

"Then shake off this fantasy, Nancy," Thoral urged. "Grome is not a dream. It is some kind of alternate reality or a different dimension, but it is real. Remember all those years ago on Earth? There were numerous stories where things like this happened. *The Chronicles of Narnia*, *The Wizard of Oz*, *Coraline*, *Alice in Wonderland*." The brothers turned back to Nancy.

"Those were *stories*, Thoral," Nancy countered. "And technically, *Alice in Wonderland* is a story about a girl having a dream and so is *The Wizard of Oz*. Kind of."

"But Grome is *real*," Thoral returned forcefully. "Its people are real. Everything that has happened to us is real. We can find another way to leave if we do not like it, but it is not our world to do with as we like." The Dark Brothers lowered their blades, their arms tired.

Nancy faltered, her eyes wide and frightened.

"No, please," she begged. "It cannot be real. All the horrors … all the pain … You do not know the things that happened after … after … You do not know the things they did to me … You do not know what it was like to lose our … our baby … my baby… " She faltered, unable to continue.

"I am so sorry," Thoral whispered.

Nancy sagged, and a single sob wracked her red-robed body. Her pale, haunted face was marred by unbearable pain, and a lost look came into her eyes. Thoral closed the distance between them and placed a hand on her cheek. She snuggled into his embrace, crying hard.

"It will be all right," he whispered, hugging her tight. "I am with you now. The nightmare is over."

Nancy stiffened. She looked up into his face, and her expression hardened. A terrible despair shone in her mauve eyes, as if someone had just fired a flare gun inside the cavity of her skull and the glow of the purple flare was leaking out through her irises.

"You aren't real either, are you?" she gasped. And then she started talking to herself. "Of course he isn't real. I am a fool. He's just another part of my nightmare!"

"Nancy," Thoral began, but she pushed him back with the full force of her own prodigious hand strength so that he stumbled and almost fell.

"KILL THEM!" she shrieked to her men. "START WITH THE GIRL, BUT KILL THEM ALL OR FEEL MY FURY!"

All of the Dark Brothers who had drawn their daggers leapt into action. They knew too much about the Heartless One's wrath to ignore an order like that. The rest of them tried to look busy, while edging toward the back of the room.

"NO!" Thoral bellowed and raced toward the helpless Nalweegie even as the men grabbed for him. He leapt over them like a gazelle or a kangaroo, cleaving a guy's head down the middle as he sailed up onto a table. From there he sprang to the table to which his princess was bound, but a Dark Brother was already throttling the life out of her.

Thoral swung *Blurmflard*, whistling through the air, the pink fire of its magic glow flaming to light. The priest's head left his shoulders with such force that it smashed an onrushing brother in the face so hard that it killed him, the guy behind him and the guy behind him. The brother behind those three got a concussion, and the guy behind him got a bloody nose.

While his attackers were still reeling, Thoral sliced through Nalweegie's chains as if they were made of licorice and pulled her up beside him. He put her behind him, shielding her with his body, even though he realized his odds of protecting her were pretty low as long as he was surrounded.

"Go for the Heartless One!" Brad shouted from his shoulder. "If you kill her, the others will flee. Cut off the head and the body dies."

Thoral glanced over at his wife as he fended off a wave of new attackers with *Blurmflard*. She was within easy leaping distance, just standing there, apparently talking to herself.

"What are you waiting for? Take her out," the fish ordered. Thoral steeled himself to jump, but at that moment Nancy started to cry again and buried her face in her hands. The warrior hesitated and another group of Dark Brothers swarmed him, grabbing at his and Nalweegie's legs. He laid into them full force and reduced them to mincemeat. By the time he'd finished them off, Nancy had started some kind of spell. A second later, a shield of green, shimmering energy enveloped her.

"Dang it!" Brad shouted. "She's cast an impenetrable-shield spell."

More evil brothers swarmed Thoral, even though the pile of dead ones was getting pretty high around the table. Actually, the new round of attackers had a slight advantage because the dead bodies were like a ramp that they could just run up. So they did that.

Thoral whirled *Blurmflard* in a glittering pink arc, chopping through the first couple of attackers, but one Dark Brother ducked under the blade and threw his arms around Nalweegie's legs. She cried out as she tumbled back and Thoral had to spin and grab her around the waist to prevent her from falling off the table. This, unfortunately, created an opening in his defense that the other Dark Brothers immediately exploited. They threw themselves at his legs and grabbed at his arms, hampering his movements with their sheer numbers. He staggered under their onslaught and his mighty sword chopped the table in two so that it caved in at the middle like a V. Everyone tumbled into the cavity except for two brothers who were standing at the far edges and were flung into each other, breaking both their necks.

A new group of Dark Brothers pounced. Thoral, Nalweegie and Brad disappeared beneath their frenzied charge. The Heartless

One cried out behind her impenetrable shield as she saw Thoral go down, although it was impossible to tell whether she uttered a cry of triumph or anguish. She watched the seething knot of Dark Brothers with what could have been delight or horror until they exploded away in all directions. Thoral had grabbed one of them by the ankles and was swinging him around, helicopter-style, in order to knock the others away. When he had cleared a ten-foot circle, he let go, flinging the brother he had been swinging right into Nancy's impenetrable shield. She flinched as the hapless brother was vaporized in a pink cloud. Once the mist of blood settled, she locked eyes with Thoral. For just a moment, she wore a hurt expression, as if she had not expected him to fight back. Then her face hardened and she grimaced in rage.

"FOOLS! IDIOTS! MORONS!" the Heartless One screamed at her minions. "Do I have to do everything myself?" Apparently, that was a rhetorical question because she didn't wait for an answer. She fired a barrage of magic beams from behind her shield.

Thoral covered Nalweegie with his body to protect her from the magic while Brad braced himself to be burned to a cinder. Nothing happened to them. The magic beams hit the dead bodies of the fallen Dark Brothers, and they glowed with a hideous green light.

"Crap!" Brad squealed. "She's reanimating them."

It was true. The severed, glowing bits of the dead priests were reattaching themselves, and the reassembled dead bodies were struggling back to their feet. They shambled toward the companions, moaning, gurgling and making gross squelching noises where their guts were spilling out.

"Don't let them bite you," Brad cautioned. "It's really unsanitary."

Thoral didn't need to be told twice. He started edging back from the oncoming zombies but found himself ringed by the living-dead Dark Brothers.

"Thoral, my love..." Nalweegie groaned. Her face was deathly pale, her emerald eyes glazed, her broken arm twisted and swollen.

She struggled valiantly for a moment and then passed out, sagging to the floor.

Thoral caught her one-handed and slung her slight form over one of his massive shoulders. Although her weight was not much of an encumbrance, she made an excellent target, as if the warrior had just draped himself in elfish princess armor. He tried to turn himself sideways to minimize her exposure. It was no good. The zombies were coming from all directions now.

"Great," Brad grumped. "Could this get any worse?"

As if in answer, the doors at the back of the dim-lit Great Feasting Hall banged open and more Dark Brothers raced into the room.

"It took you long enough," the Heartless One snapped at them. "Did one of you bring my deadly crossbow, *Thwump*?"

A Dark Brother came up behind her shield and knelt, offering up her wicked, murderous bow. It was a nasty piece of work, made of black iron and wood with a big black stirrup and crank. It was already drawn, and a bolt lay at the ready. The Heartless One took it without so much as a thank-you and raised it to her shoulder, sighting down the flight groove in the barrel and through her impenetrable shield.

"She's got a—" Brad started to shout the warning but was cut off.

THWUMP! The crossbow grunted its name as it hurled its deadly bolt at an unsuspecting Thoral. The warrior had such preternaturally good reflexes that dodging the heavy projectile might have been a possibility if he had seen it coming. His attention was instead focused on trying to keep a particularly aggressive zombie from biting Nalweegie's calf in half. The pesky undead warrior had grabbed the elf maiden's attractive leg and was hungrily and relentlessly lunging for a juicy mouthful of princess flesh. Just as the unwitting warrior realized the zombie had slipped past his blade and was about to bite down, the crossbow bolt caught the reanimated priest in the back of the head and tumbled him to the ground.

A spark of hope kindled in Thoral's striking violet eyes at the thought that his wife might have had a change of heart.

"Blast it all!" the Heartless One cursed. She was just a lousy shot. She began cranking the crossbow for another bolt, and the zombie she'd hit picked himself off the floor and started at Thoral again with the pointy end of the bolt protruding several inches from his forehead.

"We might be in a spot of trouble here," Brad noted. "If you have any other secret weapons or anything that I don't know about, this might be a great time to use them."

"I am afraid I do not," Thoral said through clenched teeth as he sliced a zombie in half at the waist.

"Incoming!" Brad yelled as the Heartless One's crossbow discharged another quarrel. It would have struck the reanimated priest Thoral had just bisected, except that he'd sliced off the zombie's top half. Instead, the bolt buried itself deep in the warrior's side.

"This is inconvenient," Thoral growled.

Watching the earthling's crimson life essence spurting out around the shaft, Brad knew that was a significant understatement.

"Do you have any more golden healing pudding?" the fish demanded, already sliding down Thoral's arm toward his belt pouches.

"Yes," the warrior grimaced, driving back a trio of zombies. "I am not really fond of puddings, but it is in my turquoise pouch. The one with the nice needlework around the top. And bring enough for Nalwee—" He was cut off as another crossbow bolt thuddered into the rectus femoris muscle of his upper leg, piercing him so deeply that it came out his biceps femoris at the back.

"Ouch," Thoral said.

Although Brad was sorry to see his friend hit again, the new crossbow bolt did make a good perch for him to stand on as he fumbled with Thoral's belt pouches. He lowered himself onto it and made a grab for the swaying turquoise bag in among the tangled mass of pouches, all swinging wildly as the warrior danced and dodged in the deadly ballet of battle.

"Ouch again," Thoral noted as the fish shifted his weight on the shaft and more blood squirted out of the wound.

"Sorry," Brad called up, missing the pouch. His head swayed side to side as he tried to match the timing of the dangling bag. "Almost got it!" His pectoral fins twitched in anticipation as he prepared for another try. Even as he went for the bag, another bolt whistled in. The Heartless One had been aiming for one of Thoral's piercing violet eyes. The missile was again off its mark and instead knocked a chunk out of Brad's left fin as it struck the turquoise pouch, tearing it from the warrior's belt and the fish's grasp.

"NO!" Brad gasped.

"Actually, that could have been much worse," Thoral noted, considering the pouch's proximity to his privates. He was unaware that the pouch had been lost. "Did you get the pudding, Brad?"

"It's gone, Thoral," the fish informed him, starting to climb back up to his shoulder as yet another wave of zombies closed on them. The sound of the Heartless One's clicking crossbow crank echoed in the room.

"Oh," the warrior murmured, almost to himself. "I was kind of counting on that pudding." If he hadn't already been desiccated because the Goomy Crystal had sucked most of his soul out of him, he probably could have lasted another few hours. As it was Thoral wasn't in such great shape. Burdened with Nalweegie and pierced by multiple arrows, his breath was coming a bit ragged now. His arms were beginning to tire, his head light from exertion and loss of blood. He was slowing.

"YOU WERE ONCE MY HEART!" the Heartless One screamed, sighting down the flight groove of her crossbow barrel at Thoral's chest, right at the spot where his noble heart thundered against his ribs under his sexy leather vest. "NOW MY HEART IS GONE!" She concentrated on the crossbow lessons her wizard mentor, Yiz, had given her all those years ago. Yes, Yiz was just a part of this stupid dream, she thought, but even dreams can be educational. She centered herself, exhaled slowly and squeezed the trigger.

For once, her aim was true.

CHAPTER THIRTY-FIVE

Damned Symbolism

You are no doubt thinking something like "I'm not falling for that again. Thoral never gets killed. Probably a zombie gets in the way. Or he happens to collapse out of the path of the bolt at just the right moment. Or he catches it in his unnaturally even white teeth. Or it will turn out it's not really Thoral again." None of these things happened.

The crossbow bolt flew straight and true, right from *Thwump*, right into the real Thoral's real chest where it stabbed through his flimsy leather vest and knocked him backward as if Dorgpust, the powerful mule god of the powerful mules of Grome, had kicked him. Brad was flung from his side, Nalweegie spilled from his shoulder and Thoral smashed up against the wall. Ironically it was right at the exact bloodstained spot where Necrogrond had been driven by Thoral's bullet.

Brad tucked and rolled, tumbling across the floor until he banged up against an overturned bench. As he lay panting and unable to rise, the koi's frantic gaze came to rest upon his friend. Thoral slid down the wall and crumpled to the floor. His hands clutched the shaft of the Heartless One's crossbow bolt as it protruded from his chest. His handsome face wore an expression of shock and astonishment. His violet eyes were wide and bewildered. He resembled a pincushion with the three bolts sticking out of him, each at a different angle. *Blurmflard* lie glimmering on the floor beside him. The pink glow of the blade throbbed feebly, then winked out.

"YESSS!" the Heartless One screamed in surprised glee, fist pumping the air. "Did anyone see that? I got him! I totally got him!" The Dark Brothers all paused to take in the sight and nod appreciatively. Even the ones who had been questioning their allegiance to the Bad Religion were nodding. Even some of the zombies nodded–the ones who still had heads anyway.

"Thoral?" Nalweegie croaked. The pain of landing on her broken arm had jolted her back to consciousness. She was lying in a twisted heap a few feet from Brad, her emerald eyes fixed in anguish on Thoral.

"He is dead, elf," the Heartless One said heartlessly. A bitter smile gnarled her otherwise gorgeous lips. "Which is exactly what you are about to be. Boys, make a path. I think I will kill the girl and the fish myself."

The Dark Brothers scrambled out of Nancy's way. She waved her hand and lowered her magic shield, then started toward Nalweegie.

That was, of course, the moment Thoral had been waiting for. Summoning all his remaining strength, he hurled the crossbow bolt at her. He wasn't dead. Somehow.

The bolt lobbed up, went about five feet and then fell to the ground where it stuck in the eye of a severed head. The head groaned. It didn't have any hands to pull the arrow out. Unfortunately, not getting killed had not improved Thoral's weakened condition. He was still on the verge of passing out from blood loss, physical trauma and general abuse. He flushed in embarrassment at his weak throw.

"This is ridiculous!" the Heartless One huffed at him. "I can't believe you're still alive." Then she realized how enfeebled Thoral was and a harsh smile crawled across her face. She strode to his side and grabbed him by the chin, forcing him to look up into her face. Thoral made a halfhearted grab for her throat, but she fended him off easily.

"How did you survive?" she demanded and tore open his leather vest, inconsiderately popping off the expensive ivory buttons. Her intake of breath was audible around the room as she saw what had spared him. The bolt had struck the silver locket nestled against Thoral's hairy chest, hitting it right in the heartshape formed by the two leaping dolphins. The pendant was crushed as if it had been struck by a hammer and there was a big red welt where it had shielded Thoral's chest.

"What are the chances?" Thoral coughed, spluttering blood with the words.

"Damned symbolism!" the Heartless One growled, but she looked shaken. She didn't like dolphins, so she hadn't been fond of that pendant. Once she'd lost it though, she had missed it every single day. She made a visible effort to get hold of herself and then yanked the locket from Thoral's neck, breaking the silver chain. She stood staring at it for a long moment.

"Nancy," Thoral said weakly.

"Shut up!" she roared at him, stuffing the necklace into a pocket of her crimson robe. Then, still holding Thoral's chin in the other hand, she drew forth a ceremonial dagger. Because it was just ceremonial, it wasn't razor sharp or anything, but it was the only dagger she had on her. Given her prodigious hand strength, she figured it would do the job.

"Let us see how you get out of this," she hissed and pressed the blade to Thoral's manly jugular, preparatory to slicing his throat. Brad struggled to rise but could not. Nalweegie attempted to drag herself toward her love but could not. Thoral merely closed his astonishing violet eyes and a smile touched his lips.

"Often I have wondered about death. Will it truly bring an end or just a transition to another world?" he mused.

"Don't be so noble and brave," the Heartless One cried, her knuckles white on the hilt of her dagger as she held it to the point where his rugged jaw curved to join his manly throat. How long had it been since her lips had brushed that exact spot? How long since she had felt the steady rhythm of his pulse throb against her cheek as she nestled in his powerful arms? Her hand trembled.

Thoral blinked his eyes open. "I thought you were going to slit my throat," he said.

"I am," the Heartless One grumbled. "I just need a second. Don't rush me."

"Take all the time you need," the warrior offered.

The Heartless One adjusted her grip on the dagger and pressed it tight against Thoral's throat again, though her hand continued to shake.

"For some reason, this is harder than I—" Her words were cut off as an arrow caught her in the back of her left shoulder. It hit with such force that it made her drop the dagger and spun her around to face the shooter.

King Elfrod sat astride Warlordhorse, an elfin longbow in his hands, the string still vibrating. A host of a hundred warriors, some astride horses, others on foot, parted around him like a wave as they thundered through the door of the dim-lit Great Feasting Hall. Nimrodingle led the combined charge of Elf Force and a full company of the Reefma city guard.

"You have got to be kidding me!" the Heartless One shrieked in pain and frustration. Elfrod and his fighters did not look as if they were in a joking mood. Taking into account her own wound, the superior numbers of the attackers, how many of her dark acolytes had already been snuffed and the abuses she had subjected Nalweegie to, the Heartless One chose the better part of valor. Her hand darted out and grabbed *Blurmflard*.

"I guess I will have to kill you some other time," she told Thoral.

"Mayhap," he whispered.

Then she whispered the magic word Yiz had taught them both, the word that Thoral had long ago forgotten. It was *fruitbat.* There was a massive slurping sound and she vanished, teleported away with the blade.

Without her to hold up his chin, Thoral keeled over, dead.

CHAPTER THIRTY-SIX

Unjust Desserts

Hours later, Thoral cried out, clawing his way to consciousness, tangled and strangling beneath a heavy, black death-shroud.

Actually, it was a frilly white comforter. Technically, his heart had stopped and he had been legally dead for a few seconds back in the Fortress of the Bad Religion before Elfrod got to him and revived him. Now he was in a cozy bed in a room in the Inn of the Gruesomely Gashed Gnome, his wounds cleaned, bandaged and mostly healed by the golden pudding. He reached for *Blurmflard*, but the blade was not beside him. He sat up, gasping for breath as if drowning on the memories that flooded his brain. As his startling violet eyes came into focus, he saw that Elfrod sat in a high-backed chair facing him. Brad was perched on the headboard of the bed, his fin in a sling. Warlordhorse was there too, his noble tiger-striped head sticking in through the window.

"Where is Nalweegie?" Thoral begged, his voice cracking as he realized she was not there. "Does she still live?"

"Neigh," Warlordhorse nickered.

"NOOOOOO!" Thoral cried, burying his face in his hands.

"Calm yourself," Elfrod soothed, shooting a severe look at Warlordhorse, who rolled his eyes in embarrassment. The horse had just been clearing his throat. "She lives."

Thoral sagged with relief.

"She was in here nursing you most of the time you were unconscious. She left when she saw you were starting to come around," the king informed him.

"Because she's kind of mad about your wife," Brad added.

"Mad?" Thoral asked, his brow furrowing. "I am confused."

"So is she," Brad said offhandedly. "I kind of tried to explain the stuff you told me about you and Nancy, but Nalweegie seemed put out by the whole discussion."

"Why? I chose her over Nancy." Thoral struggled to work it out. "What cause has she to be angry with me?"

"There's no figuring women," the fish noted wisely.

"They are all crazy," Elfrod agreed. Even Warlordhorse whinnied an assent from the window.

"I am right outside the door," Nalweegie cried from the corridor. She burst into the room and stalked up to the foot of the bed. Her pretty face was flushed with anger, her arm bandaged and in a sling. Elfrod had healed her bones with elf magic. "And I am not crazy. You never mentioned you had a wife."

"I thought she was dead," Thoral objected. "And I did mention it to your father."

"He did," Elfrod confirmed, nodding sagely.

"You did not mention it to *me*," the princess said, her voice cold. "And last I checked, you were romancing *me*, not him."

"The omission was clearly…" Thoral trailed off. "Brad, what is that word that means when one has made an error or omission due to carelessness or lack of forethought?"

"An oversight," Brad supplied.

"The omission was clearly an oversight," Thoral admitted.

"Was it also an oversight that you appeared so happy to see her? That you showed her such affection? That you hugged her and let her nestle against your manly chest? That you hesitated when you had a chance to kill her?" the princess asked.

Thoral sucked air through his teeth.

"Princess," Brad began, coming to his friend's defense despite his better judgement, "you've got to keep in mind that Thoral was overcome by surprise. He had no idea his wife was still alive and also the evil mastermind controlling the Bad Religion. The last time he saw her she was good and also the mother of his infant son. Seeing her again was a lot to process on the fly."

Warlordhorse launched into a long, whinnying speech in support of Thoral, noting that he himself had been so shocked to see Nancy alive again that he had almost thrown Lord Elfrod. Although his words were well intentioned, they just sounded like neighing to everyone else.

"Quiet, horse." The princess shushed him after he had gone on for a full minute. "This is between Thoral and me." She turned on the warrior again. "You had a baby with the Heartless One?"

"She was not heartless at the time," Thoral started.

"Why did she not kill you?" Nalweegie demanded, cutting him off. "She had a knife to your throat and plenty of time to kill you. Why did she not?"

"You would rather that she *had* killed me?" Thoral asked.

"It would have been reassuring if she had," the princess huffed.

Even Warlordhorse rolled his eyes.

"Of course I wouldn't have wanted her to kill you," Nalweegie snarled. "She could have tried harder though. At least then I would have known that there was nothing between you."

There was an uncomfortable silence.

"There isn't anything between you, is there?" Nalweegie asked, her voice catching in her pretty throat. Her emerald eyes searched his violet ones for reassurance.

"There will always be a connection between us," Thoral sighed. He was not very good at understanding when to hold back information. However it was clear from Nalweegie's expression that this had been the wrong thing to say, so Thoral tried to stammer out a clarification. "I mean, I no longer love her, but we are both from another world and—"

"Ah, yes!" Nalweegie shouted. "When were you going to share that little gem? I have already forsaken my betrothed in favor of a human barbarian, for which I am sure to be roundly scolded by the council of elves and their busybody husbands. How pleased they will be to learn that you are not even from this planet!"

"I did not think—" Thoral began.

"No! You did not think. You did not think at all, you great oaf." Nalweegie stamped her foot in anger. "Is your alien race even compatible with mine? Can we…can we even…" She flushed. "Can we even…mate?" She whispered the last word.

Thoral turned red to the roots of his tawny mane. King Elfrod fidgeted in his rocking chair and pulled the misplacement compass, which Thoral had returned to him, out of his pocket so he could pretend to be examining it. Warlordhorse actually pulled his head out of the window in order to leave the room.

"Whoa! Put a cold towel on the back of your neck, Princess," Brad exclaimed. "I think we can save the…the mating discussion for another day. It's a little premature to be picking out baby names while the Heartless One is out there planning on quaffing the Pudding of Power to end the world and destroy Thoral, you, your father and every other living thing in the bargain. Unless we get our act together and stop her, it won't matter whether you and Thoral are…compatible or not."

"This fish speaks wisdom," Elfrod jumped in, eager to change the subject. "We must address the issue of stopping the Heartless One as soon as is elfishly possible."

"How can we stop her?" Nalweegie demanded. "We know not whither she went nor whither the pudding rests."

"Actually," Thoral interjected, "I do know whither she went. The magic blade *Blurmflard*, lent to me by my wizard mentor, Yiz, was enchanted to teleport its bearer to the mage's cabin in the midst of the withered wood near the Western Wastes in Fligryngen."

"That is many days' ride from here," Nalweegie noted. "Certainly by the time we get there the Heartless One would be long gone on her quest for the pudding. As she is the only one who knows its accursed resting place, it does us little good to know her starting point."

Everyone fell silent and dejected. Elfrod fiddled with his misplacement compass for a moment before looking up.

"Actually," the king admitted, "I know the last resting place of the Pudding of Power."

"What?" the other three gasped in unison. Warlordhorse poked his head back in through the window at that moment, chewing a mouthful of grass, wondering what he'd missed.

"The pudding was lost when Lord Mauron was defeated," Nalweegie cried. "No one has seen it in a thousand years."

"A thousand and two years this fall," Elfrod corrected her. "I was there when the pudding was taken from the Dark Lord by Emperor Doug of Chowder, and Mauron lost control of the Bracelet of Evil."

"No way," Brad said in wonder.

"It is even so," Elfrod affirmed. "When Mauron evaporated, it was my counsel that the pudding should be washed down the black drain in the Veil of Blurch where it was cooked. Emperor Doug refused. Haughty were the great men of Chowder in those days, and none more so than its fancy king. Doug's mind was too easily corrupted by the pudding's evil ingredients. In his folly, he claimed it as his 'just dessert' and decided to save the foul snack 'for later.' While I could not convince him to destroy the pudding, I did talk him into hiding it. The two of us interred it somewhere safe and secret, swearing many oaths not to try even the tiniest bite without splitting it each with the other. And then, not surprisingly, Doug was killed by a ravening barfart while trying to sneak in without me to eat the whole pudding himself."

"So you really do know where the pudding rests?" Thoral asked.

"Indeed," Elfrod answered.

"Then what are we waiting for?" Nalweegie demanded.

"The Great Pudding of Power lies hidden in the ice caves beneath the citadel of Chowder in the dread land of Flurge," the elf king informed her. At the mention of the citadel, everyone got such a chill that they all broke out in goosebumps. Except Brad. Fish can't get goosebumps. He did shiver though.

"Then to Chowder we must go," Thoral pronounced, rubbing his arms to warm himself. His words hung in the air like doom.

"I will make arrangements with the innkeeper for us to leave at first light tomorrow," Elfrod said sagely. "It is a long journey, and we will need proper supplies."

"Lay in enough provisions for me as well," Nalweegie said, her voice fierce. "I am going with you."

"To Flurge?" Elfrod barked, incredulous.

"Yes, to Flurge," Nalweegie threw back.

"One does not simply walk into Flurge, my daughter," Elfrod said in a theatrical whisper. "It is a terrifying, dangerous, dread place, crowded with the twisted spirits of the dead and overrun by monsters like barfarts, mertalizers, and stinkasters. It drips with darkness like a burlap bag full of black paint. The very air is a smelly fume. I myself am only willing to return there because Thoral is going."

"I am going too," Nalweegie said, her lips tightening into a determined line. "I … I have had a prophetic dream in which I went to the citadel with you all to prevent the Heartless One from getting the Great Pudding of Power."

"Really?" Brad demanded.

"Yes," Nalweegie answered. She wouldn't meet his eyes. "Why would I say I did if I did not?"

"Oh, I don't know," the fish speculated shrewdly. "Maybe you aren't too keen on letting your ticket out of your arranged marriage run off on a grand adventure where he's likely to bump into his long-lost wife without you?"

"Brad…" Thoral cautioned, glaring at the fish beside him on the headboard of the bed.

"I'm just saying," his companion shrugged.

"How dare you!" the princess huffed.

"Well, exactly when did you have this dream?" Brad asked.

"I need not explain myself to you, *fish*," Nalweegie retorted.

"I am curious as well," Elfrod declared. "Last we spoke, you made no mention of this dream, and yet it is so portentous I cannot believe you would have kept it from me. When did you have this dream?"

"Oh," Nalweegie flushed again. "Well…I had it just hours ago when I was in the healing slumber as my arm bones were getting fixed. It was so vivid. I dreamt that I sat upon the floor of a cave in the dread land of Flurge right beside Thoral. In my dream–which I really had– Thoral was telling me how sorry he was that he hadn't listened to my advice about not getting his head chopped off and … and telling me how sorry he was that he had loved another before me and…and then he got distracted by…by a little animal. Yes. A talking hamster or a bird or something. That's a kind of detail I wouldn't make up. I mean, why would I add a detail like Thoral being distracted by a talking hamster or bird if I hadn't really dreamt it? That's exactly like one of those weird things that happen in a dream. And, Father, you were…you were singing a song. Yes, you were singing a song. A nonsense song. You were singing it to a cup or a chalice or some other kind of dish. There's another one of those crazy dream details that makes my account seem true. Because I'm not making it up."

"So you saw all that?" Brad demanded, unable to keep the suspicion out of his voice. "And what was I doing?"

"You were…you were…not feeling well because…you had a severe attack of gas," Nalweegie replied. "It was most unseemly."

Now it was Brad's turn to seethe.

"So I am clearly destined to go," Nalweegie concluded.

"My princess," Thoral objected, "dream or no dream, I cannot allow you to go."

"Do not 'my princess' me," Nalweegie growled, turning on him. "And do not think that all is forgiven. I am still miffed."

"Nalweegie," Thoral tried again, "I cannot allow you to expose yourself to such danger. You are too precious to me."

"Nor do I feel this is a good idea," Elfrod noted. "You are my daughter and the sole heir of the line of the elves of Creekenvalley."

"I don't like it either," Brad piled on. "Seems like it's just going to be a pain in the neck and distract Thoral. No disrespect intended, your highness."

Nalweegie narrowed her eyes at them all. "Alas, your objections matter not," she told them, crossing her arms in front of her chest, "for I am Nalweegie, Princess of Creekenvalley."

There was a long silence. Thoral, Elfrod, Brad and Warlordhorse exchanged looks.

"Are you…are you trying to pull a Thoral?" the fish asked, his voice heavy with astonished disbelief.

"I would not dream of it," the elf said haughtily. "I am pulling a Nalweegie."

CHAPTER THIRTY-SEVEN

The Gruesomely Gashed Gnome

Later, after the arrangements had been made and the others had left Thoral to catch a few hours of much needed sleep, the warrior lay tossing and turning in the darkness. Despite all of Elfrod's admonishments to rest, Thoral could not. His mighty fist clutched the bedsheet beside him, knotting in the fabric where *Blurmflard* should have been. In all his years of drunkenness, wandering and despair, the magic blade had been his only constant bedfellow. He felt worse than lost without its uncomfortable, poky presence. But now the sword was with Nancy, wherever she was.

A lump rose in Thoral's throat as images from his recent encounter with his lost wife forced themselves on his unwilling brain. She was so different now, so harsh and twisted by whatever horrors she'd been subjected to after they were separated. Even so, he had been able to see the ghost of the woman he had loved haunting her face. His violet eyes welled with unshed tears. It was his fault. It was *all* his fault.

Thoral reached for his belt pouch on the nightstand and took out his iPhone. The battery was already down to sixty-five percent, but he didn't care. He opened up the photos app and was greeted by an image of Brad, dazed from the flash used to take the picture in the dark throne chamber of the hideout of the Bad Religion. Thoral had taken the photo to satisfy the fish's curiosity about how the camera worked. There were half a dozen shots of the koi, the first few with him flinching in terror from the bright strobe of the flash, the last few with him pulling ridiculous faces. The warrior swished his finger across the screen repeatedly until he was confronted by a much younger version of himself, beaming as he held *Blurmflard* aloft. He hadn't looked at this or any of the older photos in at least ten years. The picture brought back bittersweet memories. He'd been so happy when Yiz had lent him the sword, positive that nothing could go wrong as long as he had the magic blade at his side. Thoral swished his finger across the screen and brought up a smiling version of himself hugging a sweeter though concerned-looking Nancy while she held their swaddled infant son in her arms. He remembered the picture well. Yiz had taken it just before Thoral set off for the Walking-Door Tree. Nancy had begged him not to go. The next picture was of the baby, nestled against Thoral's well-muscled forearm, smiling in his sleep.

The mighty warrior sniffled, his lower lip trembling. He fumbled in the dark for the skin of wine he always kept handy to dull his nightmares, forgetting that he did not have one at the ready because he was trying to give up drinking. Out of habit, and focusing on his inability to locate the wineskin, he uttered the magic word that made *Blurmflard* glow. He suffered through a few heartbeats of confusion when its comforting, rosy light did not suffuse the room. Then the loss hit him afresh– like a ten-pound bag of onions. It was too much. Sobs racked his powerful frame and he wept like a child.

"No more shall die on my account," he blubbered. "I must set out now…alone…"

There was a soft knock at the door and Thoral choked back his tears. The barbarian wiped his eyes as he sat up in the darkness.

"Go away," he grumbled, unwilling for any of his companions to see him weeping. The door creaked open, however, admitting a warm glow of candlelight that revealed the short, hunched form of the gruesomely gashed gnomish innkeeper. He was clad in an ankle-length nightshirt and a droopy nightcap.

"Your pardon, Fist Wielder," the gnome croaked, his one eye glittering as he peered at the barbarian. "I thought I heard the sounds of vomiting as I passed by your door. Do you require a bucket?"

"No, I am well," Thoral said, attempting but failing to produce a reassuring smile. The gnome nodded and started to close the door, then hesitated on the threshold.

"As with so many times in the past, Mighty Fist," the old gnome wheezed through his patchy gray beard, "you look as if you need a drink."

"I am...I am fine," the warrior protested, but his voice faltered.

"Come, share one drink with me and tell me your troubles," the innkeeper persisted. Thoral was torn. The innkeeper took another half step into the room, raising his candle to light his crooked, gap-toothed smile. "I have a fine mulled wine that will warm your belly and lift your spirits."

"I suppose that a single drink will not hurt," the barbarian conceded.

***

Half an hour later, Thoral was putting away his seventh large tankard of mulled wine.

"Does it not seem like more than mere coincidence that my long-lost and presumably deceased wife should return just after I declare my love for the princess Nalweegie," he hiccupped, "and that the two of them should immediately be at each other's throats? Literally."

"I don't believe in coincidence," the grizzled and gashed innkeeper said, his voice grave.

"I cannot believe it either," Thoral huffed, missing the gnome's point. "What are the odds?" He chugged down the contents of the tankard and the gnome refilled it from his steaming wine pot. Thoral was feeling so gloomy that he wasn't even tempted to smile at his host's chubby little ring-clad fingers.

"How do you feel about the princess now that your wife has returned?" the innkeeper probed. The barbarian shook his head.

"Well...she is crazy..."

"Your wife...or the princess?"

"My wife," Thoral said. He rubbed his handsome face with a calloused hand. "and mayhap, the princess as well. For example, she now insists that she must accompany us to Chowder, which makes my problems a thousand-and-two-fold worse."

"How so?" the innkeeper questioned. The barbarian sighed and closed his bloodshot violet eyes.

"Always it seems, harm befalls those I love because of my poor decisions," he whispered.

"You love the princess?"

"Mayhap," the warrior moaned. He laid his head on the rough-hewn table, caught a whiff of mildew and sat back up. "How can I subject her to the danger of my affections? All those I love perish or are destroyed. Yiz is dead, my son is dead, my wife is insane. How can I risk dooming Nalweegie with my love?"

"That is a very interesting perspective," the old gnome said, eyeing the anguished barbarian. "Many look on love as a gift or a blessing rather than a curse."

"I suppose my feelings matter not anyway," Thoral mused. "The princess is furious with me because of Nancy. As long as she does not return my affections, she may be safe."

"Poppycock!" the gnome snapped with a ferocity that startled his massive drinking partner into sloshing his wine. "If you love her, then you should let nothing stand in the way of your happiness. You should ask her to marry you. That's a great way to smooth over minor relationship quarrels. That or having a baby."

"Oft have I heard the opposite asserted," the warrior replied, his noble brow creased in puzzlement.

"By fools!" the gnome retorted. "Love is not a rational thing, so there is no sense in trying to be sensible about it. Have another drink."

"And what of the fact that I am still married to the Heartless One?" Thoral asked, holding out his half full tankard for freshening.

The innkeeper waved a stubby hand in the air, dismissing the question as he poured the wine. Thoral drained his tankard again and slammed it down on the table.

"Answer me this, gnome: How can I ask her to wed even as I lead her to almost certain doom at the very gates of the most dread ruin of Grome? Especially now that I have lost the magic blade lent to me by my wizard mentor?" Thoral buried his face in his hands. "What if Nancy uses *Blurmflard* to kill Nalweegie? That would be unbearable. Or…or what if Nalweegie somehow kills Nancy? That would be...What would that be? Or what if they…what if they are *both* destroyed?"

"What other option do you have?" the gnome asked.

"I must needs foreswear love, leave at once and recover the pudding on my own. Face Nancy alone."

The innkeeper frowned, his one remaining eye glittering under the bulging scar tissue of his ruined brow.

"Do you think that would be wise?" he asked, refilling Thoral's tankard from his steaming pot of wine.

"I…I do not know," the warrior stammered. "Mayhap."

"Have you ever noticed this mark on my face?" the gnome asked, indicating his ravaged countenance. It wasn't really possible to miss the vast damage to the gnome's face. There was a huge, ragged scar the width of a deck of playing cards that began at his mangled hairline. It continued across his eye-patch-covered right eye socket through the puckered hole that had been his nose. It terminated in the bald patch of beard on the left side of his face, where that part of his chin must once have been. It was a very eye-catching disfigurement that pretty well eliminated the possibility of even guessing what he might have looked like before receiving it. There was much speculation among the patrons of the inn as to the cause.

Thoral blinked at him. "Yes," he said. "I suppose I may have noticed some scarring."

"I got this gash by doing exactly what you are thinking of doing," the gnome confided.

Thoral shook his head, trying to clear the fog of the wine.

"I do not follow..."

"Many years ago, I faced a choice just like your own," the innkeeper insisted. "In fact, your whole situation is eerily familiar. You see, I was not always a lowly innkeeper. No one now living knows this tale but—"

"Wait! Are you from another world?" Thoral blurted.

"What?" the gnome replied, frowning with the small part of his face still capable of making expressions. "From another world? No."

"Oh, sorry," the warrior apologized. "I...well...go on."

"As I was saying," the gnome began again, "I was once a mighty hero, just like yourself. I too fell in love with a princess, just like yours, only to discover on the eve of our union that my long-lost wife, whom I had thought was dead, had become evil and was intent on destroying me."

Thoral sat, dumbstruck. "Verily?" he asked.

"Yes. It would seem like quite an amazing coincidence, if I believed in such things. You see, I too was set to embark on a quest with an array of brave companions—a talking pony, some dwarves, a psychic camel. Our mission was to recover an ancient and unspeakably evil chocolate truffle believed pilfered from the candy box of the gods. Like you, I was torn by indecision and doubt. And like you, I decided I must deny my love and go alone to meet my destiny. That decision turned out to be the *most horrible mistake of my life.*"

Thoral's eyes were wide. He gulped down the contents of his tankard. The gnome refilled it and pressed on.

"What a fool I was! As it turned out, my quest had been foretold and I was supposed to marry the princess and attempt the quest only *with* my companions. Apparently, there was a prophecy and everything. But fearing for the lives of my friends and my love, I went alone and spat in the face of destiny."

"What happened?" Thoral asked in a whisper, sloshing his drink with a trembling hand.

"Just as I reached the truffle, I was ambushed by my crazy wife."

"No!" The warrior shuddered.

"Had I been with my companions, had I embraced their help and been supported by the power of love, we could have triumphed. As it happened, my wife caught me unawares and snapped me with a wet magic bath towel. That brutal snap flicked my eye from its socket, scattered my teeth like chickenfeed and left me this gruesome gash for a face. While I lay there insensible, she seized the chocolate truffle and used its dark power to wipe out my entire country and everyone in it, including my princess and all of my companions. My once fair land was devastated. It is what we now know as the Western Wastes."

Thoral just sat there with his mouth hanging open.

"So if I were you, I would declare my love for the princess, ask her to marry me and leave with her and your other companions to recover the pudding," the gnome concluded. "But, you know, that's just me."

CHAPTER THIRTY-EIGHT

The Fellowship of the Pudding

The sky churned and boiled with dark clouds, grumbling like the swollen, upset tummy of an incomprehensibly big gray monster crouching over the land of Flurge. From this vaporous beast fell a steady drizzle like icy-cold drool or icy-cold sweat or some other icy-cold liquid that might fall from a vaporous creature. Beneath the belly of the beast, a line of thirteen mounted companions trotted across the colorless and squelchy foothills of the Hazy Mountains beneath the shadow of Mount Crotchety: The Fellowship of the Pudding. Brad had come up with the name.

A brooding and hungover Thoral raced at the head of the Fellowship atop Warlordhorse. After the night in the inn, he'd begun drinking again. Though he had taken the gnome's advice about the quest, in the two weeks since they had left Reefma he had not redeclared his love for Nalweegie or asked for her hand. Not only was he still debating both the wisdom of such a move and his own feelings for the princess, she had so far remained aloof and rebuffed his every attempt to reconcile.

Brad rode with Thoral perched atop Warlordhorse's tiger-striped head like an orange hat. Rain was streaming from his scales and into Thoral's face— not improving Thoral's mood at all. The fish was the only one of the companions enjoying the rain because it made him feel somewhat as if he were swimming. Well, he supposed it did. Swimming was an art he had never mastered. Beside them rode Lord Elfrod astride his delicate talking black stallion, Blort. Neither one of them was even damp because Elfrod was wearing his magic Ring of Looks. Thoral had his ring in his belt pouch to appease Brad, so the warrior and Warlordhorse were drenched. Behind them came Nalweegie on her unicorn, Flug. The cold rain served only to amplify her beauty by artfully plastering her raven hair to her high forehead and bringing a touch of red to her milky cheeks. The six warriors of Elf Force brought up the rear, led by Nimrodingle.

All of the humanoid companions of the Fellowship were swaddled in elfish cloaks to protect themselves from the rain as well as from the sight of the evildoers and monsters and such that hung out around there. The cloaks were woven with a tricky technique so that they shifted color to match nearby hues. The elves typically wore them to dinner parties because they would go with any outfit or complement one's eyes, although they were also handy for blending into the countryside on secret missions.

As the Fellowship thundered on through the rain, Blort was explaining a little of the history of the citadel of Chowder to Warlordhorse.

"So you see, Warlordhorse," Blort said in Gromish, his raised voice unexpectedly cultured and urbane for a talking horse, "the citadel of Chowder was once the shining epicenter of the Kingdom of the Good Alliance in the last days of the Fifth Age of Grome, back before everything went to hell. During the reign of Emperor Dandy, son of Fancy, son of Grund the Hamfist, son of Narwall the narwhal rider, son of Eggensammer the Tenth, the treachery of Mauron began."

"Neigh," Warlordhorse nickered in disgust, tossing his head as he trotted.

"Yes," Blort agreed, sounding testy about the interruption. "Mauron was the chancellor in the court of the Emperor, but he teamed with the dark pudding mage Glurpgrond to forge the Bracelet of Evil. They used that foul bangle to slay Dandy and seat Mauron upon the Throne of Everything whilst it was still warm from the emperor's buttocks. This betrayal triggered the cataclysmic War of the Bracelet during which it seemed as if all good might be extinguished from Grome."

"Neigh," Warlordhorse whinnied.

"Stop interrupting now," Blort scolded. "This story is long enough without you slowing it down. So...Where was I? Oh, yes, Mauron had one weakness. The Bracelet of Evil was so mighty a weapon that it drained the very lifeforce of any who wore it. At first, Mauron countered its damaging effects by eating babies and taking lots of vitamin C. Even so, he withered. Thus Glurpgrond began cooking the Great Pudding of Power in the vile land of Splerph. Consuming the pudding would render Mauron invulnerable and allow him to access the full might of the Bracelet of Evil. By happy chance, Emperor Dandy's son, Doug (who was heir to the Throne of Everything) and his best friend, Lord Elfrod, smelled the evil pudding's chocolaty aroma as it was nearing completion. They joined their mighty armies together for one final attack.

"They met Mauron's evil host on the field of Sklounge, at the Great Crag, and fought a battle the likes of which the world had never seen before and we hope it will never see again. While the battle stretched into its fifth hour, the Bracelet of Evil began to exhaust Lord Mauron. As the dark one's strength failed, Glurpgrond informed him that the pudding was ready and he raced back toward Mount Grundle to eat it. Elfrod and Doug reached the pudding seconds before he did and Elfrod snatched away the chalice of pudding as Mauron grabbed for it. When the Dark Lord came after him, Elfrod tossed the chalice to Doug. When Mauron turned his attention to Doug, the last king of Chowder threw the pudding back to Elfrod.

"Thus ensued the most portentous game of pig in the middle ever played. A keep-away in which the fate of all of Grome hung in the balance. Fortunately, Elfrod and Doug managed to keep the pudding from Mauron's clutches just long enough that the Bracelet drained him completely and he evaporated. All that was left of the great and terrible Mauron was a powdery black residue that they sealed in an unopenable envelope, which they mailed to a far-off land. The pudding should have been destroyed then. But at the moment Mauron boiled away, Doug happened to be the one holding it and therefore claimed it as his right.

"Eventually, Glurpgrond led the scattered remains of Mauron's armies of monsters, their ranks swelled with the deranged spirits of the dead, into Flurge. Chowder was overrun by evil. Thus ended the line of kings, and with it much glory vaporized out of the world. To this day, Flurge remains a dread and spooky place and the citadel stands in crumbles at its sparkly, rotten heart."

"This is a sad tale you tell, Blort," Nalweegie called in her sweet, musical voice. She had urged her father's unicorn up beside Thoral and had eavesdropped on most of the black stallion's account.

"Indeed, my lady," Blort returned. "The world is a sad place." As horses go, Blort was something of a downer.

The group trotted on in wet, contemplative silence while the disquiet sky grumbled above them and flicked out ominous blue tongues of lightning.

"And what of your world?" Nalweegie asked of Thoral when the silence had become oppressive. "Is it also a sad place?"

Thoral gave her a long, searching look. He was trying to ascertain whether she was really interested or just setting him up for another argument. She had ambushed him in this way three or four times already since their departure from Reefma. "I liked it," Thoral allowed.

"What did you like about it?" Blort chimed in before Nalweegie could say anything else. "What was different?"

"Yes, tell us of your world," Brad encouraged.

The princess scowled, but even she couldn't help looking a little interested.

"Well," Thoral began, casting his mind back thirty-odd years, "one could always get a cold drink, even on the hottest day, or a hot shower even on the coldest. And most people smelled nice because they bathed every day and washed with perfumed soaps specially designed for their bodies and other soaps specially designed for their hair. They applied ointments to their armpits to prevent excessive sweating and washed their clothes with scented fabric softeners." He paused, sighing, before continuing. "And there were rinses to make one's breath smell sweet, and there was toilet paper for the wiping of one's behind after using the privy. Not just of one variety either but many varieties to cater to people's individual desires for softness or strength or some combination of the two. There were even damp tissues for that purpose. And there were amazing drinks created from sparkling water comingled with sugar, spices and herbs that invigorated and refreshed those who imbibed them. These drinks came in such an assortment of flavors as to stagger the imagination. And the foods! Long have I struggled—with little success—to duplicate crispy-crust pizza in the land of Grome. There are no tomatoes here."

"We have tomatoes," Nalweegie objected.

"What you call tomatoes on Grome are what we call kumquats in my world," Thoral explained.

"So your tomatoes are different? What are they like?"

"I cannot describe them, but they are better for pizza than kumquats," Thoral said, frowning. Then he pressed on. "Beyond traditional foods, the number of desserts and snacks available in my world was mind-boggling. A person could actually subsist on salty, sweet or savory treats. Most people I knew led lives of such leisure that physical activity was taught in schools, and people exercised as a pastime so that they would not grow too fat watching…um…"

"Watching what?" Brad asked, thoroughly engrossed.

"There is no word for it in any language of Grome," Thoral noted. "You might call it a magic seeing box or a window through which one watched enchanted stories. We called it television. We watched shows and played games on the television."

"Telewision." Nalweegie struggled to pronounce the word.

"Yesssss," Thoral breathed. "Only, I transpose the sounds of my *V*s and *W*s because of my outlandish accent, so it would actually be pronounced tele*vision* rather than tele*wision.* Whatever the pronunciation, I cannot even begin to explain how mesmerizing and engrossing it was. I used to get home from school and spend the entire rest of the day watching television or playing video games."

"You stood atop this magic box to play games?" Elfrod asked.

"You know what," Thoral said, his face brightening, "I can show you! When next we make camp, I will show you a television show. I think I have some on my iPhone."

"The iPhone!" Brad exclaimed to the others. "It is a rectangle that makes the most stirring music."

"Were we not so concerned with drawing unwanted attention, I would be playing its music aloud even now," Thoral agreed, smiling and nodding his head. "There is little more invigorating than riding fast with awesome music blaring."

Now Warlordhorse nodded, whinnying and tossing his head in agreement, so that Brad was almost thrown off. In their early days together, on their quest for the Walking-Door Tree, the mighty stallion and Thoral had galloped around to the music from the iPhone. It was indeed, electrifying.

"That is another thing that I miss from my world," Thoral said, barely seeing the countryside around him for the memories inside his head. "In my land, most people owned metal horseless carriages able to attain speeds faster than a cheetah with no effort from their passengers. The passengers were able to recline in comfort and listen to music, play games, or watch shows. These vehicles were so safe and efficient that the primary threats one experienced within them were boredom and motion sickness."

"Your world sounds like a heavenly paradise," Nalweegie marveled. She bit her lower lip, wondering how she might ever compete against a woman who had shared such experiences with Thoral or against the memories of a world so fantastical.

"Indeed," Thoral replied, still focused inward so that hc did not notice the outward signs of her discomfort.

CHAPTER THIRTY-NINE

The Walking-Door Tree

The Fellowship of the Pudding made camp in a secret cave as night fell. There were way too many nocturnal monsters in the area to travel after dark. Elfrod led the group to a cavern that they otherwise would never have found. The elfish king had spent a lot of time in Flurge in the old days, horsing around with Emperor Doug when the heir to the line of Eggensammer was still just a teen, so he knew where there were all kinds of good places to hide and smoke a pipe. The cave was dry and so roomy that even the horses could come inside. That was a good thing because the proud and noble Blort would have thrown a hissy fit if he had to stand in the rain. The Fellowship soon changed into their pajamas and got a fire going, around which they hung their wet garments. Meanwhile Brad and Nimrodingle cooked up some dinner and the Elf Force ladies groomed the horses.

"If we keep to a fast trot," Elfrod said sagely, warming his hands over the flames, "we should reach the citadel of Chowder before noon tomorrow."

"Do you believe we have moved swiftly enough to beat the Heartless One?" Nimrodingle asked as she split some gluten-free elfish buns with the ancient dagger *Dangload*, forged in the fair lands of the west for the wars between the elves and the Poojas back in the old days. She positioned the buns on a rock near the fire so that they would toast up just right while Brad expertly turned a couple of spits full of weenies.

"I believe we have," Thoral said, setting aside the wineskin he'd been nursing and drawing a rough map on the sandy floor of the cave with his finger. "The ruined cabin of Yiz is much farther from the citadel than Reefma is, and Nancy would have arrived there wounded and without a steed." He traced a path from the cabin to the citadel with the pointer finger of one hand and a path from Reefma to the citadel with the other. "Even if she made straight for Chowder the minute she arrived, and allowing for the fact that she is traveling lighter than we, our fellowship should still reach it first."

"She seems to have all kinds of weird magic," Brad noted. "What if she's teleported to the citadel already?"

"Nancy was ever a fast study in the ways of magic," Thoral conceded, "but her teleportation was a trick of *Blurmflard* that could only take her to Yiz's cabin. I do not think Nancy could magically get to Chowder, or she wouldn't have used the sword to escape."

"Do you have to keep calling her Nancy?" Nalweegie accused. "The uncouthness of that name stings my pointy ears."

"Sorry," Thoral grumbled. There was an uncomfortable silence in the cave. He took another big pull from his wineskin.

"Weenies are ready!" Brad called.

***

After the Fellowship had feasted until their bellies were full and the fire was beginning to die, Thoral bade them all gather around him except the two unlucky elves that had to stand watch. They were the two teenage members of Elf Force. One was actually Nimrodingle's daughter, Dimsel. The commander had pulled a lot of strings to get her into Elf Force, so Dimsel was always getting assigned extra duty so that her mom would not be accused of favoritism. The other was a pal of Dimsel's named Futon.

"Futon?" Thoral said, a smile playing across his manly lips. The barbarian had never heard the elf called by name before.

"Yes?" Futon replied, assuming Thoral was just trying to get her attention.

Thoral cracked up. He tried to conceal his mirth but failed.

"What's so funny?" Futon asked, first of the barbarian and then of the others as the warrior giggled and snorted.

"It's something about your name," Brad told her. "Don't let it bother you. He's just drunk."

"Futon is a pretty common name," Futon noted, sounding a little hurt but only making Thoral laugh harder. "I don't see what's funny about it. I am Futon, daughter of Crouton, daughter of Tampon, daughter of Wonton."

Thoral spluttered.

"Yeah, well," the fish shrugged, "there's a whole bunch of popular names that make him crack up like this. Futon, Tofu, Twinkie, Dinkie…"

Thoral could barely contain himself.

"Kleenex, Lasagna, Thong, Swiffer, Urinal…"

The warrior totally lost it.

"I guess they sound like words from his world," the fish concluded, casting a disapproving glance Thoral's way.

"Your pardon, good Futon." Thoral mastered himself, though his eyes were watering and his face flushed. "I mean no offense. It is as the fish says. Thine service on guard duty this night is much appreciated."

Futon still looked wounded as she left the cave. Dimsel went with her, shooting, a dirty look at her mother over the guard duty assignment.

When the guards had taken up their posts, Thoral produced his iPhone and turned it on. Even Elfrod oohed and aahed at the colorful buttons as Thoral paged through his list of songs, debating which to play. He finally settled on a playlist and started it up.

"Twist and Shout" by the Beatles blasted throughout the cave, amplified by its acoustics and an amplifying spell Thoral knew. Everybody freaked out, even the horses. Futon and Dimsel ran back into the cave to see what was going on. Thoral had to pause the song to let everyone collect their wits. He started it over at a lower volume.

Everybody freaked out again, this time in a good way. None of those born on Grome knew quite what to do with their bodies in reaction to the pulsing sound. They tapped their feet, bobbed their heads or bounced in place. They had all been raised on tamer, staid music and only knew how to dance in an elaborate, courtly style. So Thoral cut loose with some moves he dimly remembered from a dancing video game.

As he gyrated, the blonde-maned barbarian grabbed Brad, put him on his shoulder and shimmied around the sandy floor with the fish. After a moment, he set Brad down so the fish could dance on his own. Thoral took Elfrod by one hand, spinning him into motion, too. As the dignified king of the elves danced in a most undignified way, Thoral pulled each of the others (except the horses) into action in turn until only Nalweegie was left. The princess locked eyes with the warrior as he approached her. Her alabaster cheeks flushed. Without a word, he put his hands round her waist, hoisted her into the air and spun like a madman until she threw her head back and laughed for the giddy joy of it. When "Twist and Shout" ended, the iPhone launched into "Do You Love Me" by the Contours. The cave resembled a dorky middle school dance party, with everyone gyrating, whooping and giggling.

When "Do You Love Me" was over, everyone was panting and a little embarrassed. Nalweegie, relaxed and smiling in Thoral's embrace, suddenly remembered she was supposed to be mad at him and wriggled free. His face fell, then he shook himself and smiled again.

"Who would like to see television?" he asked.

Everyone gathered round. He encouraged them to settle into their sleeping furs in case they got tired while watching. As they nestled down, he went through the short list of shows on the iPhone, feeling great pangs of nostalgia at each title. By the time his audience was ready, he had settled on an episode of a reality series about a cake baker and the trials and tribulations of his family-run bakery in New Jersey.

The entire group watched, rapt and awestruck, for the next few hours as the bakers created an apple-themed cake for an apple orchard and the owner of the bakery battled with his sister, who felt slighted when he did not devote enough attention to making her birthday cake. The episode itself was only twenty-two minutes long, but Thoral had to pause to translate what was being said and to explain countless details of what was going on and the interpersonal relationships between the people. By this point, he had also consumed enough wine that he was slurring his words and often needed to repeat himself.

"I am staggered by the strange wonder of your world," Elfrod said when the episode was done. "So much effort and artistry devoted to cake! Can we watch another one?"

"I think not," Thoral said. "'Tis bedtime. We have much to do tomorrow, and the battery on my iPhone is running low," he hiccupped.

"Please," the Fellowship begged, including Futon and Dimsel, who were technically still supposed to be on watch. They had sneaked back in once the show started.

"Come on, Thoral," Brad said. "Let us start one. Just five minutes."

"No, my friends." The warrior's voice was sympathetic but firm. "We must get our sleep. We can watch more episodes when we have recovered the Great Pudding of Power and returned safely back to Creekenvalley."

"Can we at least listen to "Twist and Shout" again?" Elfrod pestered.

Thoral held firm. There was a bit of grumbling, but everyone was actually pretty tired. They banked the fire and settled down to sleep.

***

An hour later, Thoral was still awake and brooding, staring into the red-orange darkness created by the dying embers of the fire. His wineskin was empty. He heard a rustling sound beside him, and someone moved close.

"Thoral, art thou still awake?" Nalweegie whispered, her warm breath tickling his ear.

"I am," he whispered back.

For a long moment the princess was quiet beside him, wrestling with her thoughts. "You must long to go back," she said finally.

Thoral frowned in the darkness. "I have thought about going home every day since I first arrived," he said. "Mostly at night. Because the beds here are so uncomfortable in comparison. Oh, and every time I use the privy or run into someone who stinks. Also on Grumsbydays, because I first came here on a Grumsbyday, which is called Tuesday in my world."

"Is there a way for you to return?"

"Yes," the warrior sighed. "My wizard mentor, Yiz, told me of a tree with a door in the trunk that is a portal back to my world. It is called the Walking-Door Tree because it wanders about. It is some kind of birch or other broad-leafed deciduous hardwood."

"The tree the Heartless One spoke of?"

"I found it once, soon after my son was born," Thoral said. "A wandering gypsy mentioned to Yiz in passing that she had seen a tree with a door in it. As soon as he told me, I set out and found it just where she said it would be. It was amazing, an ancient, gnarled thing with a wooden door right in the middle of the base of the trunk. I recognized it. It was the door to the room in which Nan—I mean, the Heartless One—and I first stumbled into Grome."

Nalweegie smiled slightly in the darkness, pleased that Thoral had remembered not to say the *N* word.

"You did not go through?" she asked.

"No," Thoral sighed. "Yiz's cabin was attacked just as I found the tree. I should have teleported back to the cabin, but I'd forgotten the magic word. I raced back to try to help. I was too late. My son and Yiz were killed, and I thought the Heartless One had perished too. I was never able to find the tree again after that, although I have searched far and wide for it. Lately, I have begun to suspect that someone may have chopped it down and used it for firewood or something."

"I am sorry you did not find it again," the princess whispered. "Truly."

"Thank you," Thoral whispered back. "Had I found the tree, I would not have met you and that would have been…a bad thing." The warrior felt the princess's small hand slip into his large one.

"What if you were to find it now?" Nalweegie wondered, squeezing his hand.

"I…," Thoral began. "I guess I would—"

"Would you two knock it off?" Brad complained, startling them both. "I'm trying to sleep over here."

CHAPTER FORTY

The Yellow Road

The companions of the Fellowship were crabby as their steeds picked their way along a treacherous trail on the desolate slopes of the foothills of the Hazy Mountains in the shadow of Mount Crotchety. Nobody had slept well on the uneven floor of the cave. Thoral would have drained a full wineskin in a single draught, but his stores of alcohol were limited, so he was restricting himself to drinking mostly at night. As it was, he had a massive headache. Moreover, Nalweegie had started sniping at him the minute she got up, angry that he hadn't answered her question from the night before although unwilling to admit the reason. The evil gloom of Flurge, coupled with its continuing cold drizzle and its strange odor, did not improve anyone's mood by a single smidgen.

The air about the Fellowship was tinged with the faint scent of dark chocolate tainted by an ominous note of coriander or some other spice that unsettled Thoral's stomach as he tried to eat. The companions breakfasted on jelly toast as they rode, dribbling jam into the horses' manes and increasing the grumpiness of their mounts. Thoral distracted himself from wanting to drink by brooding on the mistakes he had made since coming to Grome and on the lives those mistakes had cost. It wasn't a healthy diversion. He wondered how things might have been different if he'd remembered the magic teleportation word or if he had known Nancy had survived the attack by the Grode. He sighed because he wasn't very good at introspection and took another bite of his toast.

"I still don't know why you couldn't have eaten in the cave," Blort huffed.

"I don't know why you are complaining," Brad grumped from his perch on Thoral's saddlehorn. "Elfrod's Ring of Looks would keep your mane jelly free even if he were using you as his personal napkin."

"I speak for my brothers who cannot speak," Blort said, narrowing his eyes in anger at the fish. "As all good talking creatures should."

"So, you're calling me a bad talking creature?"

"If the shoe fits," the horse snorted.

"You know perfectly well I can't wear shoes," Brad snarled, clenching his pectoral fins into the fin equivalent of fists, which on a fish, are technically referred to as *finsts*.

"Gentle beasts," Elfrod interrupted them, "still thy bitter tongues and remember thy friendship. You are out of sorts because of the evil scent of the Great Pudding of Power, nothing more. Ever has this been its way, poisoning the hearts of the noble with irritability and crankiness so that they fall to quarreling amongst themselves."

The fish and the horse eyed each other sheepishly.

"Sorry," Brad said, unclenching his finsts.

"As am I," Blort replied.

Just then, group leader Nimrodingle held up a hand to signal a halt.

"What," the commander of Elf Force asked as Elfrod, Thoral and Nalweegie rode up beside her, "is that?" She pointed into the distance at a thick ribbon of yellow that marked the gray ground like an unmoving river from one end of the horizon to the other.

"Yonder lies the ruin of the road of yellow bricks that leads to the city of Chowder," Elfrod noted sagely.

"Yellow brick road?" Thoral sputtered.

"Yes, ever were the men of Chowder vain and fancy," the king of the elves explained. "The yellow road was built at the height of their power and at ridiculous expense. It was my plan to intersect the road here and follow it the rest of the way to the citadel as the terrain will get increasingly treacherous the closer we get to Chowder."

Thoral shifted in his saddle and stared at the road uneasily.

"What troubles you?" Nalweegie asked, her emerald eyes searching his handsome face.

Thoral did not reply, but urged Warlordhorse to a sudden gallop, making for the road.

When the others caught up to him, the warrior had already dismounted and was kneeling beside the wide expanse of the yellow brick road, peering at it while Brad stood atop Warlordhorse's noble head with a puzzled expression.

"In my world," Thoral answered, "there was a famous story in which a girl was transported to a magical world in which a yellow brick road, uncannily like this one, led to a great emerald city."

"Clearly, this is not that road," Elfrod noted, "as this one leads from the volcanic Mount Grundle to Chowder, a city made of white and pink quartz."

"Yet it seems more than a touch uncanny that I, a man from another world, should encounter a yellow brick road on my journey to a crystalline city, regardless of the exact color of that city."

"I'll allow it does," Elfrod said sagely. "What meaning do you make of this?"

"I know not," Thoral grumped, getting back to his feet and sighting down the crumbling road, first one way and then the other. "This is not the only such oddity. The Sea of Tears on the eastern shores of Grome shares its name with a sea in a children's book from my world. And there was a whole series of stories of the tentacle-faced god, Cthulhu, on my world as well."

"Oh, I hate that god," Nalweegie shivered.

"Perhaps he was also a god of your world?" Brad speculated. "Who is to say whether gods are restricted to just one world?"

"In my world, he was just a story. A character invented by a writer of fiction," Thoral said.

"Weird," Elfrod acceded. "I have twice narrowly thwarted the apocalypse of his awakening, so I am pretty sure he is real here."

"Like this yellow brick road," Thoral said, stamping one iron-toed boot on the bricks.

"Many times have I trod its cheery cobbles in happier days," Elfrod confirmed.

"It is things like this that make me wonder..." The barbarian trailed off.

"Wonder what?" Elfrod asked.

But Thoral did not answer. He stood staring down at the yellow brick road, silent and troubled, while Nalweegie stared down at him, silent and troubled. There was a long, troubled silence.

"Well, all right then," Nimrodingle announced. "We've still got a ways to go, and we certainly don't want to be hanging about the Citadel of Chowder once darkness descends."

"You speak aright," Elfrod said, shivering. "It would be far better for us to get in and out of Chowder with that pudding while the sun yet shines. Only evil stalks the dead streets of crumbling Chowder after nightfall, and there are a fearsome number of moths which have a tendency to tangle in one's hair."

Thoral sighed, but vaulted onto Warlordhorse's saddle.

The Fellowship resumed their trek, now trotting along the pocked and potholed expanse of the yellow brick road, all eyes peeled for any sign of trouble.

CHAPTER FORTY-ONE

The Dead City

All that morning the fellows followed the crumbling ruins of the yellow brick road through the humps, hummocks, hillocks and buttocks of the gray and withered land of Flurge, with their eyes and mouths watering at the ever-increasing stench of the place. The powerful aroma of molten chocolate with hints of coffee and notes of full-bodied fruit was heavy in the air. While these would not normally be considered bad smells, the strong whiff of cumin that pervaded everything poisoned the other scents and made it clear that their origin point must be pure evil.

As if the grumbling ash-colored sky, the icy drizzle and the sparse and twisted foliage wreathed in ground-crawling fog were not ominous enough, the companions also encountered a significant number of bones scattered about in the weedy gray grass. At first these were merely occasional shards or splinters, but the shards and splinters progressed to partial skeletons, then to full skeletons, then to piles of full skeletons, then to piles of piles of full skeletons. While all grew depressed and nervous at the sight, Elfrod seemed most affected. He often winced at the towering mounds and sometimes even mumbled to himself.

The companions could not see far along the bone-littered road because of the combination of misty rain and lumpy terrain. After several hours, many among them fell to expecting the sight of the quartz citadel over each new rise. Since none but Elfrod had seen it before, the anticipation was high and the disappointment escalating.

"Are we there yet?" Brad called to Nimrodingle as she neared the crest of another hump just ahead of the others. It was the tenth time the fish had asked that question and everyone was tired of hearing it.

"No," the commander of Elf Force snapped, frowning.

"Weren't we supposed to be there by lunch?" Brad asked Elfrod, a note of accusation in his voice.

"Quiet," Nalweegie grumped as the group plodded to the top of the rise.

"*You* be quiet," the fish retorted, imitating her voice.

"Insolent fish!" the princess spat.

"Spoiled little—"

Everyone gasped. They had crested the hill and below them, sparkling in the dim light of the overcast sky like a giant pink-glitter-painted Easter egg perched on the white-quartz heart of the dead city of Chowder, lay the shattered crystal dome of the ancient citadel. The gigantic ruins dwarfed the surrounding landscape as a literal giant might literally dwarf a literal dwarf or some other small magical creature. Although the city and its proud citadel had been abandoned for a thousand and one years and although most of the structures were tumbled-down wrecks marred by weeds and rude graffiti left by various monsters, the engineering, skill and craftsmanship with which Chowder had been wrought were still breathtaking.

"What is that word," Thoral said after a full minute of silence, "that word one exclaims after a particularly shocking incident? It is a word that can also be used to halt the progress of a horse."

"Whoa?" Brad suggested, unable to take his eyes from the ruin.

"Whoa...," Thoral whispered.

***

The companions of the Fellowship of the Pudding did not even take the time for a hasty lunch, despite the fact that it was well past noon by the time they reached the great wall of Chowder. The overpowering chocolaty stink of the place was strong enough that one felt full just breathing it and the strangely spicey overtones were giving them headaches and making them feel as nauseated as if they had just gorged themselves on ten pounds of candy and then spun in circles.

"We must hurry," Elfrod urged as he sat astride Blort in the vast, crumbling opening that had been the main gate to the city. "The entrance to the ice caverns is within the Citadel itself and there's no telling what, if any, opposition we may meet as we approach. I expect we shall not reach the Citadel without some combat." He turned his ancient, glinty eyes on his daughter.

"Fair Nalweegie," he continued, "I urge you to turn back here and return to the cave in which we took our last rest. You have more than proven your valor on this quest and I am loath to risk your life by having you enter this dread place. I will send half of my Elf Force back with you as your personal guard."

"Wither you go, so goest I," Nalweegie said, inclining her chin to look down her nose at her father. "What evil opposition this Fellowship faces next, so next I must also face. Whatsoever goest down, I am up for it."

At that, Thoral drew a regular-nonmagical sword that Elfrod had lent him to replace *Blurmflard*, the king of the elves drew his magic blade, *Krandarthnak*, and the warriors of Elf Force nocked arrows to their bows.

"Just out of curiosity," Brad asked, eyeing the gigantic blocks of quartz that had once composed the walls, now cracked, ruined and scattered, "what kind of opposition are we talking about here?"

"Various monsters," Elfrod said, his eyes still locked on his daughter. "Barfarts, stinkcasters, bogey monsters, mertalizers, ghosts. That ilk."

"I hate that ilk," Brad complained.

"These beasts are largely nocturnal," Nalweegie noted as she clutched the hilt of her thin elfish blade, *Whisper*.

"Yes," Elfrod nodded. "If we can recover the pudding and be away before sunset, I pray we might avoid the bulk of the evil forces that dwell here."

"Got it," the koi said. "Let's move."

Without further discussion, shooting wary glances every which way, the companions passed through the gate. A chill fell upon them like a cold, damp beach towel as they rode under the shadows of Chowder's walls. Thoral could no longer help himself and sneaked a swig from a fresh wineskin. Brad shook his head in disgust.

The signs of the cataclysmic fall of that once-fair city were shockingly evident all about the companions. The massive iron portcullis that had blocked the way lay in a twisted, rusted heap atop a large collection of splintered bones, bits of rent armor and busted weapons that were everywhere mingled with the powder of shattered quartz.

"Almost we held them back here," Elfrod said, his voice catching in his throat as Blort picked his way through the wreckage. "Then the foul Pudding Mage, Glurpgrond, used his vile black wand to unleash a blasting spell upon us that blew down the great gate as if it were … something easily blown down…" He trailed off and his sea-green eyes sparkled with tears uncried as a chocolate breeze stirred his noble hair. Perhaps it was just the light, but he looked older and more frail, his face gaunt and tired.

Over the course of the next hour, as the Fellowship passed various remnants of ancient carnage and destruction, the elf king kept up a steady stream of narration of the brutal events of the night Chowder fell. He seemed compelled to do it, as if unable to hold back the terrible memories, and he kept fidgeting with his misplacement compass, as if trying to distract himself from the horrors of his memory.

"This is where Glurpgrond's evil dragon, Chubbilard, cornered and cooked the city militia. It steamed them like lobsters in their enchanted and otherwise impenetrable armor. We did not see that coming until it was too late," he confessed, pointing out lumps of melted metal and the vague silhouettes of scores of men scorched onto the otherwise white stonework where two mighty buildings came together.

"And here is where the fair and just Lord Trundle Truefriend was gutted like a pig. His mighty sons, Trigg and Gingle, were strangled to death with their father's entrails by Glurpgrond as they tried to lead a counter charge," he said. With a trembling hand he indicated the dry, cracked basin of what had been a large fountain atop an age-worn flight of quartz stairs. There was a once-lovely statue of a fair maiden at its center, now crudely defaced with a painted mustache and beard. "I tried to save them, but Glurpgrond did kick me mightily in my testicles so that I, and my testicles, had to withdraw in order to recover. I will never forget the terrible look of glee upon his evil visage.

"And here is where Glurpgrond's mertalizers ate the knights of the Order of the Goat. Alive. They did not even cook them. I can still hear their gurgling and tortured cries as those feral beasts tore quarter-pound mouthfuls of flesh from their throats."

He made a half-hearted gesture toward what appeared to be the ruins of a small keep. "And this is where two hundred men of the Legion of the Defenders of the Throne were hacked into quarter-inch cubes by one of Glurpgrond's whirling-blade spells. The very air was fogged with the pink clouds of their vaporized blood and entrails so that it was hard to see one's own hand before one's face. It was so repellent to be breathing the mist of our fallen comrades' essential fluids that everyone still alive was vomiting buckets. I will ever remember the smell of that soup of the entrails, blood and bile of good men." He shuddered as the group rode along a stretch of city street, the white cobbles of which were stained black and red. Blort made gagging noises. He was a mighty battle steed, but he had a sensitive stomach. Thoral sneaked another swig of wine.

"And here is where Glurpgrond ordered his crazed bogey monsters to fall upon the sweet and helpless little children of the—"

"Hey, Elfrod," Brad interrupted the king of the elves. "I think we've got the picture. Sounds really, really bad. Any chance you might spare us the rest of the details?"

"Oh. Of course," the elf said, a slight tremor in his voice. He remained silent and brooding as he led the companions deeper into the heart of the city. And always, the shattered pink dome of the citadel crouched above them on the hill that marked the center of Chowder like a cracked pastel Easter egg.

CHAPTER FORTY-TWO

The Citadel of Chowder

"I like this not," Nimrodingle whispered as the Fellowship stood at last before the gaping maw of the ruined entrance to the fallen citadel of the ancient city of Chowder. The sun was slanting toward the horizon through a break in the drizzle, casting long and creepy shadows, and the leader of Elf Force adjudged that they had only four hours remaining until sunset. All eyes turned from her to the king of the elves.

"I like it not too," Elfrod agreed. "But nor do I like better the other option before us."

"Nor do I like the other thing too also," Nimrodingle said solemnly.

Everyone except Nimrodingle and Elfrod glanced around at everyone else in some confusion.

"Which other thing?" Brad asked.

"The other thing which we like not," Elfrod said, frowning.

"The turning back and trying to get the pudding tomorrow thing?" Brad tried to clarify.

"Indeed," Elfrod replied. "Half my heart wouldst counsel that our best chance still lies in pressing onward whilst just over one quarter of my heart wouldst argue that we have taken too long and should tarry no more in this dread place but come back tomorrow morning." He paused and his sea-green eyes turned to Thoral's violet ones. "What thinkest thou, mighty Fist Wielder? This is your quest to lead."

Thoral winced. He didn't want to make life-and-death decisions for his companions. This was why he had wanted to come alone.

Now he was wracked by the responsibility. He took a brazen pull from his half-empty wineskin. How many times had he decided for others and led them to their dooms? Coincidentally, he had just been thinking about Trenton and that guy, Tofu, both of whom died because of his mistakes. And there were countless other guys whose names he'd never known. Like that guy who was beheaded in Thoral's place in the temple of the Bad Religion. He sucked down another mouthful of wine.

Thoral had a tendency to think about people who'd died because of him whenever he had free time. Since there hadn't been much fighting on this trip, he'd had far too much time to devote to his regrets. But all of the companions of the Fellowship were staring at him now, and he didn't like to come across as wishy-washy or indecisive. If only the universe could send him some sign to help him decide. Why was his path not made clear? He blearily eyed the dim ball of the sun, sinking lower in the overcast sky. The weak shadows it cast stretched toward his friends like evil, black skeleton hands of death, if hand bones were black instead of white. Then a sullen red comet streaked across the sky and vanished behind the city. Then a black cat streaked across the path. Then a raven fluttered down and landed on his shoulder.

"Nevermore," it croaked, its beady black eyes glinting. "Nevermore."

Thoral met its gaze, considering. The voice of the Gruesomely Gashed Gnome sounded in his ears: "*Had I been with my companions, had I embraced their help, we could have triumphed.*"

"Let us press on," the warrior gruffed, brushing the bird away. If the universe would not send him a signal, then he must cast the die himself.

"So be it," Elfrod assented, and they rode into the citadel. The retreating raven's caws resounded like evil laughter as it circled skyward.

If the city of Chowder was a wonder even in its ruin, the great Citadel was a double wonder with a cherry on top. The companions gasped as one as they rode through the front door. Giant pillars of pure pink quartz cunningly sculpted in the shape of flamingos towered a hundred feet over their heads and held up the remains of the shattered dome. Thoral dismounted Warlordhorse and strode to the middle of the vast chamber, which was suffused in pink light from the translucent quartz. He turned in a slow circle with his mouth open as he took in the exquisite detail. Every inch of the remaining walls and ceiling was embellished with glittering carvings of pigs, starfish, naked mole rats, coral snakes, newborn mice, earthworms, river dolphins, naked babies and other pink creatures frolicking and gamboling amongst a dizzying forest of pink flowers, mushrooms and fluffy clouds. It was evident that Glurpgrond's force of vile monsters had tried to deface as many of these decorative elements as possible, but everything above ten or fifteen feet was still almost untouched because the evil giants had been busy with something else that weekend.

"Gosh," Thoral breathed.

"It is so…pink," Nalweegie whispered.

"And even more amazing than the legends tell," Nimrodingle sighed.

"Meh," Brad grumped from Thoral's shoulder. "It's a little girly for my taste. Is it just my imagination or is that chocolate smell even more cloying in here than it was outside?"

"Queen Tinsel, wife of the first High King Eggensammer, commissioned the decoration of this Great Foyer," Blort explained, ignoring the fish. "It took two hundred gnomish gem cutters two decades to complete the sculptures. When they were finished, she said she hadn't realized the quartz was going to be so translucent. She wanted to have the whole thing redone in pink topaz, which would be more transparent. The dispute with the king of the gnomes over whether that should be considered a billable change order or a free make-good was part of what soured the relationship between the gnomes and the line of the kings of men.

"A lesson for us all," the horse concluded in a superior tone. No one was sure what he meant, but they didn't have time for a lecture, so no one asked him to clarify.

The others dismounted now, and the members of the Fellowship led their horses across the remaining expanse of the Great Foyer of the Citadel of Chowder in silence. They paused at the far side of the hall before a partially collapsed opening in the pink wall. Beyond this entry, the roof must have been intact, for they could see only a few feet into the space behind before all was swallowed by darkness.

"Through this door lies the throne room of the Kings of Men," Elfrod told them, breaking the oppressive silence. "The chamber bears so many protective enchantments woven into its very stones that it remains unbroken even after all this time. The secret entryway to the ice caverns below the Citadel is hidden just behind the Throne of Everything. No comely creature has crossed this threshold since I led the retreat through it into the caverns to make our escape when the Citadel fell. I suspect little remains of the throne room's ancient splendor." He dropped his eyes in sadness.

"So could we have skipped the city of Chowder altogether and just come in the way you left, through the ice caverns?" Brad asked.

"No," Elfrod shook his head. "We destroyed the exit behind us as we fled to prevent Glurpgrond from pursuing us. Long had I hoped that he perished in the magical blast with which we sealed the tunnels."

"He didn't?" Brad asked.

"Sadly no," the king sighed. "About two centuries later, his evil Glurpgronders, the nine-and-a-half Black Riders, began galloping about on their skeleton-ghost horses searching for the envelope with Mauron's remains in it so that the Dark Lord could be reconstituted."

"Like some kind of evil powdered-juice drink," Thoral observed darkly. Although no one else had any idea what a powdered-juice drink was, they all got the gist.

"Dang," Brad said.

Elfrod then ordered his soldiers to light their elfish lanterns and ready themselves to enter the throne room.

"Do you see how the elves use lanterns instead of torches?" Brad whispered to Thoral from his perch on the warrior's shoulder. "That's because elves are smart." He tapped the side of his head with a fin. The barbarian frowned and sucked down the last of the wine from his skin, squeezing it to make sure he got every drop.

"If only I had *Blurmflard*, the magic blade lent to me by my wizard mentor, Yiz. I could light the way with its pink emissions," Thoral grumped, wiping his chin.

"Where did you lose that again?" Nalweegie asked. "Oh, yes, I remember. Your psychotic wife took it from you when she was trying to kill the three of us."

"Thanks, Princess," Brad said, all mock cheeriness. "That's very helpful. You know, maybe to pass the time you'll tell us about this other guy you were supposed to marry."

"Enough, Brad," Thoral grumbled.

"No, actually, I'm happy to tell you about the man my people were planning to saddle me with, fish," the princess shot back. "Not that it's any of your business. Let's see. He wasn't much to look at. He was scrawny, with a weak chin and no discernible personality—"

"Nalweegie," Elfrod sighed.

"Apparently, he was fabulously wealthy though. Isn't that right, Father?" the princess asked bitterly. "And I guess that was all that mattered as long as Creekenvalley was facing bankruptcy because you lost the keys to the treasure vault."

The king's countenance darkened, but Nimrodingle interrupted before he could make a retort. "I hate to cut such a healthy conversation short," she said. "We are wasting what little time we have."

The king turned without uttering a reply and held his lantern aloft. Thoral fell in beside him clutching his substitute blade. Brad still stood upon Thoral's massively muscled shoulder, and Nalweegie moved behind her father and her partially estranged love.

"If we are to be ambushed, this seems the most likely place for it," Elfrod cautioned.

Knuckles white on their lantern handles and the hilts of their swords, thews and sinews tensed for battle, the members of the Fellowship stepped through the door.

By the steady, consistent light of the lanterns they saw that no enemy force awaited them. The chamber was small in relation to the giant pink foyer they had just crossed, and it was round so that no shadowed corners provided hiding places. It was empty except for a thick layer of dust, scads of bones and the great chair that hulked at its center. The gargantuan pyrite Throne of Everything sparkled in the lantern light. It was a mammoth seat, as if proportioned for a giant. It was formed from a single piece of iron pyrite thrusting up through the stone floor. The Fellowship approached it, awed to be in the presence of such a legendary artifact.

The famous seat of the power of ancient Chowder was rough, misshapen and very uncomfortable looking. The seat was so high that even Thoral would have required a stepladder to mount it. The throne was a natural formation, a chunk of iron pyrite that happened to be in the approximate shape of a chair.

"It was said that when Eggensammer first found this stone, he took it as a sign that he was meant to rule," Blort said, sounding awed. "Unable to budge it, he had the whole Citadel of Chowder built around it."

"There were once many cushions to make it more comfy," Elfrod noted sadly. "They have either been pillaged or have rotted away with the passage of the centuries."

"What's that inscription?" Brad asked, pointing a fin toward a scrawl of age-worn runes chiseled into the top of the throne.

"'With noble butt upon this seat, the very world lies at thy feet,'" Thoral answered.

King Elfrod raised his eyebrows at the warrior.

"Few living still read High Gromish," the elf noted, his voice touched with surprise and admiration.

"'Twas the language I was taught when first I arrived in Grome," Thoral explained.

"Lift me to the seat," Brad urged Thoral with a grin. "I want you to take a picture of me with your iPhone."

As the fish crouched to spring onto the throne, Nalweegie stopped him. "That inscription is more than a boast," she explained. "It is also a warning."

"How so?" the koi frowned.

"This throne is infused with eldritch magics and baleful sorcery," Nalweegie cautioned. "If any butt but a butt of royal descent descends upon this seat, the sitter will be burned to a cinder within a heartbeat."

Brad's eyes went wide. "No way!" the fish exclaimed in a shaken voice.

"Verily," Nalweegie returned. Elfrod raised his eyebrows at his daughter, who winked back at him.

"I noticed that wink," Thoral said frowning. "I was trained as a noticer."

"Fine," Nalweegie scowled. "It's not infused with eldritch magics and baleful sorcery. But you shouldn't sit in it, Brad. It's disrespectful."

"Because I'm a fish, Princess?" the fish demanded, puffing out his chest and balling his finsts.

"Because you're an insolent fool," the princess retorted.

"Please, do not call my faithful friend a fool," Thoral grumbled.

"And I'll thank you not to chastise the princess of Creekenvalley, drunken barbarian," Nimrodingle barked, her hand resting on her sword hilt.

"Do not call my slightly estranged love a drunken barbarian, you joyless taskmaster," Nalweegie cried, her face flushing in anger.

"Do not call my mother a joyless taskmaster, you spoiled child," Dimsel shouted, pushing between her mother and the princess.

"Do not speak to her highness in that tone," Nimrodingle scolded, grabbing her daughter by one pointed ear.

"Leave Dimsel alone, you controlling hag," Futon spat, lunging for her commander.

"STOP!" Elfrod's echoing shout cut them off just short of coming to blows. "Friends! Fall not victim to the evil incitements of the vile pudding this close to success," the king implored. "It chokes the air with its foul scent and poisons the mind with evil impulses. We have no time to waste in pointless argument."

"Don't call my arguments pointless, you sanctimonious pr—" Brad started to retort. Thoral clamped a hand over the fish's mouth before he finished.

"Elfrod is right," the warrior said. "My apologies, one and all. I have no quarrel with you and beg your pardon for any slights against thee."

Everyone who had gotten all fighty was pretty embarrassed. They took a moment to apologize sheepishly before they all moved around to the back of the throne. Immediately behind it, a jagged-edged black hole ten feet in diameter gaped in the floor. From this hole, wisps of icy-cold mist smelling of chocolate and cumin spurted and puffed, like fog bubbles from dry ice in water.

"This entryway doesn't look very secret," Brad noted, shivering as he peered into the opening.

"Glurpgrond and his villainous monsters must have broken the secret door when they chased us," Elfrod concluded. "Such a shame. It was built at great expense, by the finest craftsmen so as to be nearly invisible when it was shut. Oh, well. Let us hope the spiral stair to the caverns is still intact." He swung his lantern over the hole and its silvery light revealed granite steps clinging to the rough-hewn stone walls that descended in a corkscrew configuration as far as the light penetrated. The stairs sparkled with frost and were littered here and there with bones and bits of broken weapons.

"Still intact," the elf king confirmed. "Let us go." He motioned the others forward with his lamp, but the group hesitated. The stairs did not look inviting.

Thoral took a deep breath and moved to the top step, Brad perched on his shoulder. The warrior felt the stab of the icy-cold stone even through the soles of his knee-high, iron-toed boots.

"Should we maybe let someone with a lantern go first? You know, because they'll be able to see where they're going?" Brad hissed in his friend's ear, purposely loud enough for everyone to hear.

Thoral eyed the gathered group. "I shall lead," he grumbled. "I have no need of a lantern."

"Great," Brad said, shaking his head. "That's great. How drunk *are* you?"

"Watch your step, Warlordhorse," the warrior cautioned his faithful tiger-striped steed as the stallion followed close behind. "I know you have trouble with both steps and heights."

Warlordhorse nickered but started the long clomp down, eager to show off his fearlessness to Blort despite his inner-ear issues and a bad case of nerves. Truth be told, he was pretty happy to have been brought inside, even if it meant going down a slippery spiral staircase. Generally speaking, he was left outside during adventures and so missed out on a lot of the excitement.

Nimrodingle ordered Dimsel to go next, and she started down the stairs grumbling to herself about unfairness, her lantern held aloft so that its bright glow might reveal any missing steps. Futon followed behind her friend. Nimrodingle came third, rolling her eyes at her daughter's complaining. The remaining ladies of Elf Force followed, leading the rest of the horses, including Blort and the unicorn Flug.

"Father," Nalweegie said, putting a delicate hand on Elfrod's forearm to hold him back as he moved to follow. There was a slight edge to her voice. "I am somewhat puzzled."

"What troubles you, my daughter?" he asked, his brow creasing in concern.

"Before we left Reefma, you went on at length about what a dread and terrible place Flurge was and how unlikely we would be to survive it. 'One does not simply walk into Flurge,' you said. 'The land is overrun with monsters,' you said. 'The very air is a smelly fume,' you said. Yet we have simply walked into Flurge; we have encountered neither beast nor monster, not even a moth. Although the air does smell, it has done little to hamper our quest except make us grumpy. Were you just trying to scare me off?"

Elfrod met her smoldering emerald gaze and held it a long moment. Then he shrugged. "Verily, I had expected much danger," he said, "but we have come so far unchallenged that I am beginning to wonder if I did not overestimate the difficulty a smidgen. Perhaps dread Flurge is not so dread any longer." Turning away, he began the descent into the ice caverns, fidgeting with his compass while Nalweegie glared at him. She stomped her foot once in consternation before she followed, the last to enter that ominous hole.

CHAPTER FORTY-THREE

Ashes and Tears

Of course, that's when they were attacked. Bogey monsters came swarming up out of the darkness, shrieking and slavering as they threw themselves upon the members of the Fellowship with insane fury. There must have been a hundred of the apelike, guinea-pig-faced creatures, some armed with ancient weapons scavenged from the ruined city, others using fang and claw. Thoral met the onslaught first and was relieved to face a problem he could chop in half. The sword Elfrod had lent him was no *Blurmflard*, but it proved sufficient to separate the first wave of bogey monsters from their rodent-like heads.

The second wave came without a moment's respite. Although many of them met their end at the point of Thoral's blade, he'd had enough wine that two of the monsters managed to surge around and past him, carrying the fight upward to his companions. Warlordhorse reared and kicked, sending the pair of bogeys screaming to their deaths as they plunged from the stair. Then the mighty steed lost his own footing on the slippery steps and fell as well. He disappeared over the edge with a wild, echoing whinny, his hooves striking sparks off the stone.

Only Thoral's unnaturally swift reflexes saved the horse. The barbarian was a blur as he threw himself onto his belly, slid to the edge of the frozen steps and grabbed Warlordhorse's ear with one hand as the mighty stallion plunged into the darkness. The warrior grunted with exertion as the full weight of the horse tore at his powerful sinews. He used Warlordhorse's own momentum to swing his friend like a living pendulum and fling him back onto the staircase, upright. The stallion crashed painfully against the wall of the shaft and staggered, almost tumbling down the steps, but he regained his balance.

Unfortunately, the bogey monsters had used those brief moments when Thoral was distracted to swarm past him. The cacophony of battle rang up and down the stairs now as the barbarian scrambled to his feet. The loss of his sword in the rush to save Warlordhorse didn't faze him. Monsters pressed in on him from all sides, thirsting for blood. He laid into them with the full force of his flying fists, adrenaline surging through his veins and burning off the fog of the wine. He punched a hole through the hairy chest of a large and brutish bogey so that his hand came out the back and squished its still-beating black heart against the face of the one behind it. With his other fist, he smacked the jawbone off another bogey. It gurgled in agony as it tumbled off the slick staircase and fell into nothingness. Thoral roared at his attackers, his unnaturally even white teeth flashing in a crazed smile, his eyes seeming to glow with purple fire. They fell back, cowed by his ferocity.

Brad, clinging to the collar of Thoral's leather vest with all his might, felt a surge of relief as he saw the monsters retreating. His triumph was short lived. The barbarian crouched, his muscles tensing. The fish realized a split second before it happened what his friend was about to do and screamed in terror. His cry echoed in the frozen darkness as Thoral launched himself from the steps out into the dizzying darkness. There was a stomach-wrenching moment of free fall, and then they crashed down one half turn of the stairs lower and onto the top of the retreating bogey horde. The koi was shaken loose by the tremendous impact and fell to the icy steps at Thoral's feet as the warrior crushed the bogey monsters to the ground. Brad rolled back to avoid being trampled and then leapt toward the wall of the shaft as Thoral chucked hapless monsters over the edge willy-nilly, his massive body steaming in the cold air.

Thoral was beginning to enjoy himself when he heard Nalweegie's battle cry from above. He craned his neck to look over the heads of the surrounding monsters and up the stairs. What he saw made his superheated blood freeze like ice in his veins. Bogeys were battling his companions all up the spiral, and a group of five or more had raced past the rest and were backing the princess up the stairs, slavering at the thought of eating her. She had drawn *Whisper* and a look of fierce determination shone on her face. But Thoral saw what she could not; a lone bogey had come out of a secret door above and was slinking down the steps behind her.

"Nalweegie! Behind thee!" he roared. She didn't hear him over the sounds of battle. He whirled and tried to race up the staircase toward her, but his attackers were so thick around him that they hampered his progress, even though many were now trying to flee. "Nalweegie!" he screamed again, watching in helpless horror as the descending bogey closed the gap between itself and the princess.

"Thoral!" a voice cried from the stairs near his feet.

It was Brad. As the warrior turned toward the sound of Brad's voice, the fish leapt from the step, over the heads of the bogeys and into the barbarian's arms.

"Give me your iPhone," the fish commanded.

Thoral didn't waste time being puzzled. He'd fought beside Brad too many years to question him, regardless of how bizarre his requests might seem. Instead, he plunged one hand into his belt pouch while slaying monsters with the other and pulled out the phone. He fumbled it to the fish, who then jumped into his hand.

"Throw me at them," the koi barked, gesturing toward the top of the stairs where the monster was now poised to pounce on Nalweegie. "THROW ME!"

Thoral cocked his mighty arm, instantly and intuitively calculating the distance and force required. He released the koi like a football and the fish flew through the air in a tight, dizzying spiral.

"AAAAAAAARRRRRGGGGGHHHHH!" Brad shrieked, his stomach lurching as he hurtled upward. Despite the massive g-force and his own insane barrel rolling, he clutched the phone as tightly as his fins would allow and willed himself not to drop it as he activated the camera app.

He knew this was Nalweegie's only chance. He wasn't fond of the princess and he understood that it would clear up a bunch of looming issues if the bogeys were allowed to take care of her, but he couldn't just let her die without trying. She was important to Thoral and he knew his fearless friend would go into a massive, drunken funk if she were killed before his very eyes. Thoral always got so emotional when people died.

Princess Nalweegie was unaware both of the bogey about to leap on her from behind and of the fish flying toward her until a brilliant, strobing flare rent the darkness like a streaking comet. She screamed in surprise at the flash and then a second time as the bogey monster, blinded by the dazzling explosion of light from the camera, sailed over her shoulder and plunged shrieking to its death.

Brad managed two more rapid flashes before he slapped down onto the icy steps and slid into the wall of the shaft, jarring the phone from his flippers. The brilliant explosions of light did their job, stunning the monsters in front of Nalweegie for a few, precious moments. She leapt on them with her thin blade while her father hacked into them with his long sword, *Krandarthnak*, from behind. The bogeys' death screams resounded in the darkness, and then the stairs went quiet. They had been the last of the beasts standing.

Thoral pushed his way out from under a pile of dead bogeys and climbed back up the stairs toward Brad and the princess. He gave Warlordhorse a reassuring pat on the cheek as he passed the tiger-striped steed. He checked in with each of his companions as he climbed. Miraculously, they all had survived. Futon let out a whoop of exultation and Nimrodingle slapped Thoral heartily on the back as he went by. But the barbarian's expression was dour. When he neared the top of the staircase he found Elfrod bent over Nalweegie's prone form while Brad lay panting on the steps beside them.

"My princess!" the warrior cried, taking the last few steps two at a time.

Elfrod turned toward him, and Thoral saw with a surge of relief that the king was merely casting a healing spell on a large cut on his daughter's forearm. The barbarian knelt beside Nalweegie and took her wounded arm in his mighty paws, his eyes locked on hers.

"'Tis only a scratch," the princess told him, pulling her arm from his grasp and breaking eye contact. "I am fine."

Hurt colored Thoral's expression.

"*I* could use a little help," Brad groaned. Thoral, who was lost in his own emotions, didn't hear. "HELLO!" the fish yelled. "I'M INJURED HERE!"

The warrior snapped out of his reverie and turned his gaze to the koi. "Brad…" he stammered.

"Oh, yeah, remembered me, did you?"

"My apologies, Bradfast," Thoral said sheepishly. "I just—"

"Did you *throw* Brad at them," Futon asked in awed disbelief, as she pushed her way up behind Thoral with Dimsel at her side. The young soldiers, flushed with exertion and triumph, were unable to suppress their huge, dopey grins. It was obvious this had been their first real fight, and they were battle drunk.

"He threw the fish right at them," Dimsel confirmed, giggling.

"Actually, the fish *volunteered* to be thrown," Brad corrected her.

"That was genius!" Futon exclaimed. "Total genius!" She slapped Thoral on his broad back and let out another whoop that echoed and reechoed in the inky shaft. Everyone patted everyone else on the back, except Brad, whose scowl deepened.

"You are the man, Thoral!" Dimsel gushed.

"We should call you the *Fish* Wielder from now on," Futon proclaimed. Dimsel broke up laughing. "Fish Wielder," Futon repeated, and the two teens tried to high-five. But their hands missed.

Futon slipped on the icy steps and plunged over the edge. Thoral's amazing reflexes kicked in again, and he leapt with all the speed of a praying mantis to save the elf, snagging the hood of her cloak. There was a loud tearing sound, and his hand came up holding only a torn scrap of fabric.

"Aaaaaaaaaaaaaaaaaaaaaaaaaaaaaaaaaaaaahhhhhhhhhhhhhhhhhh hhhhhhhhhhhhhhhhhhhhhhhhhhhhhhhhhhhhhhhhhhhhhhhhhh hhhhhhhhhhhhhhhhhhhhhhhhhhhhh—" Futon's cry stretched, stretched, stretched, and then cut off with a sound like a watermelon dropped from a skyscraper. There was a distant flare of orange-yellow light deep in the shaft.

"FUTON!" Dimsel screamed over the edge. "FUTON!" There was no answer.

***

Thoral was still clutching the hapless elf's hood when the Fellowship reached the bottom of the dead-bogey littered staircase. They found only a pile of ashes and blackened bones where Futon's body had struck the frosty stone floor. Elves were so awesome that they often burst into flames and burned to dust when they died. Everybody was pretty broken up about the accident, but Thoral took it the hardest—even harder than Dimsel.

"I should have grabbed her ear," the barbarian mumbled, tears streaming down his cheeks.

Nalweegie hesitated for a moment, then put a comforting arm around her slightly estranged love's massive shoulders. He melted into her arms and was racked by sobs. Overcoming an initial moment of surprise, she cuddled him ardently. Where his stoic strength had done little to move her, his childlike tears struck her to the heart.

Brad leapt off Thoral's shoulder to escape being squished. He glared at his friend. "You always do this," he huffed from the icy floor.

"I should have grabbed her ear," the warrior whispered.

"Her ear probably would have torn off, too," Nalweegie soothed, her breath steaming in the frozen air. "There is no more time to mourn her passing now. Help me."

She released the big barbarian and knelt to the floor where she began scooping Futon's ashes into a bag so that their fallen comrade's remains could be scattered in the chuckling waters of the Glimmerwimmer River that giggled through the heart of Creekenvalley. That was the age-old custom of their people and the reason no one drank from the river anymore. All the elves joined her. Thoral helped too, still weeping and sniffling. As they scooped the ashes, Thoral's hand touched Nalweegie's. She gazed up at him, her emerald eyes a-smolder.

"Do not weep, brave one," she comforted. "Do not weep, my love."

"Life is too short for more wasted moments and mistakes," Thoral sniffled, pink tear tracks streaking the ash coating his cheeks. He took her small, soft hand in his own, massive, calloused one, his startling violet eyes downcast and his lower lip trembling. "This needless death has made me realize that I love thee with my whole heart and—"

"What are you doing, Thoral?" Brad asked, his worst fears confirmed as he noticed what was going on. "Don't say anything else. At least wait until you're sober."

"…and I am so sorry," Thoral pressed on, "so very sorry that I upset you and that I did not do this immediately when first we declared our love for one another and—"

"Ixnay, ixnay," the fish cautioned, frantically making that throat-cutting gesture that people make when they have suddenly realized that someone they know is about to do something tremendously stupid.

"and I want…," the barbarian stammered, "I want you—"

"Thoral!" Brad hissed.

"Hush, fish!" Nalweegie snapped. "Let him speak."

"I want you to be my bride if you will—"

He did not finish his proposal before he was bowled over. The elfish princess threw herself upon him. Futon's collected ashes puffed out around them in a cloud as the bag was squished between them. The slender princess knocked the mighty hero onto his back, smothering his powdery face with ardent kisses, her ashy fingers twining in his golden locks as the dust of their companion billowed around them. Brad staggered back, choking.

"Oh, Thoral, my Thoral," she sobbed. "Yes!"

"Nalweegie, my Nalweegie," he moaned.

"Dang it, Thoral!" Brad groaned, shaking his head.

The couple rolled around in the settling cloud of Futon's ashes while everyone else who'd been involved in the clean-up operation rose to their feet feeling really uncomfortable.

The making out continued.

"How long are you going to let this go on?" Brad demanded of Elfrod. The king rolled his noble eyes sagely.

CHAPTER FORTY-FOUR

The Pudding of Power

"Our time grows ever shorter," Elfrod snarled about ten minutes into the kissing, after it had become plain that clearing his throat was not going to be enough. Nalweegie and Thoral broke from their impassioned embrace and looked woozily around as if awakening from a shared dream.

"Oh," Thoral said, taking in the circle of cranky, ash-dusted faces staring down at them. "Your pardon, my friends." He and Nalweegie struggled to their feet and began dusting each other off before remembering it was Futon's ashes that coated them.

Elfrod eyed the couple with a sour expression. "So, I suppose...I suppose that congratulations on your engagement are in order," he said. It was more than a little awkward. He didn't sound like he meant it. "May I suggest that we leave noble Futon here? She would have wanted us to press on." He wasn't sure that Futon would have wanted that at all, but it would have taken a dozen cleaning people with brooms several hours to gather the remains of their fallen comrade. Thoral nodded, squeezing Nalweegie to his side. Everybody else piped in with their own half-hearted congratulations. A few of the Elf Force ladies even patted Thoral on the head. This was a sign of rejoicing and respect among the elves. Nimrodingle gave Nalweegie a little hug. Only Brad held back.

"So does this mean you're going to retire from adventuring?" the fish demanded from the cold stone floor, unable to keep an accusing note out of his voice. "Just throw in the towel on your carefree life as a wanderer and become a prince in Creekenvalley or something?"

"Brad," Thoral began, as he beamed down at his little friend, but the fish cut him off.

"Nevermind," Brad snapped, throwing up his fins in disgust. "I get it. We'd better get moving. We can celebrate the death of our partnership later." He stalked off into the darkness, then realized he had no idea which way the pudding lay. "Can we get moving now, your majesty?" he snarled at Elfrod.

The companions pressed on; most of them somber, cranky, shivering, ash-coated and apprehensive in the chocolate-and-cumin-reeking cold darkness of the ice caverns. The scent was so oppressive now that they felt as if they were being smothered by frozen dark-chocolate pillows. Elfrod led them forward, marking his way by the grotesque rock formations revealed in the light of their lanterns. Under different circumstances, the companions might have been awed by the wonder of the caverns. Untold eons had sculpted the rock into blobby, multihued pillars of living stone that glistened from ceiling and floor, forming countless small chambers linked by winding, cramped tunnels. Nobody was keen on it at the moment though. Instead, they trudged along, feeling oppressed by the weight of the gagillions of pounds of stone pressing in around them like the walls of a tomb. All except Nalweegie.

"I love thee," the princess whispered to Thoral as they walked. "Ardently. I cannot wait to be thy lady wife."

The mighty barbarian blushed and punched her in the arm. He made sure to mitigate the force of his massive sinews so as not to smash her bones to powder.

"And I love thee," he whispered back. The die was cast. He had proposed. He was just going to have to find some way to keep her alive.

"I am certain thy love is great, but I suspect I love thee more," Nalweegie almost giggled.

"No, I love thee more," Thoral objected.

Everyone heard them. You can't whisper in a cave like that without everyone hearing. Brad started clenching and unclenching his finsts while grinding his teeth.

"No, I love thee m—"

"Oh look, a fork in the tunnel," Elfrod announced, as loud as he deemed still polite. He paused for a moment at a junction in the path, shining his lantern back and forth between three possible paths forward.

"You remember the way to the pudding, right?" Brad demanded, eyeing a looming rock formation that looked like a gargantuan fish skull.

"Of course, of course," the elf king assured him. "Well, I believe I do. Hold here a moment." With that, he walked a few feet down the right-hand tunnel of the fork until he disappeared around a bend.

"Can you not use the vibrations of your koi whiskers to locate the pudding?" Thoral asked the fish.

"For your information, Thoral," Brad came back at him, "my koi whiskers don't work well in caves. After years of adventuring together, you'd kind of expect that one friend would know that about another. Maybe I read too much into our association."

"I believe our path lies in this direction," Elfrod announced as he returned. He led the way into the right-hand branch with the companions trailing him. They walked down a twisting tunnel that descended at a sharp angle for several minutes. They passed a number of outlets and offshoots, turning here or there until everyone was thoroughly confused except Elfrod, who pushed on at a confident pace as if following some inner compass.

Eventually, they came to a place where the floor was slick with frozen water and they had to crouch to fit between it and the icy ceiling. The passage also narrowed so that they had to go single file. The further they went, the narrower and lower the passage became until Warlordhorse, by far the largest of the steeds, got stuck. He whinnied in distress and struggled to force his way through, but found that he could go neither forward nor back. Everybody behind the horse bumped into the person in front. When Nalweegie bumped into Thoral's back, his massive sinews were so hard that she actually got a bloody nose. Nimrodingle didn't bump into anyone because she was in front of Warlordhorse. In fact, she was the one who had been directly in front of him and had to call Elfrod and Brad to a halt when she noticed the tiger-striped steed was no longer breathing on the back of her neck. Doubling back, Brad told Warlordhorse to hold still and threaded his way between the horse's massive hooves to check in with the others.

"Your horse is stuck," the fish observed to Thoral, his voice tinged with bitterness.

"He is not my horse. He was lent to me by my wizard mentor, Yiz."

"Fine. Your wizard mentor's horse is stuck," Brad snapped.

"Mayhap," the warrior replied.

"There's no mayhapping about it," Brad growled. "He's just stuck."

Thoral eyed the koi with sadness, then threw his shoulder against the mighty horse's bottom. He pushed and strained, his face flushing and cords of muscle standing out from his neck. Nothing happened. Brad rolled his eyes in disgust as the warrior continued to strain. Finally, with a pop like a cork coming out of a bottle, the mighty stallion was squeezed through the choke point, his hooves sliding on the icy floor. Warlordhorse rolled his eyes and snorted. He tossed his head in fear as he slid to a halt on the other side. Thoral slipped through the opening and patted the horse's flank. He took Warlordhorse's snout in his hands and nuzzled his muzzle.

"Who is a good and noble steed?" the warrior asked. "Who is a good horse?" Then he fed him lumps of sugar from his belt pouch.

"Your pardon, one and all," Blort interrupted, his own eyes showing white all around, his voice trembling as he eyed the opening through which Thoral had just pushed Warlordhorse. "I think I speak for all the horses when I say that we need to get out of this STUPID CAVE RIGHT NOW! RIGHT NOW! RIGHT THIS SECOND! NOW!!" He hyperventilated, pawing at the floor, his nostrils twitching.

"WHY DID YOU EVEN BRING HORSES INTO A CAVE?" he neighed. "WHAT WERE YOU THINKING?" He would have bolted if some of the companions hadn't blocked the path both ahead and behind.

It was Brad who calmed him. The koi climbed up the stallion's foreleg and onto his back. He patted Blort's neck with a fin.

"Hey, big guy," the fish soothed. "I don't mean to change the subject, but I was wondering what these caves were used for. I asked Nalweegie. She doesn't know anything."

"What?" Blort sputtered.

"I've got no idea what these caves were used for. It seems as if they must have been used for something and nobody here is smart enough to tell me. Ah, I bet you don't know either."

"Of course I know, imbecile," the horse snapped. "The kings of the line of Eggensammer used these caverns to house their perishable food stuffs and gelatos. The caves are frozen year round and the people of Chowder were fiends for gelato. It was because of the consistent cold temperature that King Doug decided to store the Pudding of Power here, hoping that the chill would preserve its foul potency."

"That's fascinating," Brad said. "Tell me more about that."

So Blort enumerated the many other uses of the ice caverns as Brad steered him through the choke point. The delicate stallion slipped through the narrow opening with no problem. His haughty voice droned on with all the details as the tunnel widened and inclined. Thoral shot Brad an appreciative look. The fish rolled his eyes again.

Nineteen-and-a-half minutes later, as the stallion was explaining how the royal chocolatiers of Chowder liked to temper their chocolate bars in the ice caverns because the temperature was perfect for producing a smooth, shiny finish and a satisfying snap, the tunnel widened at another fork with three possible paths forward. Elfrod seemed really puzzled now, shining his lantern back and forth across the openings multiple times.

"I do not remember this," the king murmured. "I do not remember a single instance of a second triple fork on the way to the pudding. Hold here for a moment." With that, he headed off down the central tunnel.

Once he was out of sight, Dimsel shone her lantern on the floor, looking for further clues. It revealed only the skeleton of a man in an apron and chef's hat huddled between two stalagmites.

"Whoa!" Blort exclaimed, skittering back and knocking Dimsel over with his butt. The elf was still in the dumps about Futon dying, so her reaction time was poor.

"I think we're lost," Brad huffed.

"And our time is running out," Nimrodingle hissed.

"And I have to pee really badly," one of the elves from Elf Force piped up.

"And I have discovered that I am claustrophobic," Blort complained. "Severely claustrophobic." His voice started to rise again. Everyone stood around looking in distress at everyone else and at the skeleton.

"Elfrod," Thoral called down the middle passage.

Only echoes answered the companions. The cold darkness of the ice caverns pressed in on them like a frozen crowd of starving lost souls around a single, still-warm glazed donut.

"Oh, great," Blort said after a long moment, his voice edged with panic, "I was afraid something like this might happen. These caverns go on for miles and miles. Many a gelato maker and chocolatier of ancient Chowder entered these caves never to return. Like this poor gentleman." He touched the skeleton with one delicate hoof and the bones collapsed to the floor with an echoing clatter that made everyone jump. "Once lost, it is virtually impossible to find one's way out of the ice caverns. Our quest is doomed and this frigid tunnel will be our tomb unless we start seeking the exit immediately."

"Don't panic. We have enough food and water to last for two days if we strictly ration it," Nimrodingle said, ever the stoic.

"For horses as well?" Blort demanded. Nimrodingle dropped her gaze to the uneven floor.

"I thought not," the horse spat.

Thoral was silently trying to calculate how much wine he had left. Then he remembered he'd already polished it off.

"How long will the light last?" Brad asked.

"Oh, I didn't think of that," Nimrodingle admitted, sounding even more worried. "Maybe another day, if we take to using a single lantern at a time."

"So we will die of starvation in the dark," Blort blurted. He was about to freak out again when Elfrod stepped back into the tunnel. Thoral caught a brief flash of brass as the king tucked something back into his pocket.

"This way," the elf lord said cheerily and headed back down the central branch.

Thoral fell in behind him. "Are you following your misplacement compass to the pudding?" the warrior asked him in a low voice.

"Not exactly," Elfrod answered. "Although I am following the compass."

***

Twenty minutes and twelve seconds later, the Fellowship stood before a brass door. The portal was green with verdigris and engraved with an intricate ice-cream-cone motif.

"This is the door to the pudding chamber," Elfrod announced with a confident smile. He had his misplacement compass in his hand and the needle was pointing at the portal.

"Does it seem to anyone else like this whole 'dread land of Flurge' thing has been a little too easy?" Blort asked, frowning.

"Tell me about it," Nalweegie answered, shooting a look at her father as he reached out to turn the ornate doorknob. Blort grimaced.

"Do you know what would be ironic?" the horse asked. "If we opened the door and the pudding was gone or the room was full of monsters or the Heartless One was already in there or something. Or if the door was booby-trapped so that a massive explosion blasted the first person to go through and sealed the chamber forever or something."

Elfrod pulled up short. "Right as I am reaching for the door you say this?" the king demanded.

"Sorry," Blort apologized. "It just occurred to me. It's probably fine."

"Well then, you open the door."

"I'm a horse," Blort noted, stamping his hooves. "I'm not that great with opening doors designed for humans."

"You can open it with your teeth," Elfrod suggested.

"I shall open it," Thoral grumbled.

"No!" Nalweegie cried, trying to hold him back.

"It is on my account we are here," the warrior told her, looking fantastically noble as he stepped up to the door. He squared his shoulders, clenched his right fist around the hilt of his dumb replacement sword and reached his left hand toward the knob.

"At least be careful," Nalweegie cautioned, wincing.

"I am never careful," Thoral noted.

"He's Thoral Mighty Fist," Brad agreed, nodding. The others took a step back, except Brad, who shouldered his way through their ankles to the front.

"Let me stand on your shoulder," he said. "Like old times."

The warrior turned, and his violet eyes met the fish's bulging orbs. Smiling his gratitude, the big barbarian crouched down and held out a hand. The fish scrambled up his arm and into his accustomed position. Thoral stood and turned back to the door. He took a deep breath and laid his fingers on the icy doorknob, gritting his teeth against the stabbing pain of the cold. Then he pulled the door open.

A massive explosion blasted from the opening—an explosion of chocolate fragrance. It was so strong that it staggered the gathered companions like a shock wave, so overpowering that it was as if they had snorted cocoa powder directly onto their brains. Everyone reeled, their eyes, mouths and noses watering, struck blind, ageusic and anosmic by the intensity of the odor.

"Is anyone else blind, ageusic and anosmic?" Blort shouted, coughing.

"I'm blind," Brad spluttered, "I'm not sure about those other two."

"Unable to taste and unable to smell," Blort clarified.

"Yeah, then—all three," the fish confirmed.

"I am as well," Thoral noted, feeling before him with his free hand.

"Us too," everyone else added, likewise groping around.

"Follow my voice and gather close," the barbarian commanded. "Brad and I have honed our ability to fight in total darkness. If this is a trap, we will defend you all to the death." Everyone pushed in toward him until, as near as they could make out, they were gathered in a ragged huddle.

"Hark, I am getting a faint bitter taste now," Elfrod called. "Like the darkest chocolate with a faint note of… cumin."

"Me also. And I can see a little, as if through a dense brown fog," Nalweegie cried. She straightened up, realizing that she had been nuzzling into Warlordhorse's side thinking he was Thoral.

"Oh! All my senses are coming back," Blort gagged.

Then everybody threw up at once. It was gross. After that, they could all see, taste and smell again, although they kind of wished they couldn't. Because of his Ring of Looks, only Elfrod wasn't splashed with puke.

After they'd used Thoral's towel to clean up a bit, they found themselves standing at the threshold of a massive natural chamber that was lit by a soft bluish phosphorescence and dripping with cascades of glittering limestone stalactites that vaulted hundreds of feet above their heads. It was like some kind of weird cathedral built of waterfalls of soft-serve ice cream flash-frozen in place. Despite the riveting and impressive sight of this wondrous natural architecture, the eyes of every member of the Fellowship were drawn to the far end of the room. There, perhaps two hundred feet away, surrounded by countless small, sealed wooden tubs, stood a sawn-off stalagmite as wide around as a dinner table for five. Upon this formation sat a small, cut-crystal chalice half filled with creamy chocolate pudding. White fog billowed from the face of the stalagmite where the goblet touched the stone, bubbling and puffing like the vapors released by dry ice in water, almost obscuring the small silvery spoon lying there beside it.

"Behold," Elfrod intoned, "the Pudding of—" He stopped in midsentence and stooped suddenly to pick something up from the ground at his feet.

"Ah! Here we are!" the elf king said, sounding pleased, a rusty ring of keys with a dangling green-dyed rabbit's foot jangling from his hand. "My lucky rabbit's foot and the keys to the treasure vault of Creekenvalley. Long have I suspected I dropped these somewhere around here." He put them into the pocket of his cloak. "Well, this is certainly going to ease the money problems we've been having lately." He smiled with glee before noticing that everyone was staring, unblinkingly, at the pudding.

"Oh, yes. As I was saying," he continued, "behold, the Pudding of Power!

"It looks so harmless," Nimrodingle commented, her pupils dilating.

"And tasty," Brad added, his eyes glazing.

"And delicious," Nalweegie sighed.

"And yummy," Dimsel breathed.

"And chocolaty," Thoral whispered.

And before any of them were aware of what they were doing, they had started toward it along with all the women of Elf Force and all the horses. They picked up speed as they went until they were pelting toward it, panting for a bite.

"HOLD!" Elfrod cried, his voice reverberating in the chamber with kingly command and bringing them up short mere paces from the chalice. His thunderous order seemed to snap them out of the trance they had fallen into. They shook themselves as if awakening from an evil dream.

"The pudding works, even now, to befuddle you," Elfrod explained urgently, striding toward them across the chamber. "It longs to be consumed so that it may spread its darkness like an evil mayonnaise across all of Grome!"

Everyone eyed the pudding with newfound caution.

"What exactly is it supposed to do when you eat it?" Brad asked from his perch on Thoral's shoulder as the companions gathered in a loose half circle. This close, you could see that it emitted a vague chocolaty light that made all their faces look a little dirty.

"That is somewhat unclear," Elfrod admitted. "Only Mauron and Glurpgrond knew the full recipe, but this much they did share: Whosoever consumes that pudding will be infused with godlike stamina and will gain the power to withstand and control the unbridled evil of the Bracelet of Evil and thereby subjugate this world."

"Godlike stamina, huh?" Brad questioned, gazing at the pudding as if he might like to try a bite. "And that's a bad thing?"

"It all depends on the god," Elfrod answered. "Regardless, it is always a bad idea to ingest pure evil."

"Fine, whatever. Let's bag it and get out of here while there's still some slim chance we might possibly survive," the fish suggested.

At that, Thoral reached for the chalice, but Elfrod grabbed his arm and pulled him back.

"Do not touch it," he cautioned, "for there is a deadly exploding spell upon that pudding that will explode to death anyone who disturbs it."

"Verily?" Thoral asked.

"Yes," Elfrod said. "I put it there myself."

"You put a deadly exploding spell on the Pudding of Power?" Nimrodingle asked, her eyes wide.

"Yes. That was why I and the last defenders of Chowder came down into these caverns," the king confirmed. "When it was finally inescapable that the Citadel would fall, we came to put a spell of protection on the pudding so that none might touch it without exploding to death. It seemed the only way to prevent Glurpgrond from seizing it for himself. Many a brave elf and human and one talking rabbit met his doom to buy me the time to work that deadly spell." His eyes took on a faraway look and his countenance reflected a finite but substantial sadness.

"Wait a second," Brad said, cutting the elf lord's noble remembrance short. "If you put a deadly exploding spell on the pudding so that no one can touch it, what are we doing here?"

"What?" the king asked.

"Well, if no one can touch the pudding because they'll explode to death, what's the point of us coming here to stop the Heartless One from getting it?" the fish questioned. "I mean, she can't get it, can she? She'd explode to death."

"Whoa," Elfrod said, as if his mind had been blown. "I guess I did not think about that." Everyone turned and stared at the king of Creekenvalley, whose fine-boned elfin features flushed.

"You did not think about that?" Nalweegie demanded.

"Wait a second," Brad said, his bulgy eyes bulging even more than usual, "did you … did you drag us all out here just to find the keys to your treasure vault?"

"Well, I…You see, we haven't been able to get into the treasure vault in over a thousand years and we've been having some difficulty making ends meet of late and…You know, the thing no one thinks about is how much it costs to run a kingdom these days…Do you have any idea how much even a single lavish feast costs?" Elfrod stammered. "And it's not like it was my idea to come. I did not twist anyone's arm."

"Oh, this is just great," Dimsel bristled. "So my friend Futon got killed for a key ring?"

"I am in a cave for no real reason," Blort choked. "And I am a horse."

"I missed my hundredth wedding anniversary," an Elf Force lady named Sharnon

Silverbrow added.

"I used up the last wish from my magic lamp wishing I would be chosen to go on this glorious mission," another Elf Force lady named Elvenshmeer groaned. "Stupid!"

"Well, getting my keys back is important," the king tried. "The treasure vault is magically sealed so that it is literally impossible to get in there without the keys."

There was a long, awkward silence in which everyone shot accusing looks at Elfrod and he looked chagrined.

"So what do we do now?" Brad asked finally. "Just turn around and go home?"

"I suppose so," Elfrod said. He couldn't meet Brad's eyes and glanced away. He accidentally met Elvenshmeer's eyes and felt even worse. He shifted his eyes to his daughter, who was obviously steamed, so he dropped his gaze to the floor. What he saw there made his expression brighten a little. "My friends, I know it is not much consolation, but I believe these containers are full of gelato," he said, pointing at the collection of wooden tubs that lined the back wall of the chamber. "We could all have a scoop or two before we depart, if we hurry."

"So I get to eat gelato?" Elvenshmeer huffed. "That's what I get in exchange for my wish? Glorious."

"Actually, you should try a scoop," Nimrodingle suggested. "I remember we used to get shipments of Chowderian gelato in Creekenvalley when I was a little girl. It's pretty amazing. Way better than the sherbet we make ourselves. I can't see as how it would hurt if we took just a minute to have a little."

Everybody was still cranky and grumbling, but they set about opening a dozen of the five-gallon barrels, which did indeed turn out to be full of gelato. A lesser confection would have long ago turned gummy and freezer burned, but the gelato of Chowder was made with a skill now lost to the world of men. It was still smooth, rich, creamy, delicious and satisfying: the gelato of kings. Pretty soon, everyone had a spoon and was sampling various flavors or giving tastes to their horses.

"I should have just wished for this gelato," Elvenshmeer said, savoring a delightful mouthful of mint chocolate chip.

Thoral and Nalweegie shared a scoop of fudge ripple from Nalweegie's spoon. It was romantic to share, even though it meant they couldn't eat the gelato as fast as if each had a spoon. As Nalweegie fed her love a tasty bite, he sighed.

"A copper coin for thy thoughts," she said.

"I am going to swear off drinking," the warrior answered. "Now that we are to be married, I will not drink another drop. Also, I am sorry that you had to endure believing that I had been beheaded. I did not intend to cause you any aguish. In fact, I am so sorry for all that has gone awry between us of late that I cannot begin to tell you how…" he paused. "What is that word that essentially means sorry but suggests also a sincere desire for atonement?"

"Contrite," Brad suggested around a spoonful of strawberry gelato, as he sat on the edge of a tub of the same. Thoral shot him an appreciative look and the fish smiled back at him, although the smile was tinged with sadness.

"How contrite I feel," Thoral finished.

As he said this, Nalweegie's pretty brow creased with vague concern. "Your words awake in me a strange and disturbing feeling," the princess said. "They are like the echo of some dimly remembered memory I have mostly forgotten to remember."

Thoral was about to question her when he was distracted by a dark shape darting toward him from the entrance through the frosty air of the cavern.

"A moth!" Blort cried, rearing up on his dainty hind hooves. Blort had a horror of moths.

Elfrod dropped his spoon to cover his hair, but it was not a moth. It was a flying black squirrel.

"Thoral!" a desperately sweet and teensy voice squeaked as the squirrel glided to a stop and collapsed at the warrior's feet.

"Tyncie?" Thoral gasped in disbelief. "Tyncie CheeChaw CheeChee WeeWaw?"

"Thou art in deadly danger," the tiny, ridiculously cute rodent panted from the floor. "Flee! You must flee this very moment. Thou art ambushed."

"What?" Thoral roared, scooping up the swooning squirrel in one mighty fist. "Ambushed? Warlordhorse would have smelled something if there were danger."

Warlordhorse pulled his nose out of a tub of caramel gelato at the mention of his name, a guilty expression on his face.

"Ambushed by whom?" Thoral demanded of the squirrel.

"BY HER MASTER, THE HEARTLESS ONE!" a familiar voice boomed through the chamber.

CHAPTER FORTY-FIVE

The Deadly Exploding Spell

Before anyone could react, dozens of Dark Brothers of the Bad Religion materialized throughout the room brandishing wickedly curved scimitars. Even Thoral, with his lightning-fast cat reflexes from another universe, was taken by surprise. The Heartless One teleported herself behind Nalweegie. She grabbed the elfish princess by her raven locks and yanked her head back, forcing a sword to Nalweegie's throat so that the fair one dropped her spoon to the floor, where it clattered with a silvery tinkling sound. Within seconds, half the Fellowship, including Lord Elfrod, were held hostage. As Thoral went to whip *Blurmflard*, the magic blade lent to him by his wizard mentor, Yiz, from its sheath in a whistling blur, he realized he had only the crappy substitute sword, which didn't whistle or blur nearly as impressively.

"Ah-ah-ah," the Heartless One chided him, pressing the sword so hard against Nalweegie's ivory throat that she gave the princess a paper-cut-style wound, welling with Nalweegie's crimson life fluid.

Thoral seethed but backed down, realizing the sword at his love's throat was *Blurmflard.*

"What the heck?" Brad stammered, climbing out of the strawberry gelato to find multiple swords leveled at his face. He had been so startled by the sudden appearance of so many bad guys that he had fallen into the tub. Now, in addition to being surrounded, he was a sticky mess.

"Surprised, fish?" the Heartless One sneered.

"Frankly, yes," Brad said, dripping gelato on the icy floor. "Someone said there was no way that you could get to Chowder as fast as we did and that you didn't know teleportation magic." He shot an accusing look at Thoral.

"This is *my* dream. I can do anything I want in it," the Heartless One replied.

"I am so sorry Thoral, my friend," Tyncie whispered in her tiny little squirrel voice. "If only I could have warned you sooner."

Thoral set her down on the floor so he could switch his blade from his left to his right hand. Although he was ambidextrous when wielding *Blurmflard*, he favored his right hand for serious combat with lesser weapons.

"I will deal with *you* shortly!" the Heartless One threatened, narrowing her eyes at the flying squirrel.

Thoral ignored the exchange and pointed his sword right between the Heartless One's striking mauve eyes. "Release Nalweegie and I will let you live," he growled.

"You will let *me* live?" Nancy laughed. "Oh, how magnanimous! I think not."

"Meaning Thoral *won't* let you live?" one of the Dark Brothers menacing Elfrod asked from the darkness of his hooded robe. Everybody stared at him.

"What?" the Heartless One snapped.

"You said, 'You will let me live? I think not,'" the Dark Brother clarified. "Meaning you don't think Thoral will let you live?"

"No!" the Heartless One snarled. "Meaning, I do not think Thoral is in a position to be making—Why am I explaining this to you? BE SILENT!"

"Trenton?" Thoral asked, disbelief coloring his voice.

"Oh, hey, Thoral," the Dark Brother said, pushing back his hood to reveal that he was, indeed Trenton.

"But I saw you die!" Brad exclaimed. "I knelt beside your body and gently closed your eyes."

"Oh, hey, Brad," Trenton waved to the fish. "Yeah, I was in a coma for a week. They fired me from my job as a city guard though, so I had to take this job with the Bad Religion. Apparently, Thoral killed so many Dark Brothers that they were desperate for new recruits. Anyway, good to see you both again. Sorry I have to menace you and all. It's nothing personal."

The Heartless One looked as if she was suffering from a migraine.

"You be quiet," she snapped at him. "I'll deal with you after I eat the Pudding of Power."

"Sure thing, your Heartlessness," Trenton said with a little hand gesture indicating that he was locking his lips.

Nancy shook her head in disgust then turned back to Thoral. She took a second to compose herself, and the evil smile returned to her face. "Here is how this is going to work," she gloated to her husband and his companions. "You will all lay down your weapons and surrender. Once I have consumed the Pudding of Power, I will spare your lives so that I may bend you to my will and make you serve as my slaves while I locate the Bracelet of Evil."

Brad, Elfrod, Nalweegie, Nimrodingle, Blort and most of the other good guys exchanged stealthy looks.

"Sure thing," said Brad. He turned to his team, giving them a big wink while trying to sound super glum. "OK, guys, I know you don't want to give up, but I guess the Heartless One has beaten us. Dang! Let's all lay down our weapons and let her eat that pudding." He winked again, for emphasis.

"Oh, yes, I am really distressed to have to do this," Nimrodingle said, sounding convincingly upset as she laid her sword on the floor. "Brad is right. We must surrender and let the Heartless One eat the pudding, even though we don't want her to." Every one of the companions exchanged stealthy looks now, except Thoral.

"We cannot surrender," the barbarian objected, his knuckles white on his crappy sword's hilt. "We cannot let her take the pudding. She intends to destroy Grome."

"Thoral!" Brad growled. He fixed the warrior with his bulging eyes and when he was sure he had Thoral's full attention, he winked again. "I know this is terrible, but we'll just have to let the Heartless One eat the pudding, regardless of the *explosive* consequences." Thoral's brow creased in puzzlement. Then the fish gave him another very pronounced wink. The barbarian finally understood.

"What's that you're doing with your eye?" the Heartless One demanded of Brad.

"Nothing," the fish assured her. "I just got some gelato in it."

"Whatever," the Heartless One snapped. "My patience is at an end. Surrender now, or I will slaughter little Princess Husband-Stealer." She pinched Nalweegie's ear so hard that the princess screamed.

"Fine," Thoral cried. "We surrender." He let gave a loud sigh of resignation and made a show of setting his sword on the floor at his feet. The rest of the Fellowship laid down their arms, too.

The Heartless One smiled in wicked triumph. She handed Nalweegie off to one of her men, sheathed *Blurmflard* and walked toward the chalice of pudding, a smile curving her ruby lips.

"Wait!" Thoral called as she neared it, a look of anguish on his face. The Heartless One stopped short and looked back at the warrior. So did all of his companions.

"What are you doing, Thoral?" Brad asked through clenched teeth. "Let's let the nice lady eat her pudding."

Nalweegie narrowed her eyes at Thoral.

"Please, Nancy," the barbarian begged. "Stop. That pudding is evil, and it will make you evil. Well…more evil. Do not eat it. It is madness."

The whole room seemed to hold its breath. A flicker of indecision passed across the Heartless One's face and she hesitated.

But then she recovered her composure and went back to looking evil. "Still on that 'stop this madness' thing, huh? Well, sorry, Teddy. I'm eating that pudding." She stepped to the stalagmite table and stood before the chalice, bathing in the brown glow of the Pudding of Power. Reaching down, she took up the silvery spoon. Everyone watched, trying hard not to wince. Thoral's face was a mask of agonized inner turmoil.

"Now," said the Heartless One, turning to Lord Elfrod, "if you will kindly remove the deadly exploding spell, we can get on with this."

Everyone gasped.

"You know about the deadly exploding spell?" Brad groaned.

"Of course, fish. Why do you think I went to such trouble to lure Lord Elfrod here?" Nancy asked. "The Goomy Crystal told me that Elfrod had placed the deadly exploding spell on the pudding when first I used the last of the Voodoo Stones to learn the whereabouts of this most powerful of confections. And the crystal also revealed that Lord Elfrod was the only one who could remove the spell."

"Wait a second," Brad said, turning his exasperated gaze to the elf king. "You can remove the spell? I thought you said we just had to turn around and leave."

"I suppose I can," Elfrod answered, looking embarrassed. Again. "There didn't seem to be much point in taking the pudding away as long as it had the spell on it. I mean, that spell has protected it for a thousand and two years."

"So," Brad struggled to keep his voice level, "let me see if I've got this straight. You put a deadly exploding spell on this pudding when you first abandoned it. That spell would have protected the pudding from the Heartless One for all eternity if we'd just left well enough alone. She never would have been able to eat it. Instead, you lead us into the heart of the dread land of Flurge, one of the most dangerous places in all of Grome, thereby giving the Heartless One the only possible means of getting at the pudding we were trying to stop her getting at."

Elfrod nodded sheepishly. "That seems about the size of it," he admitted.

"Dummy," the Heartless One mocked.

"You hold on, too," Brad told her. "Explain to me how this plan of yours to lure Elfrod here made the slightest bit of sense."

"Well, I orchestrated everything so that Elfrod would find his misplacement compass," Nancy said, "and then he'd come here to recover his keys. That's why I ordered my servant Necrogrond to capture Princess Nalweegie the first time and gave him the compass to put in his treasure horde. Did you think that was just a coincidence?"

"Oh, this is classic," Brad growled. "So the one thing we absolutely needed to do to stop you was to *not* come here to stop you. All we had to do was stay away and you would have failed."

"Exactly," Nancy gloated.

"What a monumentally dumb plan!" the fish complained. "Elfrod didn't even rescue Nalweegie. Thoral and I did, which meant that we found the compass. What if we hadn't given it to Elfrod? What if he'd been a little smarter or in a little less financial trouble? Your plan was utterly stupid. There's no way it should have worked."

"And yet, here we are," the Heartless One sneered. "So who is the idiot?"

"Maybe this *is* just a dream she's having," the fish said, shaking his head in disbelief.

"So, Lord Elfrod," Nancy snarled, "remove the deadly exploding spell, or my man will kill your only daughter."

All eyes were now on Elfrod. He was red with embarrassment. "Fiddlesticks," he said. Then he nodded, defeated. "You leave me no choice."

The Dark Brother released him, and the lord of the elves trudged to the stalagmite table. He stood before the pudding and chanted an incantation in ancient Elvish, tracing complex sigils of power in the air with his pinkie fingers. His sea-green eyes rolled up until just the whites were visible. The tempo and pitch of his words increased until it sounded as if he were singing a nonsense song to the chalice. A tremor passed through his body, and with a great cry, he fell to the ground.

"It is done," he whispered, then buried his head in his hands.

The Heartless One eyed him.

"Really?" she demanded.

He peeked up at her through a crack between his fingers and nodded, but she wasn't buying it.

"Fish," she ordered, extending the silver spoon toward Brad, "you will take a small taste first or your companions die."

"Why me?" the koi demanded.

"You are the smallest. If you explode, it will make the least mess." She pointed at the fish and then at the pudding.

Brad was clearly frightened, but he climbed up onto the table and took the spoon in one trembling fin. He shot a frightened look at Elfrod, whose expression was unreadable. Then he shifted his gaze to Thoral, who clenched his mighty fists and raised his eyebrows in a mute question. Brad shook his head just a fraction to prevent the warrior from attacking. He took a deep breath to steady his nerves, dipped the spoon into the pudding and scooped up a tiny bite. With that, the chocolaty smell in the room intensified a hundred-fold, causing everyone to stagger.

"Here goes nothing," the fish whispered. Before he could chicken out, he licked the spoon clean.

"HOLY CRAP, THAT'S DELICIOUS!" the fish shouted, his voice magnified like the voice of a god, his eyes wide, his body seeming to glow from within like a golden lantern shaped like a fish. Everyone watched him closely, unsure what other effects the pudding might have. For the moment, nothing else happened.

"Okay, fine," the Heartless One said after another few seconds had elapsed. "Give me that spoon."

As she reached out to take it, the fish clutched at his belly. He doubled over with a great cry and fell writhing, to the tabletop.

"What is happening?" Thoral roared. "Brad? Are you all right?"

The fish could not answer. He flopped in paroxysms of agony and then went rigid, his belly swelling. He gasped and blasted out a single, stunningly loud fart that echoed and re-echoed through the cave as if the foundation of the earth had cracked.

"You did not remove the spell," Nancy accused, leveling a finger at Elfrod.

The king shrugged. "'Twas worth a try," he admitted.

"Brad!" Thoral screamed, approaching his longtime companion. "BRAD!"

"Remove the spell. NOW!" the Heartless One demanded. "Or the fish will explode and I will kill you, your daughter and everyone else."

"Even us?" Trenton asked. A fortune-teller had warned him that he would either die on his first adventure with the Dark Brotherhood or he would become one of the greatest heroes of Grome, whose legend would be the stuff of a trilogy of epic poems and songs. So he was kind of concerned.

"No, not you," the Heartless One yelled at him in annoyance. "Them."

"Of course not us," Trenton scolded himself. "Idiot!"

Throughout this exchange, Brad's belly continued to swell and he continued to fart and belch, although none of his subsequent emissions rivaled the first one. The Dark Brother holding Nalweegie yanked her head back, exposing her throbbing jugular to the edge of his scimitar. Thoral looked from Nalweegie to Brad and then shot a pleading look at Elfrod.

"All right," the elf king shouted. He pointed both pinkie fingers at the chalice of pudding and said, "Cancel!"

Brad belched thunderously loud again and then the swelling was gone. He sat up, amazed.

"All better," he said. Thoral sighed with relief.

Nancy stood before the pudding and raised her spoon in gloating triumph. "And now," she said, "time to end the nightmare."

Thoral tensed, intending to launch himself at her and save the day. He wasn't exactly sure how it was going to work out, but last-minute-saving-the-day stuff usually paid off for him, so he was just going to wing it. He clenched his fists and braced his mighty sinews to leap, waiting for something to happen that would provide an opening.

As the Heartless One lowered the spoon toward the pudding, there was a ripple in the air. A short, brown-cloaked, hooded figure materialized beside her. The newcomer touched her once with a black wand and the Heartless One froze, her silver utensil poised a fraction of an inch from the chocolate surface of the dire dessert.

Thoral never hesitated. He took advantage of the distraction and sprang, his fists swinging, to grab the chalice and capture the pudding.

The newcomer gestured in the air with the tip of the black wand and Thoral was hurled back with incredible force. His massively muscled body slammed into Trenton, buttocks first, and the newly minted Dark Brother crumpled to the ground with Thoral on top of him. The barbarian leapt up within an instant, but Trenton just lay there because he was dead⊠his skull cracked like a thin-walled clay pot. Thoral noticed Trenton's passing with a pang of guilt but whirled for another try at the pudding. He would have to grieve some other time. Despite his incredible speed, he didn't even finish his whirl before the diminutive, brown-robed stranger made another miniscule movement of his wand and froze the warrior in his tracks.

"NO!" Thoral roared, straining with everything he had to break free of the spell. His mouth wasn't frozen, just his body.

"Who are you?" the Heartless One demanded. She was locked in a similar state beside the stranger.

The rest of the companions, as well as all of the Dark Brothers realized that they were frozen too.

"Who are you?" Nancy repeated.

In response, the little figure raised his chubby hands to pull his hood back.

"This better not be Necrogrond again," Brad whispered. "I'm pretty sick of killing that guy."

The little man revealed his face.

Elfrod, Nancy, Thoral and Warlordhorse all gasped in shocked recognition.

"Neigh!" Warlordhorse whinnied in disbelief.

"You!" Elfrod screamed with dread.

"You?" Thoral and Nancy cried in stunned unison.

"What?" Brad demanded. "What's going on? Who is this guy?"

Warlordhorse, Elfrod, Nancy and Thoral all tried to answer at once.

"Neigh," the horse explained.

"It is Glurpgrond," Elfrod warned.

"No, it isn't," Nancy contradicted.

"That," the barbarian roared, "is Yiz!"

CHAPTER FORTY-SIX

Preposterous Convolutions

"Indeed," the little bearded one replied with a self-satisfied smile. "You are all correct."

As Thoral, Nancy, Elfrod and Warlordhorse exchanged confused looks, the gnome drew *Blurmflard* from the sheath at the Heartless One's side. He gave the blade an appraising look and tucked it through a loop in his wide, black patent-leather belt. "Remind me not to lend you anything again, Thoral."

"How can we all be correct?" the tawny-maned warrior queried as he hung in the air, suspended halfway through a whirl.

"Because I am both Glurpgrond *and* Yiz," the gnome answered with a smug little grin. He grabbed Warlordhorse by the muzzle and pulled open his mouth to examine his teeth.

Elfrod's eyes widened in disbelief. "Of course!" the king said, stunned. "Why did I not realize? The name Glurpgrond translated into Gnomish would be Yiz."

"You've got to be kidding me," Brad groaned. "And none of you geniuses figured that out until now?"

Everybody was quiet. It was clear that they hadn't. Blort was most embarrassed. He was fluent in Gnomish. Glurpgrond released Warlordhorse's face and chuckled in a cute but evil way, his chubby cheeks flushing.

"I have been waiting for this moment for more than thirty years," he giggled. "Ever since I summoned Teddy and Nancy out of their own universe and into this one."

"Summoned us? What are you talking about?" Thoral demanded.

"You did not summon us," Nancy interjected. "This is my nightmare. I know how it happened. Teddy got us sucked into an alternate universe and you just happened upon us as we were being attacked by a pack of ravening barfarts."

"Enough with the crazy nightmare stuff, Nancy. This isn't a dream. It is a reality I orchestrated," the little gnome said, his eyes glittering. "Wasn't it convenient that I showed up at just the right moment to save you?" He looked merrily back and forth between their stunned faces as realization dawned in their eyes.

"And win our trust ..." Nancy whispered.

"And become our mentor and father figure ..." Thoral breathed.

"All part of the plan," Glurpgrond told them. He paused and examined the odd group of the Fellowship and Dark Brothers with a mischievous glint in his eyes. "Everybody sit," he commanded. "I have a little gloating to do before I kill you all." He waved his wand again and everyone was lifted into the air and then forced into comfortable lounging positions, even the horses. They drifted to the floor around his feet, like a group of children with their war steeds getting ready for story time. He gestured with the wand, rearranging them into an order he found amusing. He settled Brad in Thoral's lap, Nancy by her estranged husband and Nalweegie in her father's lap beside her rival.

"We've got to get his wand while he's gloating," Brad whispered to Thoral while Glurpgrond was distracted with moving the others around.

"Yes, but I cannot bestir myself," Thoral whispered back. "Canst thou?"

"Not so much," the fish answered. "We've got to figure something out, or we're all dead."

"I will figure something out, or something unexpected will turn the tables," Thoral said with certainty. "That is how this kind of situation usually—" He was going to say more, but just then the gnome finished his artful placement of the others and addressed the group.

"The problem with leading an army composed largely of insane monsters is that they don't appreciate the ingenious nuances of an evil plan," Glurpgrond sighed. He took a second to climb up onto the stalagmite table and settled himself on it. "Okay. Let's see. It all began about a thousand and seventeen years ago, when the Goomy Prophecy was revealed and the High Scryer of the Prophets' Guild of Reefma wrote it down in the Book of Doom. Elfrod and Nalweegie, I know you both know it." He shot a look at the king of the elves of Creekenvalley and his daughter.

Elfrod and Nalweegie exchanged nervous glances.

"Come on. One of you recite it, or I'll turn you all to powder," the gnome encouraged.

"I too know the Goomy Prophecy of Doom," Blort volunteered. He cleared his throat and began:

"When all the signs align aright,

One shall emerge from the darkness, led by a gnome.

A mighty pudding shall be consumed

To wear the bracelet and all defeat,

And sit the throne his butt upon."

"Not really very poetic, is it? Sounds clunky," Glurpgrond critiqued. "But enough to get me started on my plans for vengeance and world domination. I recruited Mauron to make the Bracelet of Evil. We brewed the Pudding of Power so he could wear the bracelet. Of course, when I picked Mauron as my candidate for Dark Lord, I had no way of knowing that it was not he who was destined to rule all of Grome. I didn't even figure it out when you, Elfrod, and your stupid friend, King Doug, evaporated the Dark Lord on the very eve of what was to be our great triumph." He shot a threatening look at Elfrod, his eyes glittering.

"At first, I was devastated by the defeat. How could I have failed? I'd followed the instructions in the prophecy to the letter. So I figured maybe I could fix it. I went after the pudding you and Doug took from Mauron. That's when I discovered that you'd put a deadly exploding spell on it. My only consolation was that you had dropped your misplacement compass and the keys to your treasure vault in here when you were booby-trapping the pudding. Once I figured out what they were, it was kind of fun to watch you spend yourself into debt.

"Of course, watching someone descend into bankruptcy over the course of decades doesn't hold a candle to running the world, so I shifted my efforts to recovering Lord Mauron's remains. I created the Glurpgronders, my nine-and-a-half black riders. I used the Dark Brotherhood to place my agents everywhere. I scoured the land for that darned envelope you put Mauron's dust in. And I tried to break the spell on that pudding." He pointed at the chalice.

"I spent seven hundred and ten years on the whole reviving-Mauron thing. The envelope proved to be all but unopenable when we found it, and when we did get it open, there was still the deadly exploding spell you had placed on the pudding. I warned Mauron about it and he still blew himself right back to dust the minute my back was turned. After I'd gone to such trouble to reconstitute him. Boy, was I miffed! Then, just as I was getting ready to throw in the towel, I heard a rumor. Just a whisper really, that your ten-year-old daughter, Nalweegie, had a dream in which were revealed secret lines to the Goomy Prophecy of Doom." He paused for dramatic effect and looked around at his prisoners, most of whom were interested in spite themselves. He tweaked his wand a little and made them all lean in.

"Secret lines! Imagine my surprise," the little gnome exclaimed. "Nalweegie, would you be so kind as to recite the whole prophecy as you dreamed you read it? It's okay. I've known the missing bits for three hundred and six years now." He gestured to the princess, inviting her to recite the longer version.

Nalweegie squirmed, but recited in a clear, high voice:

"When all the signs align aright

And the Fatal Pink Comet lights the night,

One shall emerge from the darkness, led by a gnome,
Born here of no mother nor father of Grome.
A mighty pudding shall be consumed,
But not by the guy who had been groomed
To wear the bracelet and all defeat.
Another guy will get that treat
And sit the throne his butt upon.
Just to be clear, 'tis not Mauron."

The little gnome clapped his cute, chubby hands in mock applause, still clutching his wand.

"Bravo, elf princess," Glurpgrond said. "Although, at the time I read those words, I was ready to wring your little neck. I could have used that information a thousand years earlier. But there it was. Only a child born into this world from parents of another world could eat the pudding and harness the full power of the Bracelet of Evil. Mauron was a dead end." He shook his head.

"How preposterously convoluted! If there's one thing I've learned in this life though, it's that you can't fight prophecy. So, time for a new plan. I devoted the next two hundred and seventy-six years to figuring out how to open a portal to another world so that I could summon a man and woman to sire the whelp I needed. I sacrificed much to pull that off and at last I succeeded, only to find that the two I had pulled through were mere children—and scrawny, ugly ones at that. No offense, you two." He made a conciliatory nod toward Thoral and the Heartless One.

"But I…It was my fault we came to Grome," Thoral said in a hoarse whisper. "I thought we were pulled through because I opened that underwear drawer that my mysterious uncle forbade me to open."

"Yeah, that was hilarious," Glurpgrond chuckled. "You were so wracked by guilt. I could hardly keep a straight face whenever you mentioned it."

"Teddy," the Heartless One said, her voice catching in her throat. "I always blamed you. I gave you such a hard time about how it was all your fault…"

"Also hilarious," Glurpgrond noted, "but totally incorrect. Anyway, I'd been expecting a couple of grown-ups ready to make a baby and instead I got you two kids, who didn't even seem to like each other. You fought all the time. So I made do. I started feeding you powerful puddings to modify you physically so that you'd become superhumanly attractive. I gave you enormous-muscle puddings. I gave you glossy-hair puddings. I gave you cat-like-agility puddings and sexy-voice puddings and animal-magnetism puddings and prodigious-hand-strength puddings."

"So that is why you made us eat all that pudding," Thoral exclaimed. "You soured me on puddings forever."

"It worked like a charm!" Glurpgrond congratulated himself. "You blossomed into such awesome, irresistible specimens that you couldn't help but fall in love with each other. In fact, the only unexpected side effect was that your eyes turned those strange shades of purple, for which we have no word on Grome. Even that seemed to make you more attractive in an odd way."

"Your eyes aren't naturally purple?" Nalweegie asked.

"They used to be blue," Thoral conceded, "back when I was but a skinny and normal-looking boy."

"Within a handful of years, you became much as you look now and as planned, you fell in love and I encouraged you to marry," Glurpgrond said. "It was when you conceived the child and the birth drew near that I first realized I might have refined you a bit too well. You see, you'd both become so superheroic that I was concerned I might not be able to dispose of you without risking my own life or the life of the child. I then made my alliance with the grode and hatched the plot to trick Teddy into leaving so that I could kill Nancy and take the infant."

"Does it bother anyone else that these plans seem so needlessly convoluted and so unlikely to succeed?" Brad asked.

"You sent the beast that killed my child?" Nancy cried, anguish making her voice crack.

"You set the grode upon my wife and my infant son?" Thoral demanded.

"That is correct, Thoral," Glurpgrond gloated. "After first ensuring you would be gone. I thought I'd done an awesome job of setting everything up so that you would arrive at the Walking-Door Tree, the grode would attack and you'd witness the deaths of Nancy, your child and myself. I figured that would be so devastating you'd jump through the door and return to your own world."

"See that? He's making my point right there," Brad commented.

"I'll give you that one, fish, because of course, Nancy didn't actually die and Teddy didn't return to his world. Miscalculations that have plagued me these twenty-one years."

"The grode didn't kill our baby?" Nancy whispered, stunned.

"No. I needed your baby," Glurpgrond told her. "Pay attention! I've already covered that. I had to raise your baby to be evil and train him in the ways of darkness so that he would be ready to rule once I figured out how to get at the pudding."

"What have you done with my son?" Nancy sobbed. "You vile, vile jerk!"

"Ah-ah-ah," Glurpgrond chided her with a grin. "No need for name calling! Anyway, once I found out you'd survived, I saw to it that you were taken prisoner by the Dark Brotherhood and brainwashed into becoming a member of the order so I could use you in the event that I needed you."

Brad just rolled his eyes this time.

"Sorry for all the physical and psychological torture, by the way," the gnome said to Nancy, but he didn't sound or look very sorry at all. She burst into tears.

Thoral roared in fury, fighting with every ounce of his will to break the spell that held him but to no avail. He remained seated, criss-cross applesauce.

"And you, Teddy," Glurpgrond continued when the barbarian had shouted himself hoarse. "I tried everything I could think of to kill you. I even had the grode lure you into a trap. Would have succeeded too if it weren't for Warlordhorse. Spectacular escape incidentally. After that, you turned into such a drunken wreck that I didn't think I had to worry much about you anymore. I did, however, keep a secret watch on you so that I found out when you began seeking the Walking-Door Tree once more. You know all those years you've spent trying to find it again? Well, I chopped it down the minute I learned you were after it so that you couldn't escape this world without my knowing." He reached into a small pouch at his belt with one chubby hand and pulled out something that was too big to have fit inside. "I used the wood to make this spice rack and burned the rest to ash," he said with a chuckle. "Not only do I use the spice rack to store my cumin; I also figured it would be a slap in the face when you found out."

As the barbarian glanced toward the spice rack, a shock went through his body. His striking violet eyes widened a fraction before he redoubled his efforts to escape. He made a spectacle of himself. His face was red, his veins throbbed at his temples and throat, and it looked as if his massive sinews would burst with the strain. Glurpgrond stared, fascinated. Elfrod closed his eyes to block the sight of the mighty warrior's suffering while Nalweegie struggled to get off her father's lap and come to her love's aid.

"You wasted so much time searching for that tree, so desperate to get home," Glurpgrond gloated. Then a crafty look crossed his chubby face. "I could send you back, you know," he continued silkily. "I think the rack would still work as a portal to your Earth, and I will happily send you back. You'll have to go knowing that you have sentenced all of your friends to die and everyone on this world to utter servitude. What do you say?"

"I'll go," Nancy cried. "None of this is real anyway. Let me wake from this nightmare."

"No, crazy lady, the offer doesn't apply to you," Glurpgrond sneered. "It's only for Teddy Mighty Fist because he's such a righteous hero and understands that this is all true. What say you, Earthman?" The wizard's greedy stare probed the warrior's eyes, seeking an answer. He was not the only one breathlessly awaiting Thoral's response. Nalweegie, Brad, Warlordhorse and even Nancy all knew of the barbarian's deep desire to return home.

"If…I…were…free…" The warrior grunted each word as he struggled. He sounded like one trying to speak while suffering an incredibly constipated bowel movement. "I…would…break… thy…wand."

"Yes, duh," Glurpgrond chuckled. "That was a lot of effort expended to say something stupendously obvious even for you, Teddy. But you are not free, and now you've thrown away your only chance to get home, and you will never be free again. I worked very hard to craft this spell, taking into account the superhuman abilities of you and Nancy as well as the superelven, superfishy and superhorseish abilities of all of your companions. The Dark Brothers Nancy brought with her don't count for anything, but I've even factored in their wimpy abilities. See, I've been following your progress all along and pulling the strings to orchestrate this moment. I've been close enough to you to have slit your throat on many occasions, Thoral. I've watched you tossing in your sleep, whimpering in the grip of your pathetic nightmares. I've known most of your plans the minute you confided them in your fish friend. Yes, I've thought of everything."

"You…have…missed…something…" Thoral strained.

"No," Glurpgrond frowned, considering the possibility. "I have missed nothing! You are caught in *my* mighty magic fist, Thoral Mighty Fist. You'll be the one missing things! Like your wife, your friends and your ladylove. The only real question is, once you've watched me enjoy my moment of ultimate triumph, what order do I kill the others in so as to maximize your pain and suffering?"

At these words, Thoral's strength seemed to fail him. He would have collapsed if he'd been able to. Instead, he seemed to deflate in place. His body wracked as he drew in heaving breaths. Glurpgrond watched him closely. Something about the warrior's outburst troubled the gnomish wizard, but he couldn't decide exactly what.

"Please, Yiz," Nancy begged, drawing his attention. "After all you have put me through if you won't send me back, please tell me, what you have done with my sweet baby?"

"You'll be happy to hear that he is well. Thriving in fact. Although I've ensured that he hates you with a burning passion and has no idea you are his mother." Glurpgrond chortled, rubbing his short-fingered hands together. "Would you like to say hello to him? It's just about time he ate this pudding and took control of the whole world anyway." He set down his wand on the stalagmite tabletop, reached into the same small leather pouch from which he'd drawn the spice rack and laid his chubby hands on something within. Then, so quickly it was hard to say exactly how the physics worked, he yanked from the bag a six-foot-tall, scrawny, blue-eyed, red-haired, weak-chinned twenty-one-year-old dressed only in a loincloth. He set the newcomer on the floor with his back to the group. The young man swayed on his feet, disoriented and more than a little motion sick. He was holding a half-eaten banana.

"Dad, I have asked you not to do that without warning me first," the young man complained around a mouthful of fruit, his voice a bit high-pitched and whiny. "I was right in the middle of something." He seemed to become aware of his surroundings at that point and turned to take in the room. He swallowed audibly.

"Prince Sugarin?" Nalweegie and Elfrod exclaimed in unison.

"Nalweegie?" the boy gasped, looking embarrassed. He turned on Glurpgrond. "Dad! I am in my loincloth."

"You know this guy?" Brad demanded of the elves.

"He was my betrothed," Nalweegie whispered. "His riches were to save my father's kingdom."

"Yes, and it would have saved me a load of trouble if you had married him like you were supposed to," Glurpgrond huffed. "I went to considerable lengths to set up the marriage. I even had Necrogrond trick Nancy into believing it was her idea to have him capture you so that my mighty son here could kill him, rescue you from his clutches, recover your father's misplacement compass and win the affections of you both. But then Thoral messed everything up."

"I'm not even going to roll my eyes anymore," Brad said, shaking his head in disgust.

"Thank you for standing me up at our wedding feast, Princess," the boy sneered. "By the way, I didn't want to marry you anyway. My dad told me I had to."

Nancy, who had not taken her eyes from her long-lost son since his reveal, let out a gigantic sob as if her heart were breaking.

He stared at her, his brow creasing in puzzlement. "Dad, who are these other people?"

"These are those bad guys I was telling you about. The evil ones who are trying to destroy the world. The ones who murdered your mother."

The young man scowled and eyed Thoral, the Heartless One and the others with undisguised contempt. Tears streamed from Nancy's striking mauve eyes as she stared at the boy, as if trying to hug him with her gaze. Thoral refused to look at Glurpgrond or his son and instead kept his own purple orbs trained on some point behind them.

"Teddy, Nancy and the rest of you evildoers who don't already know him," Glurpgrond smiled, "I'd like you to meet my son. He is not actually named Prince Sugarin. Sorry for the deception. His real name is Glurpgrond Junior."

"Glurpgrond Junior?" Brad asked, incredulous.

Nancy let out another sob.

"Nice touch, eh?" the gnome chuckled.

"Do not make fun of my name, evil fish," the young man growled, leveling the remains of his banana at Brad. His watery-blue eyes were narrowed in irritation. "Father has warned me of your vile and nasty mockery."

"Don't let them distract you, Junior," Glurpgrond soothed him. "I've finally recovered that pudding we talked about, and it's time for you to eat it so that you can save the world and we can kill these bad guys."

The boy turned and glanced at the pudding. His face brightened. "Chocolate!" he said. "My favorite!" He picked up the chalice in one hand and the spoon in the other. "Hey, did someone already sneak a taste of this?" he asked as he scooped up his first bite.

"Wait. Look at me," Thoral called, urgency roughening his voice. "Before you taste that pudding, know this: That man is not thy father."

"What?" Junior asked, turning from the pudding to the barbarian. "Of course he's my father. What are you talking about?"

"What is he talking about?" Brad demanded from his seat on Thoral's lap. "Glurpgrond is a tiny, chubby old gnome, and you're a six-foot human. How the heck could he be your dad?"

Junior eyed Glurpgrond, and puzzlement creased his brow.

"Pay no attention to them, son," the gnome ordered, but he was no longer smiling and there was a slight edge to his voice. "Just be a good boy and eat your pudding."

"HOLD!" Thoral commanded. "Look at me. Look right into my eyes with all of your focus. Do not be distracted by my gorgeous features, my luxurious blond mane, or my chiseled bone structure. Look past these things and concentrate on the general shape and cast of my face. Squint if you have to. Do I remind you of anyone? Take your time. You look too, Glurpgrond."

"No. You don't remind me of anyone particularly," Junior said. He squinted and cocked his head to one side.

"OK, enough of this," Glurpgrond huffed. "I think I'll just zap you into silence for the eating of the pudding. Now where's my wand?" The gnome had reached for it on the tabletop while glaring at Thoral, but his questing fingers did not find it. He frowned in annoyance and dropped his gaze to search for it in earnest.

"What the—!" Glurpgrond snarled, taking in the empty tabletop. He picked up the spice rack to make sure the wand hadn't rolled beneath it. Nothing. He turned toward Junior.

"Did you touch Daddy's wand?" he asked, brandishing the spice rack in his anger.

"What? No!" the young man responded, indignant.

Now panic touched the gnome's face, and he whirled on Thoral. To Glurpgrond's surprise, the warrior and all his companions were still sitting there, frozen.

"OK, what are you up to?" Glurpgrond demanded. "Where is that wand?"

"If I had it, I would snap it right now," Thoral said with great deliberation, as if explaining it to someone who did not understand. "Or bite it right in half, for that would break the spell and free us all."

"Why do you keep talking like that?" the gnome growled. He jumped off the table edge to stalk toward the barbarian.

"No reason," Thoral answered, with a slight a smile.

Glurpgrond stopped in his tracks and held up a finger for silence. There was a very faint crunching or gnawing sound.

"Oh hey, Dad, I found it!" Junior said, following the sound with his eyes. "There's like some weird squirrel thing chewing on it behind the stalagmite."

"EAT THE PUDDING!" Glurpgrond shrieked at his stolen pseudoson. "NOW!"

"BITE, TYNCIE! BITE!" Thoral bellowed.

A second later, before a confused Junior could get the spoonful of pudding to his lips, there came a distinct, crisp cracking sound, as if someone had snapped a pencil in half. Bitten it in half, actually, with her supercute buckteeth.

"NO!" Glurpgrond shrieked a second time, fury and terror comingling on his chubby face.

"SON!" Thoral roared as he sprang to knock the pudding out of Junior's hands, finally free of the immobilization spell. He balled his mighty fists, moving considerably more quickly than a cheetah because of his pudding-fueled superreflexes. The only one who rivaled his speed was Nancy. She leapt at the same moment, intent on snatching the pudding from the boy.

"NOOOOOO!" Glurpgrond shrieked a third time. He was a shrieker. Because he was very self-centered, he assumed that Thoral and Nancy were leaping to attack him. It didn't occur to him that they would have any other target. If he had been fast enough, he would have drawn *Blurmflard*, the sword that he had lent to Thoral so long ago, but he wasn't fast enough. He only had time to throw up his arms to shield himself before the two earthlings collided with him on their way toward Junior. He didn't even have time to drop the spice rack clutched in his chubby hands.

As they struck, Thoral caught a glimpse of Nalweegie out of the corner of his eye. His beautiful elfin princess was springing to her feet, her pretty face flushing with triumph and excitement. He felt his love for her surge through his being. It felt like a massive, disquieting sucking sensation at the center of his soul, as if someone had just stabbed him in the solar plexus with a vacuum-cleaner hose.

"NALWEEGIE!" he cried. It wasn't love he was feeling. His breath was squeezed away, and he felt himself falling or flying forward like a dust bunny sucked at high velocity into a vacuum cleaner.

And then he realized what was happening. He screamed and wept and tried to claw at the darkness welling all around him to stop himself. But it was too late. As he spun into nothingness, he had a last glimpse of the ice cavern and his friends, his ex-mentor, his son, their expressions frozen in shock and horror, even little Tyncie CheeChaw CheeChee WeeWaw who still clutched the broken bits of Glurpgrond's wand.

CHAPTER FORTY-SEVEN

The Last Straw

There was a massive *bang* as Thoral exploded out of the underwear drawer of a rickety old dresser, kicking up a flurry of men's white briefs. As they rained down, he was followed by Nancy, who also blasted into the deserted spare bedroom of his uncle's mysterious mansion. They shot ten feet through the air and landed with a loud *whump* on a four-poster bed that banged against the wall and released a billowing cloud of dust, obscuring everything.

"No!" Thoral squeaked, struggling to untangle himself from the blankets. He sat up and whirled toward the Heartless One but found himself staring at a sweet-faced thirteen-year-old girl who was clutching her left breast with one hand.

"No!" he squeaked again as she laughed, marveling at her undeveloped and unmarred bathing-suit-clad body. He leapt to his feet and dashed to a floor-length mirror leaning against one wall. The reflection that stared back at him was of a scrawny, thirteen-year-old boy in short pants with watery-blue eyes and greasy dishwater-blond hair. He fumbled in his pants pocket, yanked out his iPhone and hit the wake button with a trembling finger. The date and time that came up showed that it was just three seconds after the moment he had first opened the underwear drawer, found his uncle's gun and been sucked into Grome. He buried his face in his hands and wept.

There was a gentle touch on his shoulder. Nancy stood beside him.

"It's OK," she soothed. "It was just a fantasy. Just a dream. Like I always thought. We're back now. We're back in the real world."

"It wasn't just a dream," Teddy sobbed, turning to face her. "It was like Narnia or Oz or something. We were really there."

"No," Nancy said, hugging his skinny body to her own. "Narnia and Oz are just stories. Grome can't have been real. Occam's razor, Teddy. What's more likely? That we just came out of an underwear drawer after spending thirty years in a magical world where the forces of darkness were battling for control of an evil pudding and where we were married and I had a baby and your best friend was a fish? Or is it more likely that we just dreamed it all or hallucinated it all or something? Everybody has dreams, and some people have hallucinations. Those things are well documented. They happen. Going to other realities…that doesn't…I mean, if any of it was real, then what happened to our grown-up bodies? What happened to my scarlet robes and your pirate clothes? Why aren't our eyes purple or… or anything? It all seemed really real, but it couldn't have been. It had to be pretend or…or something." She sighed with delighted relief and nuzzled his cheek with her nose.

Teddy pulled away from her, sniffled and wiped his eyes with the heels of his hands. He met her hazel eyes, his lower lip still quivering a little, and she gave him a tentative smile.

"Come on," she said. "It was just pretend, and now the pretending is over. This is the end. Agree with me and let's…" She dropped her eyes, blushing. "…Let's kiss on it." She nuzzled close to him again, her breath warm and grape-popsicle-scented on his face.

It brought back memories. She was his uncle's neighbor. She had only agreed to come over because he had offered to show her the gun. His brow furrowed. "You didn't even like me," he whispered, his own face flushing despite his misgivings.

"I love you," she cooed. "I never really stopped loving you. Never." She brushed his lips with her own as she spoke, and it sent a pleasant shiver through his thirteen-year-old body.

"You said I was a wimp," he whispered, trying hard to keep his head clear. "You didn't even want the necklace I gave you. If none of it happened, then we never fell in love and you wouldn't have any reason to kiss me now."

"Don't you want to kiss me?" she breathed. "I want to kiss you…"

"I …I …"

"Come on, Teddy. I don't ever want to think about Grome or any of that again. You could be my boyfriend. So say it was pretend. Say the game is over and you can kiss me, then we'll go watch TV."

"TV," he whispered, his resolve crumbling.

"TV," she breathed. "We can watch shows and drink soda and eat chips on the couch. And then we can make out, and then we can watch more shows."

He closed his eyes and surrendered, leaning into her warmth.

"You know," a gruff voice said, startling them both, "she does make some pretty good points."

The kids turned toward the sound to find Brad, the orange koi fish, standing on his tailfins in the open underwear drawer.

"No!" Nancy gasped, sinking to her knees on the floor.

"Then again, she is evil and crazy," the fish noted, "so maybe take it with a grain of salt."

"Brad!" Thoral cried, breaking into a lopsided grin as he leapt to help his friend out of a pile of briefs. "But how?"

"I was in your lap when you jumped up. I just grabbed onto your belt and got dragged along for the ride when you guys got sucked into that spice rack," Brad explained as he and Thoral embraced.

Behind them, Nancy sprawled on the hardwood, slapping her palms on the floor as she wept. The fish and the boy stared at her solemnly.

"And hey, I guess I owe you another serious apology for being mad when you saved Tyncie's life," Brad conceded. At that, the boy's eyes went wide with realization.

"We must go back!" he cried, looking around the room as if he expected to find a door hanging in midair. "We've got to get back and stop Glurpgrond and Junior. I've got to convince him he's my son. And I've got to save Nalweegie. She's in danger. They're all in danger. We need to have a final, climactic battle in which I defeat everyone. Quick! What do we do?"

"No idea." The fish shook his head. "The only reason you got to Grome in the first place was because Glurpgrond summoned you. There might not be a way back. Even if there is, how could we ever find it? You said magic doesn't work here. You're just a scrawny little kid and I'm just a … a fish out of water. Everything is against us. There's no way we can succeed." He hung his head, defeated.

"This can't be the end," Teddy whimpered. He swallowed audibly. "It can't be. If this were a story, it would probably only be the ending of the first book in an epic trilogy."

"OK, that's the final straw," Nancy said, sitting up and wiping her nose on the back of her forearm. "First, you should probably stop saying such dumb things now that you're not a gorgeous, muscle-bound hero anymore, because it all just sounds dorky coming from a scrawny little nobody. And second, do you think that everything is all about you and you somehow deserve a happy ending where everything turns out OK *for you*? Well, it's not and you don't. You don't always get to finish things the way you planned—or even finish them at all. Think about all of the people you killed back on Grome. I bet every one of them had other plans the day they crossed swords with you, and I bet they all thought some version of 'This can't be the end' as they died. But that didn't stop it ending."

Teddy stared at her in horror, noticing the crazy glint from the Heartless One's mauve eyes kindling to life in Nancy's hazel ones as she got to her feet. She strode to the door of the room and yanked it open then turned to face him as she stood on the threshold.

"And third," she spat, "what makes you think this isn't an awesome ending? What makes you think this isn't the conclusion of the *third* book in a trilogy that was about Glurpgrond? I bet he's just thrilled with how things have turned out. And so am I. What if everything is about *me* instead of you? Did you think of that? What if the first book was about me getting to Grome, the second book was about my trials and tribulations while I thought you were dead, and the third book was the one that just finished, the one where I finally succeeded and got everything I wanted? I spent thirty years in hell, wishing every day for this exact ending. Praying for it. I've been through such terrors, such horrors. You can't even imagine. Now I'm back. I'm safe. Like it never happened. As far as I'm concerned, it can totally end like this. It should end like this. I don't want there to be any more to the story. This is my happy ending. Or at least, happy enough, so get over yourself. It's over and I'm going home!" She snarled one last line as she stalked away. "THE END!"

"No," Teddy whispered.

"What was that?" Nancy demanded, stopping short. "I didn't quite catch that."

"I said *no*," the boy replied, his voice growing stronger. "There was a time when I thought I was at the end of my story, but a very good friend reminded me that your story is never over until you give up, or until you're dead." He shot a look at Brad, who smiled back at him. "I am not dead, and I will not give up. There must be another door. We'll find a way."

"Even if there is a door, I'll stop you," Nancy hissed, her face livid. "There's no way I'd ever let you open a portal back to that hell. No matter what it takes, I'll stop you. I swear it!"

"You will *not* stop me," Teddy growled. "This is *not* the end."

"It is!" she spat back at him. "And I will! I already said 'the end,' so it's over."

"No it is not. And you will not. I *will* find a way back," he said solemnly, "for although I may not appear so right now, *I am Thoral Mighty Fist.*"

Nancy gasped as she looked at the boy who stood before her in his short pants, scrawny chest thrust out, hands on hips in a classic hero pose. Yes, in this world he was just the nerdy, wimpy new kid in the neighborhood, a worthless nobody who'd tried to impress her with Popsicles, a dolphin necklace and a sneaked look at a gun. But somehow, somewhere inside and also far off across the gulf between this reality and that other distant universe, he was still the Fist Wielder. And even Nancy knew that once Thoral Mighty Fist noted that he was Thoral, there was no point in arguing further. Everyone knew it. That's just how it was.

FISH WIELDER is J.R.R.R. (JIM) HARDISON'S first novel novel (He wrote a graphic novel, The Helm, for Dark Horse Comics). Jim has worked as a writer, screen writer, animator and film director. He started his professional career by producing a low-budget direct-to-video feature film, The Creature From Lake Michigan. Making a bad movie can be a crash course in the essential elements of good character and story, and The Creature From Lake Michigan was a tremendously bad movie. Shifting his focus entirely to animation, Jim joined Will Vinton Studios where he directed animated commercials for M&M's and on the stop-motion TV series Gary and Mike. While working at Vinton, he also co-wrote the television special Popeye's Voyage: The Quest for Pappy with actor Paul Reiser.

Jim has appeared on NBC's The Apprentice as an expert advisor on brand characters, developed characters and wrote the pilot episode for the PBS children's television series SeeMore's Playhouse and authored the previously mentioned graphic novel, The Helm, named one of 2010's top ten Great Graphic Novels for Teens by YALSA, a branch of the American Library Association. These days, Jim is the creative director and co-owner of Character LLC, a company that does story-analysis for brands and entertainment properties. He lives in Portland, Oregon with his lovely wife, two amazing kids, one smart dog and one stupid dog.

www.fishwielder.com
www.jimhardison.com

CPSIA information can be obtained
at www.ICGtesting.com
Printed in the USA
LVOW12s1600261117
557612LV00001B/55/P